AFTERMATH

TITLES BY E.A. COPEN

Judah Black Novels

Guilty by Association

Perfect Storm (novella)

Blood Debt

Chasing Ghosts

Playing with Fire

The Lazarus Codex

Death Rites

Organ Grind

The Fairchild Chronicles

Kiss of Vengeance

Other works

Beasts of Babylon

AFTERMATH

BOOK ONE OF BROKEN EMPIRE

E.A. COPEN

BOLIDE
PUBLISHING LIMITED

AFTERMATH
© E.A. Copen 2018

Cover Art by Ravenborn
Editorial: Michelle Dunbar and Clever Fox Editing.

First published in 2018 by Bolide Publishing Limited
http://bolidepublishing.com

ISBN: 978-1-9999529-1-4

In memory of Carrie Fisher,
the reason I grew up loving spaceships more than dolls.

CHAPTER ONE

Timothy

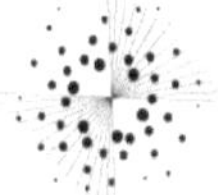

Fire swallowed the shuttle behind *Epsilon One*, sending twisted shards of metal into the Torian atmosphere. The blast was close enough that an impact warning appeared on the visor screen inside Captain Timothy Val's helmet. Timothy tapped the side of his helmet to silence the alarm and flexed his gloved fingers. He turned away from the blue hue of the shuttle's kinetic barrier flickering in the window and ground his teeth. The sensation made him cringe.

Another blast exploded, and the hue turned to static for a second. The metal plating groaned. *The shields will hold until we hit the ground.* Timothy grimaced. *They have to.*

He stood. An explosion rocked the shuttle and sent

him scrambling for one of the handholds in the ceiling. Hands shot out to steady him from both sides. When the shuttle stabilized again, he acknowledged the gesture with a bob of his head and gripped the next handhold tight, working his way down the line of men toward the exit hatch.

He stopped by Private Malor, the newest member of their team. The man sat with his head bowed, one thumb against the bridge of his nose. His gun rested against one leg. He whispered a hurried prayer and passed the circle of beads between a thumb and forefinger.

"Put those away," Timothy ordered, and shoved the assault rifle back into the private's hands. The prayer beads clattered to the floor. "You'll do more damage with this."

Malor let the gun fall into his lap, staring at it with reddened, droopy eyelids. "Is it true what they're saying?"

"Is what true?" Timothy snapped.

"That half of the 51st battalion got wiped out by rebels at Den-Mak. Here at Olarin, they're supposed to be even better armed."

Timothy frowned behind his helmet. "The fifty-first did their job, Private, and shot rebel supply lines to hell. The people at Olarin haven't seen a supply truck in weeks."

The man next to Malor shifted and leaned forward. "Don't matter how many guns they've got if they're too weak from hunger to aim."

Malor lowered his gaze to the string of prayer beads on the floor and shook his head. "Why in the hell are we even here? Since when do we put down our own people? It's not right, Captain. I'll burn for this. We all will."

Timothy knelt and picked up the prayer beads. "We're here because the empire demands it. We go where the crown commands." He tucked the prayer beads into Malor's pocket.

"It's not right," Malor repeated. "This is their home. They've got a right to defend it. They've got a right to choose to be part of the empire or not. Don't they?"

The captain picked the gun up and forced it into Malor's arms. "A soldier's job isn't to question, Private. It's to point and shoot. If you want to talk rights and wrongs, maybe you should've run for the senate."

His directive prompted nervous chuckles from the men nearby.

"I'll tell you one thing, Malor. Those rebels out there"—he pointed to the shuttle door—"they'd shoot a senator just as soon as a soldier right now. They're not your priority. Your priority is the man next to you, not the rights of the rebel shooting at you. You understand me, Private?"

Malor blinked and offered weakly, "Yes, sir."

Timothy gave the kid a firm slap on the shoulder before glancing around at the rest of his men. Most were seasoned veterans, but they were used to shooting Erolyians, not their own people. Killing a foreign invader in a strange uniform could, at least, be justified.

"We have our orders," Timothy reminded his men. He pointed to the shuttle doors on the far side. "Those doors open, you get your asses off this shuttle, or the rebels will be the last of your worries."

Another burst of fire exploded in the sky, but their roar of acknowledgement drowned out the sound. "Yes, sir!"

As they flew out of range of the planetary defense grid, the city of Olarin rose on the horizon. The earth had been overturned, a sure sign the rebels had resorted to burying mines. Five mobile mortar cannons dotted the landing zone. Several semi-circular trenches marked the other side of the minefield. Black shapes darted back and forth inside the trenches. Enemy soldiers. Rebels.

A loud buzzing sounded over Timothy's head and he moved toward the back. Everyone stood and readied their weapons. As soon as the first man moved forward and off the shuttle, there'd be room for him to shoulder his rifle and open fire. The shuttle landed to the booming of mortar shells crashing into the terrain nearby. Dirt sprayed and struck the kinetic barrier with a rhythmic clink. Timothy flexed his finger against the trigger guard and breathed in and out, focusing on the mission.

Take Olarin. Those were their orders. Fuck rebel fire and fuck the rebels. That's what Colonel Krail had said. Take the city at any cost.

Timothy clenched his hands to still the tremble in his muscles. His battle suit registered his elevated heart rate with a yellow notice. It wasn't fear. It was the familiar rush of pre-battle adrenaline. One more chance to die on his feet. There was honor in that.

The shuttle door slammed to the ground and the men in front flinched. A few let out cries of fear or pain. It was impossible to tell which. Hot plasma pelted the men in the front before they could even move. Their shields and armor took most of the shots, but even the strongest material couldn't hold up against a barrage of six or seven shots at a time. Once the shielding in their suits took enough damage, it flickered and burned out, leaving the plasma to burn holes through their armor. The barrage mowed through them in lines, hitting the man to Timothy's right and three of the four men in front of him.

Timothy gave a shout and pushed forward. "Go! Forward!" he urged, charging forward. Mortar hit to the left and right, whistling before it slammed into the ground. Dirt, debris and dark smoke erupted in a thick plume, obscuring their view in either direction. As they cleared the ramp, the shuttle exploded in a fireball of twisted metal, knocking them to the ground.

His visor lit up with impact and heat warnings. In the diagram of his suit on the right, his lower back was highlighted in red. One of the shield generators was already out.

Malor collapsed a few feet away, screaming like a madman. His visor had flipped up revealing wide, bulging eyes. Malor's jaw worked open and closed like a fish cast onto land.

Crawling on his forearms, Timothy crossed the distance between them. "Dammit, Private, you're going to get yourself killed." He slammed his hand into the side of Malor's helmet. The visor snapped down, but it wasn't enough to knock Malor out of shock.

Timothy looked around at the chaos, gripping Malor's shoulders. The heavy plasma fire hadn't let up. The line of rebels had advanced from the nearest trench under cover of men operating plasma turrets in strategically placed defense towers.

He heard a shout and turned his head toward the sound. Dirt and smoke clouded visibility, but the screaming told him everything he needed to know. There were mines in the field.

More shuttles glided into the lower atmosphere. Roughly one in four came down in a fireball, crashing to the ground and taking more men with it.

Move or die, Timothy's brain screamed. He hoisted Malor up and over his shoulders into a fireman's carry with a grunt. The private didn't weigh much, but the suit added a good eighty pounds. The extra weight would slow his progression to cover, but Timothy would not leave anyone behind—not while he still had enough strength to forge on.

The two of them made for a piece of warped and burnt out shuttle plating where two of their squad waited. A mere two yards before they were safely behind it, a mortar shell came down close enough to trigger impact warnings. Timothy's shields faltered and plasma zipped close enough that he could smell the air burn. Malor's body jerked but Timothy couldn't stop to check him, not so close to safety.

His shields flickered back up and he scrambled for cover, where he lowered Malor to the ground. The private had taken a round of plasma through his visor, turning his head into meat soup. The two men behind the plating pulled Malor's body aside and out of the way so the three of them had more room to maneuver.

Timothy shouted into the comms in his helmet, "Where the hell are those support drones?"

"Debris must be fucking with their targeting vectors," his lieutenant shouted back. "Can't get a lock. Control's rerouting them. ETA thirty secs."

"Tell them to make it fifteen, LT!"

A loud boom echoed through the atmosphere. Timothy looked up. Three black drones shot out of the debris floating and spinning above them. The drones spun at breakneck speed and fired guided missiles into the base of the defense towers. A cheer went up from the men nearby as the tower exploded in a fireball of wood and metal. Timothy chanced a peek around the shuttle plating and watched a drone slam into the closest mortar gun.

A soldier stumbled into Timothy's cover, his blue-green armor covered in mud and blood. "Are we waiting for the drones to clear a path, sir?"

Timothy ducked back behind the cover as hot plasma skimmed by. The suit sent up a warning, but didn't register an impact. "Negative. Our orders are to clean out the trench thirty yards up and hold position."

The soldier shook his head. "Don't know if you'd noticed, sir, but there's a minefield between us and them."

Timothy noted the colored stripes on the other soldier's uniform. Second lieutenant, and the nameplate read Hawk.

"Get your sergeant up there and secure us a forward position, mines or no mines. That's an order!"

"Aye, sir. We'll move on your command."

Timothy readied his rifle and took a deep breath. "We go in three … two—"

Just before he reached one, he moved out of cover, raised his weapon and fired two shots, lining the rifle up with the targeting matrix in his suit. One struck a rebel closing in on their position. The unarmored rebel fell over, clutching his leg.

Timothy's in-suit scanner pinpointed the mines on screen and flagged them as he ran. Between that and the targeting matrix, there was almost too much information to process. Garbled messages sounded on comms, rallying cries and orders to advance. His men closed on either side of him, joined by soldiers from half a dozen other companies under different commands. Every order worked in unison to one goal: forward march. Take the trench.

They cleared the minefield and Timothy broke into a run. Behind him, his men roared and ran with him. They jumped into the trench, firing rounds at anyone not in Senjelian armor.

A rebel in reclaimed bits of armor shouted and jammed the butt of his weapon at Timothy's visor. Timothy's arm shot out and grabbed the gun. He was exhausted, but the mechanized joints of the suit kicked in, giving him the strength to pull the weapon away. "On your knees!" Timothy ordered and pointed the gun at the man's face.

The rebel's hands went up, but he didn't kneel.

"I said on your knees, damn it!"

The man sank to his knees.

"Are you in command here?" The rebel's clenched jaw trembled, but when he didn't offer an answer quick enough, Timothy fired a round into the mud.

The man flinched, blinked and said, "Yes! Yes, I'm in charge!"

"Tell your men to drop their weapons. Anyone who complies will not be fired upon. Do you understand?"

"And food?"

Timothy hesitated. "What?"

"Please, sir. I'd sell my own mother for a bite. I can't help it. I'm just so damned hungry."

Timothy studied the rebels in the trench. There were only a dozen or so men left uninjured, each kneeling in the mud with their hands behind their heads. Timothy's men held them at gunpoint. Some of the rebels didn't even have rifles, only pistols and knives, and pale, thin faces.

"Everyone who surrenders will receive standard prisoner rations," Timothy promised.

Throughout the trench, the rebels threw down their weapons and raised their hands.

Timothy hesitated, not knowing what to say. He turned and surveyed the maimed and broken bodies lining the trench. Behind him, many of his men lay dead or dying. Had they come armed with bread instead of guns, Malor might still be alive.

Colonel Krail's voice buzzed over the comm. "Captain Val, I've received word of a surrender."

"Yes, sir. We still need to sweep the city though."

"Good timing. Our techs are unlocking the iris now."

The metal plates shielding the city groaned and shuddered. The sound sent chills through Timothy. Victory.

"Congratulations, Captain," the rebel officer said as Hawke secured his hands in cuffs. "Olarin is yours."

After the prisoners were secured in the trenches, their hands tied and their weapons removed, Timothy entered Olarin with a handful of men. The streets were filthy, littered with garbage and feral people huddled around warming vents. Gaunt children with hollow eyes poked a corpse in an alley, but ran away when Timothy called to them. In the skeletal remains of a playground, Timothy found a group of children swallowing painted rocks. Timothy offered them a cracker each and left the package with them, feeling guilty there wasn't enough for everyone.

"Now I know it's been a shitty day," said Hawke as he marched beside Timothy. "When you're so hungry army rations sound good."

"I've never been hungry enough to swallow a painted rock."

"Aye, Captain, but then you've never had my mother's potatoes. I remember the time—"

Hawke's speech cut off as Krail's Staff Sargent reported over the comms that Colonel Krail was outside the city. Timothy motioned for his team to follow him back to the gates.

Krail sat inside his armored transport, eyeing the city with his jaw set. The Colonel was a hard, imposing figure. Tall and clean-shaven, he wore his red hair buzzed close to his scalp. He didn't wear armor, but instead traveled with two heavily armored bodyguards. The transport parked off to the side of the main gate with Krail scowling in the back seat with the window down.

When Krail saw Timothy, he sneered and ordered his

driver to approach. "What the hell is this, Captain?" Krail said, gesturing to the line of prisoners congregating outside the gates. "I told you to eliminate the resistance, not bring them back for tea and cookies."

Timothy gave a stiff salute. "Sir, these people are on the brink of starvation. The Amasian Convention is clear. Prisoners are to be given food and shelter." He hesitated before adding, "No one is above the laws of the convention, Colonel."

"To hell with the convention! Bureaucratic nonsense and bullshit will keep their cases tied up in the courts for half a decade at the taxpayers' expense." Krail threw open the door and climbed out, towering over Timothy. "They're traitors, every damn one of them. They deserve a traitor's death."

Timothy shifted his grip on his gun. "That's not for you to decide, sir."

"Don't presume to tell me what my job is, you blue-blooded upstart. My job is to tell you assholes what to do and when to do it. If I say we execute them, you ask me how I want it done."

"Respectfully, sir—"

"Ask me how I want it done!"

Timothy clenched his jaw and stared straight ahead, refusing to answer.

Krail pulled his sidearm, pointed it at the nearest prisoner and pulled the trigger. The man fell against a wall and slid down, leaving a bright red streak behind. The rest of the prisoners began shouting and backing away. "We don't feed traitors, Val. We execute them. Now, order your men to obey my command or I'll promote someone who will."

"No."

Krail turned to one of his bodyguards.

"Congratulations. You just made captain. Show this asshole how to follow orders."

One of his bodyguards moved to hop out of the transport. Timothy drew his sidearm and pressed the barrel to her temple. "You follow that order, and you won't live to regret it." The blood drained from the soldier's face as she lifted her hands in surrender. Her eyes traveled to the Colonel, looking for support.

Timothy disarmed her and pointed the second gun at the soldiers closing in on the prisoners. They looked on, frozen. "The rest of you, step away from the prisoners." They exchanged glances, but didn't move. "That's an order!"

Krail laughed. "They don't follow your orders, Val. You're a captain. I'm a colonel, and I say we kill the bastards."

"It's a bad order and you know it."

"Last time I checked, the Senate put me in charge of operations on Toria, not you."

Timothy pointed the gun at Krail. "Then consider yourself relieved of duty."

The colonel's smile faded, and he twisted his thick lips into a snarl. "To hell with you!"

A shoulder struck Timothy's ribs, knocking him to the ground. The other soldier grabbed for the gun, but Timothy didn't let go. For several tense seconds, the two of them groped back and forth, each trying to wrench the gun away. With a grunt of effort, the other man pushed the gun away from his head just as Timothy squeezed the trigger. The transport creaked as Krail's remaining bodyguard shifted and someone let out a desperate shout.

No ... Timothy elbowed the soldier, knocking his helmet loose. He pulled a fist back and punched the soldier in the mouth. He wriggled the gun free, jumped to his feet and turned. Several men under his command swarmed Krail's transport, yanked his driver out and pushed the Colonel to the ground. He turned again. On the other side, four of Krail's men marched along the wall, firing at the prisoners. Bodies fell. People screamed. Five or six of the prisoners tried to run, their hands still bound behind their backs. Krail's men picked them off with ease and laughed.

Timothy's legs moved on their own, his mind numb. He stumbled to the nearest of Krail's men on the edge of the trench. When the soldier spun around, Timothy grabbed him by the arm and slammed a fist into his visor. It cracked, and he drew his fist back to make a second blow, but something cracked against the back of his head. Timothy crumpled, his suit lighting up with impact and injury warnings. Krail's men grabbed his shoulders and forced him face first to the ground.

"Restrain him!" The soldier who had wrestled with him for the gun spat thick blood on him and wiped his mouth clean. "He'll answer for his treason. Round up the rest of them!"

"What about the rebel prisoners?" someone asked.

The injured soldier sneered, showing bloody teeth. "Shoot every goddamn one."

They jerked Timothy up and dragged him, kicking and fighting with everything he had. He got one arm free and struck the soldier closest to him, but another ripped off his helmet. A needle stung the back of Timothy's neck. Spinning wooziness overtook him and he sank to his knees.

Everything blurred and faded into darkness.

CHAPTER TWO

Clovis

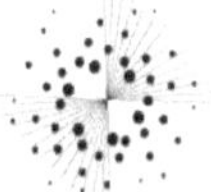

Senator Waval Clovis stepped onto the balcony of his villa and scratched at the gray whiskers on his chin. He watched the red and swollen sun rising in the sky. The whitewashed buildings drank in the pale pinks and blues of dawn. The senator pressed his ear to the railing and listened to the city's heart flutter at his touch. The offbeat murmur of the market below was always the sweetest part of his day.

One can never buy love, the senator thought. He uncorked a wine bottle and poured the first few drops over the railing, a libation to the gods of quick thieves and deep pockets. *Everything else is fair game.*

He sat down on the deep, mahogany chair, a goose-feather pillow softening the plop. With his feet swung up on the table, he tilted his head back and took a long drink.

Everything except the damn crown. No amount of gold would transfer it from Ludus's head onto Prince Annon's. The emperor's steel crown knew only the firm fist of honor, the bite of duty and the strong grasp of tradition. Why would anyone in their right mind want the bloody thing?

The empress, gods bless her, was still a sight. Clovis might have given his right eye for the honor of a grope. She was young, less than half the age of the emperor. Ludus had taken her to his bed just after the rebellion on Illion, a girl of nineteen, all chestnut curls and curtsies. Ludus put Rebos in her the same year and Annon just a year later. Twenty long years of being mother and wife to royalty had changed her heart but not her vixen face. At least those boys had the sense to take her looks and not Ludus's. For all his charms, the emperor would make an ugly corpse.

The balcony doors swung open behind him. He set down the bottle as a young woman in a faded brown dress stepped out. She carried his breakfast on a polished silver tray: a single poached egg, two bits of toast with jam and a fat, greasy sausage. His pants hung folded over her arm, and she carried a data pad in her hand, tuned to the morning news. "Chaunstance, my dear, smile for me. Sit with me. Drink with me!"

"Wine already, Senator?" Chaunstance placed his breakfast before him. "You have matters of state today."

"Wine, women and song are all matters of state, dear lady."

She folded her hands over her apron and sighed. "Should I draw up a check for Mistress Danayla or did you pay her in advance? I told her to dress and wait by the back entrance. It does your reputation no good for whores to go out the front."

"I was a man long before I was a senator. Men have needs. The voters of Senjele remember that."

"They remember you buy drinks for them and extort their extortionists." She held his pants out to him. "Your dignity, senator."

"Dignity be damned," he mumbled as he fought to get them on. The waistband was getting tight again. "I'll deal with the lady myself." He glanced at the front-page headlines. "So, they did it, did they?" He seized the data pad from her before plopping back down. "Executor bastards. He'll be a publicity mess for them."

"Who?"

"Timothy Val. He's the last of a dying breed of Senjelian men, the kind that gives a damn about this crumbling empire. A brave man might call him a patriot. A stupid one, perhaps, but a patriot nonetheless."

He glanced through the story, even though he could guess what it would say. The press had been following the rebellion on Toria since the beginning. A poor farming world, Senjele had swallowed it up fifty years ago, the last prize of the late emperor before Ludus ascended.

Toria grew almost a quarter of all the grains in the empire. When the blight hit the crops on Toria two years ago, bread prices on Senjele soared and people got angry. The Senate introduced a measure to subsidize the cost from the treasury to bring the price back down, but could only support it by raising taxes on the wealthy. Despite Clovis's best efforts, the Senate voted it down. Bread prices went up. Demand went down. Subsidies for farming worlds were slashed due to decreased output and decreased demand. Toria, which was still recovering from the blight, spiraled further into poverty and despair. It was only a matter of time before their people went the way of

Illion and rebelled, and Captain Val, gods bless him, had gotten himself stuck in the middle of it.

He swiped to the next screen to glance through the obituaries, and bit into the sausage, wishing it was more bloody than burnt. Clovis's eyes widened as he settled on one obituary in particular, that of the young Lord Governor Torbin Val.

He let the fork clatter to the plate. "Chaunstance, cancel my appointments for today."

"All of them?"

"Everything but the Senate meeting. That, I have to go to."

Chaunstance frowned and produced another, smaller data pad from her pocket. "Is there something the matter, Senator?"

He lifted his eyes from the page. She was impossible to read, even after all these years of service. He stood, stretched, and clapped his hands on his over-ripe melon of a belly. "Send my compliments to the cook and fetch me my shirt, the midnight blue with the copper buttons. I'll need my cape and hat too."

By the time he stepped onto the street, it was closer to midday. The streets were quiet for a midweek afternoon, the stalls mostly empty. There was a heaviness in the air, and it showed on the people's faces. The market felt more like a funeral. Change was in the air, and the people feared it.

He hurried through the main section of the market, stopping to order a fresh pork pie he wanted delivered to his manse in the evening. His cook could make one, but few things pleased Clovis more than tasting the wares of the small folk. They loved him for it, and his cook was pleased she did not have to slave over peasant dishes for a man of his wealth.

Slave. Now there was a word he wrestled with often. Clovis had often owned slaves. The practice was legal, though frowned upon, in the empire. It had been his custom to free them after a time. Chaunstance was a different matter altogether. He had held onto Chaunstance for more than a decade now, watching her grow from a grim-faced girl into an even grimmer woman. She ran the household so well he didn't think his estate would survive her leaving.

Clovis turned down another wide street, this one emptier than the last. The Senate building loomed at the end of the pavement, white columns splashed with crimson and gold banners standing idle in the breeze. He slipped into the Senate meeting already in progress, thankful his seat was at the back of the amphitheater.

Prince Rebos stood in the center of the room under the domed glass ceiling. The senators crowded into stacked, semi-circular rows above him.

The prince was a handsome man to look at, though Annon had gotten the better half of their mother's beauty. He was a thin man with a longish face. Brown hair, made black by oils and spices, slicked back against a well-shaped brow. Eyes of cracked jade peered out, silent and stoic. Rebos wore his mother's colors today, the royal purple doublet with silver trim. Sewn into the left breast were two arrows with their shafts crossed. The symbol of House Herrin, the now-defunct House of Empress Cylene, clashed noticeably with Rebos's crown of interlocked crescent moons. A stenographer drone floated over the prince's left shoulder. Behind the drone, half a dozen reporters yawned and doodled on their data pads.

Senator Queeran of Novaeux was yet again pleading for Rebos and the rest of the Senate to dispatch the military to Mandara to enforce order. It was only to drive up the price of Tethran, Mandara's most valuable export and Senator Queeran's biggest recent investment. The people of Senjele were not fond of the unusual, striped fruit that was all the rage in Noveaux. Senator Clovis had to admit, however, the fruit itself was more appetizing than Senator Queeran's proposal. If there was any resistance on Mandara, it was slight.

"Thank you, Senator," Prince Rebos said after someone seconded the motion. "The Senate will deliberate and vote at our next meeting."

Senator Clovis groaned.

"Now," Rebos continued, his eyes moving over the senators. He raised his voice, not because he needed to—sound carried quite well through the amphitheater—but to draw their undivided attention. "I would like to introduce a motion into the Senate for your immediate consideration."

A murmur went up from the senators. Rebos had submitted motions before, but always in his father's name. As a prince, he couldn't introduce any of his own, not yet, at least.

Rebos raised his hands and the room fell silent. "By now, you will all have heard of the tragedy on Toria and the role Captain Val played."

No. Clovis leaned forward. *Ludus had no part in this proposal.* The realization left a bitter taste in his mouth.

"This Senate would do well to remember the reason Timothy Val was on Toria." Rebos folded his hands over the podium and his face grew stern. It reminded Clovis strongly of the look Chaunstance would give him when he'd had too much to drink. Scolding. "Terrorism is not something Senjele can afford to overlook, especially home-grown terrorism. Initial reports suggest pockets of the Torian resistance were stockpiling illegal weapons—

weapons Governor Opale believes the Erolyians smuggled onto the planet."

The senators exchanged whispers. It wasn't the news that was shocking, only that Rebos would agree with Governor Opale. The two hadn't seen eye to eye on anything since the blight, especially regarding Erolyia. Rebos had always favored a direct confrontation with the neighboring empire, while Opale was firmly in the blockades and treaties camp.

Such a shift in political alliances was big news. It hinted that more deals had been made between the crown and Toria than had been made public. Decisions had been made without consulting the senate first. Executive decisions. As that realization settled into everyone's minds, the whispers swelled into a wave of demands calling for an explanation.

"High Executor Yolen has presented evidence to further back the claim that the Erolyians were supplying the rebels on Toria."

One of the senators in the front—Clovis couldn't tell who—shouted, "What evidence?"

Again, Rebos raised his hands and called for silence. "Evidence that requires further investigation and remains classified as a matter of national security. High Executor Yolen has requested the Senate approve an adjustment to the yearly budget to send two executors to Toria to investigate."

Clovis sighed. Some of this had only come out during the executors' interrogation of Timothy Val, no doubt. Clovis looked around. Every set of eyes he met turned away. The senators seated next to him shifted and toyed with their data pads. They didn't want to challenge the High Executor. Doing so would draw his attention and the last thing anyone in the Senate wanted was the highest law in the land peering into their private lives. They were cowards, the lot of them.

Clovis cleared his throat and stood with a grunt. "Your Highness," he shouted over the din of disgruntled voices.

Rebos turned his face toward the pudgy, clean-shaven senator in the back of the room.

"Is your imperial father aware of this motion?"

Rebos narrowed his eyes and lifted his head. "Emperor Ludus has given me his voice. These may not be his words, but I speak for my father in this matter."

Eloquent and short, Clovis thought. The old senator smiled. "I would be happy to second your motion, Prince Rebos, with a simple modification. We should never make such important decisions with haste. I propose a delay in voting until we convene next, after Senator Queeran's plea has taken the floor."

Senator Queeran nodded her thanks and took to her feet. "I second the motion by Senator Clovis." Even though they didn't matter, a third and a fourth cried out. He only needed Queeran's second to make it so.

Rebos pursed his lips and raised his head. "As you will, senators." Clovis beamed and remained standing. "Is there something else, Senator Clovis?"

"There is. While we are on the subject of Toria, let's discuss Captain Val's illegal incarceration."

"Illegal?" Rebos lifted an eyebrow. "I assure you, Senator, there's no question of the legality of—"

"Spare us, please." A handful of senators shifted in their seats as Clovis's voice echoed off the Senate floor. The reporters perked their ears. "We all know how it should have been handled. I warned this assembly not to send Krail. It's one thing to execute criminals but, from all reports, some of these so-called terrorists were children. Where was their legal representation? Captain Val objected to Krail's vigilante justice. Yet he is arrested for questioning poor leadership, while I stand here, a free man. Why is that?"

"You've killed no one," Rebos pointed out.

Nervous chuckles echoed through the hall.

"I've killed plenty." Clovis raised his voice over the murmurs. "So have you." He pointed to the senator next to him. The room became deathly silent. "And you. And you. I dare say each of us has the blood of Toria on our hands. If not there, some other world. At one time or another, each of us has voted to go to war, to execute, to change laws that resulted in death."

"But those votes are our jobs," said the man beside him. "It's what people elected us to do."

"And Val is a soldier. Killing is what we pay him to do. Captain Val is no traitor. You need only look at his record to see it." Clovis swiped through the data pad in front of him until he found Timothy's service record. "Star of Honor for his chivalric conduct in the Battle of Broken Lines. Distinguished service award at the Battle of Star's Haven. A Hero's Cuff for his service during the Blitz. The people view him as a hero. Just this morning, people were rallying for his release. If the beggars and the bakers are wise enough to know this is wrong, then it is unthinkable for their electorate to ignore their cries for justice."

"The Senate has no bearing on matters of the court," Rebos reminded them. "It isn't the place of this Senate to instruct a judiciary committee, civilian or otherwise, how to interpret the law."

Clovis raised his voice. "What you say is true, Prince Rebos. However, you're missing my point. We, as representatives of the people, have a responsibility to ensure this never happens again. There can be no more trials, military or otherwise, without representation, no matter the offense."

"Are you saying we should defend terrorists?" a senator across the room asked.

"I'm saying we should protect our citizens' basic rights. Timothy Val has seen no more of a trial than Krail's detainees. These days, the executors do whatever they want, whenever they want. All they do is breathe the word terrorism and we flinch. Did we not sit in these very chambers months ago and agree that we would not let fear of the unknown cloud our judgment? That's all I ask of you right now. Let us ensure that no one is above the law. Let us give every offender the right to defend himself, regardless of his crime."

Clovis turned to look at Senator Queeran. "This is a fair law, is it not? Let us appoint a committee to draw it up. Do I have a second?"

There was a heavy silence. Senator Queeran pretended to consult her data pad in a ruse to avoid looking at him. Clovis shook his head. "Is a sense of justice so rare?"

"I will give you your second."

Clovis scanned the room for the source of the hesitant support and found Senator Myran Speardant of Clevennia waving back at him. As the senator representing Timothy's home planet, his voice counted almost for nothing. When the vote fell to the floor, the measure would die. It didn't matter to Clovis. His speech had done its job. The reporters were swaying back and forth in their seats, itching for an adjournment and the interviews that would follow.

Rebos cleared his throat. "Senators, you will have the floor at our next meeting."

The Senate meeting ended and Clovis left, choosing a path to bring him close to Senator Speardant. Myran gave him a respectful nod and said nothing. Myran was a first-term senator with enough dreams of change to spin Senjele backward. For all that, the man lacked courage.

The reporters swarmed Senator Clovis on the Senate steps, all with variations of the same question. He held up his hands, silencing the roar. "Captain Val's case proves only one thing, ladies and gentlemen. The system is corrupt, top-down. Val challenged the slaughter of innocents on Toria. He offered peace and mercy when his superiors wanted blood. The aristocracy of Senjele has been living off the blood and sweat of worlds like Toria for generations and, when they needed help, we answered with violence. Captain Val recognized the foolishness behind the call to arms and the corrupt aristocracy of our empire will stop at nothing to silence him. What do I think should be done?" Clovis slammed his fist into his palm. "They ought to release him, that's what. And pin a medal on his chest for being the only man in the empire with enough balls to do the right thing. Until that happens, I will put my entire fortune into ensuring Timothy Val's defense. It's time someone stood up for him. Enough is enough."

"Senator, what about the fact that the Torian terrorists blew up an imperial building? Should taxpayers have supported the expense of a trial instead of a more economical execution?"

"Any empire claiming to be just and fair, only to turn its back on its most vulnerable citizens, doesn't get the right to determine what is just and fair. Senjele belongs to the people, not to the senate or the emperor. It's time we reminded the aristocracy of that."

Clovis pushed past them and hailed a taxi. Only when he was safely inside did he smile. He scrolled through the headlines on his data pad. The reporters had seized on his final words as if he might never speak again.

CHAPTER THREE

Timothy

The door to Timothy's cell buzzed open and two guards stepped in, blocking the light from the corridor. They were taller than the previous guards, with long, spidery limbs stretching into the blurry edges of darkness. They extended their shock batons with a jerk, switching them on. The high-pitched buzzing made Timothy flinch. The chains around his wrists clanked through no will of his own. He closed his swollen, crusty eyes. Another beating, then.

He did his best to ground himself, straining to balance on his toes against the cold floor. It was the best he could do, considering they'd strung him up so he could only just reach the floor. One man touched the baton to his foot, sending an electric jolt through Timothy's body. The other swung his weapon at Timothy's gut like a bat, as the first slipped behind him and jabbed the blunt end into the back of Timothy's neck.

They asked no questions. These ones never did. The beatings weren't about getting a confession, nor were they a punishment for his insubordination or for the murder of a superior officer. This was about following orders. As much as Timothy wanted to hate the guards, they were common soldiers following the High Executor's orders.

The batons struck his chest, arm, head and shoulders, each blow delivering an agonizing electric shock. The men beat him bloody, until the swings and jabs didn't hurt anymore, and the shocks only made him wince, whimper and jerk, instead of cry out.

Timothy did what he had been trained to do under torture, reciting the words like a prayer. *Captain Timothy Val. Service number forty-six, thirty-four, twenty-eight, nineteen.*

"Enough." A new voice boomed through the room, pulling Timothy from the brink of unconsciousness.

The beating halted. Footsteps receded as the guards retreated to their posts by the door. Timothy cracked open a blood-crusted eye and fought the blackness creeping on the edge of his vision. Another figure stood in the doorway, this one all sharp angles and points. He stepped into the room and touched a button on the wall beside the door. Timothy cringed, expecting the harsh light from the ceiling heat lamps to kick on. But they remained dark. Instead, soft fluorescent lighting buzzed on.

For the first time since being brought into the bowels of the executors' headquarters, the Bloody Keep, Timothy got a look at the room around him. It was a half circle without windows and a floor of bare concrete. A drain sat in a depression beneath him. Blood dripped from him and pooled in a crack near the drain. Timothy watched it, barely aware it was his.

Another executor scurried in without making eye contact with Timothy and set up a portable metal table and a folding chair behind it.

"Good morning, Captain."

Timothy fought to raise his head and regard the new interrogator. He was tall and willowy with gaunt cheeks, small eyes and a sharp nose. Pale, thin lips accented his slit of a mouth. Delicate fingers clutched the briefcase he placed on the metal table before him. He dismissed the other executor with a wave of his hand. "Do you know who I am?" asked the man as he pulled out the chair and sat.

Timothy rubbed his dry lips together. His voice was hoarse and deep. "High Executor Yolen."

The High Executor smiled. "Very good, Captain." He opened his briefcase and took several mundane items out of it: a photo, a tin of biscuits, a bottle of water. "And how are you today? Are you ready to give your confession?"

Timothy fixated on the water. How many days had it been since they'd given him a sip? Two? Three? The ache of dehydration had settled into his limbs. He couldn't remember the last time he'd had a piss.

Yolen rose from his cushioned chair and crossed the distance between his table and his captive in three long strides. He took Timothy's chin in his clammy hands and turned his face, first to one side and then the other. "You look like hell, Captain. It doesn't please me or anyone on Senjele to see you beaten. I've always opposed physical coercion, but the emperor approved its use. And who am I to question his will?" He dug a thumb into an aching spot on Timothy's shoulder. Timothy ground his teeth. "Even Emperor Ludus has said you can't beat a Deyne into submission."

"I'm not a Deyne," Timothy snapped before realizing he'd said it.

Yolen grinned and retracted his hand. "Your mother was, though. You trained with the Deynes, commanded a unit of Deynes in the Nautis blitz. Won a medal for it too, if I'm not mistaken. And since your father struck your name from the Val lines of succession, leaving you a Val in name only …" He shrugged. "You can dye wool any color you like—that doesn't change the fact it itches." Yolen dropped his hands behind his back and went to his table.

Timothy wanted to argue, but even if he'd had the energy to fight, Yolen was right.

"Of course, none of that matters now," Yolen continued. "All the squabbling of lords, all the money and all the titles in the empire don't matter here. In this room, we have only one worry, you and I." He lifted something sleek and silvery.

A knife, Timothy thought, though he wasn't sure. It flashed in the light for only a moment.

Yolen walked back over to him. "Do you know what that worry is, Captain?"

A game. His torturers were fond of guessing games. Guess where we are. *Guess what we want. Guess how much force it takes to crack skulls and break bones*. No matter how well Timothy played, the game never turned out well for him. The last executor bloodied his whole face for his silence and got nowhere. *If I'm going to die, I'll die knowing they had to work for every word that came out of my mouth*. He clamped his jaw shut.

"The truth," Yolen answered.

In one quick movement, he slid a keycard through a reader on the wall. The manacles holding Timothy's wrists retracted, releasing him. Weak and unsupported, Timothy crumpled to the concrete floor, knocking the air from his lungs. Fire spread from his center, followed by numbness. For a moment, he thought he preferred the shock of the batons. When the pain lessened, he realized how comfortable the floor was, although it took all his effort to roll onto his back.

Yolen stood over him, taking him in with those sunken eyes. "You will answer my questions, Captain Val."

Or what, he wanted to ask. Both knew he would not leave the Bloody Keep alive.

Timothy closed his eyes, wishing he could fade into the concrete. He should have died on Toria. Even now, with his hands free, there was no chance of escape. If he managed to get out of the room, he faced a maze crawling with executors, each loyal to Yolen. He'd have to flee the empire he loved too. Timothy found dying preferable, even if Yolen made it a long, drawn-out affair.

"I've been charged with sedition," Timothy answered. "I've got no reason to cooperate. You'll kill me no matter what."

"Let's start from the beginning. Small, simple things. Easy things." Yolen walked back and stood over Timothy again, this time with the bottle of crisp, clear water in his hand. The sight of it made Timothy lick his lips. He reached for the bottle, only to have Yolen jerk it away. "First, your father's name."

Timothy's jaw tightened. That information was harmless enough. Yolen already knew the answer. By now, the High Executor must have known every word of his file by heart. Timothy didn't want to give Yolen the satisfaction of knowing he had won, but didn't know if he was more stubborn than he was thirsty.

"Talmon Val,"

But Yolen didn't give him the water. He unscrewed the cap and took a drink for himself. "And your mother?"

"Risa Val." Timothy fought to get into a sitting position, his eyes never leaving the bottle of water.

"Of course," said Yolen, touching a finger to his chin. "She wasn't always a Val, was she? She was a Deyne before. Doesn't that make you half-Deyne?"

Timothy exploded, pounding his fists against the damp floor. "What does it matter? What does it change?"

Yolen's face spread into a mile and he held the water out. "Tell me what matters."

Timothy stared at the light refracting through the water. His tongue was as dry as sandpaper against the roof of his mouth, swollen and parched. Timothy reached for the water, the answer resting on the tip of his tongue. As his hand stretched out, Yolen's face shifted into that of his father's. At the sight of those dark, distant eyes, Timothy's arm dropped to the floor.

The High Executor sneered and stomped away to drop the bottle in his briefcase. "Let's try a new line of questioning," said Yolen, taking up a print out on photo paper. "Your record shows you took your last leave on the planet Helenia. Do you have an interest in the mining industry, Captain?"

Timothy shook his head and swayed. God damn him. If Yolen had left him tied to the ceiling, he could have looked the High Executor in the eye instead of wallowing on the floor, weak and broken.

"Surveillance says you were interested in drilling Nareen Ambren at least."

He returned and thrust the picture at him, a candid photo of Timothy and Nareen kissing in the gardens behind her home on Helenia. The time stamp placed it at six months earlier, days before a whole chapter of his life had come to a close. Judging by the grainy quality of the photo, and the aerial angle, Timothy guessed a surveillance drone had taken it.

"She's a civilian. What's she got to do with any of this?"

"Perhaps she'll be more forthcoming concerning your involvement with the rebellion. Men often let plans slip over pillow talk."

Timothy shook his head. "I didn't plan what happened on Toria. She had nothing to do with it."

"You murdered a colonel, Val. The same colonel dozens of witnesses saw you fire upon."

"It wasn't like that."

"You murdered Colonel Krail, incited dozens of men to attack Krail's men, and freed fifteen terrorists on the same day the Torian nationalist group blew up the capital building in Den-Mak and attempted to assassinate Emperor Ludus. Am I supposed to take your word that this wasn't part of a planned coup? The sedition charge is laughable. You should be labeled a terrorist along with the men you freed."

"They weren't terrorists! And half of them weren't men. They were boys … children. Women. Farmers." He ran a hand over his face. "They wanted food, access to medicine; the support Senjele promised when they agreed to join the empire."

"They destroyed the capital building with a fertilizer bomb!"

"Only after the government refused to help them treat the blight!" Timothy fought to get to his feet and strained against the chains around his ankles. Yolen stepped out of Timothy's reach. "When we liberated Olarin, there were children eating rocks." He shook his head. "You executed the men who planted the bomb in the capital building.

Why should the people of Olarin pay for their crime?"

"They took up arms against the empire," said Yolen, raising his chin. "Your men died liberating the city. Do you not want to see their killers brought to justice?"

Timothy shook his head again. The people of Olarin had been defending their home—from invaders who had promised them the glory and resources of the galaxy's largest and richest empire only to let them starve and die. Senjele had not kept its end of the bargain, and so Toria had seceded from the union. But Toria was a farming world, exporting wheat, sugar, and rice. They had only joined the empire because they didn't have the men or resources to resist the Senjelian war machine as it closed in on them. "There's no such thing as justice for the damned."

Yolen sighed. "Tell me about your argument with Colonel Krail."

"Why don't you watch the feed from your drones?"

"Because I want to hear what you have to say about it."

When Timothy didn't answer, Yolen retreated to his briefcase and rummaged through it before he returned. The High Executor grabbed Timothy's arm tight, holding it so Timothy couldn't jerk free. There was a sudden prick and Timothy turned his head to see Yolen pushing on the plunger of a syringe. His head spun, and his stomach lurched. If it hadn't been empty, he would have vomited.

"Do you feel that? That's Verifex in your veins, Captain. The sour feeling will pass momentarily, and you'll be much more at ease." Even before Yolen finished speaking, Timothy's limbs tingled as if they'd fallen asleep.

Verifex ... Timothy wondered why he wasn't in a state of panic. Like every officer, he'd been trained to withstand pain. But Verifex—the thought of having pain-inducing nanites in his bloodstream, latching onto his nerve endings to activate on command made his pulse quicken.

Yolen lifted a remote with a single button. "Let's try this again. Detail how you shot Colonel Krail."

Timothy took a deep breath to steel himself for the pain to come, concentrating as his shoulders rose and fell. It didn't matter what he said anymore. Nothing mattered. Even if the nanites bit into every nerve ending in his body, even if Yolen let them chew into him, he wouldn't give him what he wanted.

"Go fuck yourself."

Pain flooded his body. Every muscle jerked and spasmed. He opened his mouth to scream, but the sound came out as a series of desperate grunts. Pressure built at the base of his skull, in his chest, in his neck, as his body fought to compensate for the sudden flood of pain. It was a moment, the space of a lightning flash and no more. But it was enough.

Yolen deactivated the nanites with the push of a button. Timothy fell, groaning against the grate.

"It's much more entertaining when you're stubborn." Yolen's voice lorded over him. The High Executor slammed his thumb back down on the button.

Pure agony rushed through Timothy's veins again. It was fire and electricity merged. It was white-hot and freezing cold all at once. He writhed and jerked, unable to think or breathe or control anything. When the pain stopped, he collapsed. The cement floor was heaven against his hot skin. He curled into a fetal position as aftershocks rocked him in waves of pain and he wept openly.

There was no reprieve. The guards hauled him up. Yolen took Timothy's chin in his hands. "It may take longer to break you, but I will. I'll break you from the inside out."

"Then do it," Timothy said.

Yolen raised the remote, his finger hovering over the button.

The cell door opened. Yolen released his hold on Timothy as a muffled voice spoke to him from the doorway. Timothy's mind was already far away, dreaming of burning fields and hungry children, withered farmers and the unmarked graves of thousands. *What difference did I make? For all this fighting, not one thing has changed. Not one damn thing.*

"Put him back in chains," Yolen ordered with a sneer. "We'll finish this later."

The order was a welcome one. It meant an end to his torture, however temporary. But after the relief, anger and regret settled in. Yolen would be back and, meanwhile, he would hang and suffer. The end would remain where it had been all along, out of reach.

The High Executor collected his things and left the room in a hurry.

The guards raised Timothy's arms above his head, put his wrists together and chained him back up. Timothy was too weak to fight them. The chains would keep him upright, at least.

"Talk to him," urged one guard. "It'll save you a lot of pain."

Timothy blinked, surprised to hear a woman's voice. In the dark, he hadn't been able to see who was beating him. Their strikes had been so fierce, he could only imagine them as men. They'd never spoken to him before. In the unflattering executor guard uniform, with their matching hats, he still couldn't tell which one it was.

"Shut up," hissed the other guard, this one male. "Yolen will have your head for talking to him."

The woman, the one on the right, looked at the other guard. "He deserves better treatment than this, Stantis. A dog deserves better."

"Talk like that and Yolen will put you right next to him."

The two of them said nothing more to each other as they finished chaining him up. As the male guard turned to go, the woman hesitated, looking Timothy over. "Sorry," she said in the lowest of whispers.

"Come on! Let's go!"

The woman tucked her head low and exited with the other guard.

Timothy did not let himself weep again until they were gone.

CHAPTER FOUR

Cylene

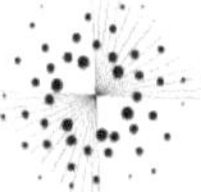

The empress quickened her pace down the gold-plated corridor. Her footsteps echoed on the marble floor as she neared the throne room, attended by two of her ladies. They were young things, with plenty of pink in their baby-fat cheeks. They would come into their full beauty soon, and she would have to send them away. The thought almost saddened her. It *was* for their own good. These girls were too delicate to survive here. Nebarius was a city of cannibals, with every man hungry to devour even the most innocent girl if it meant he had just a little more gold or power.

The youngest of the ladies, Desmanda, turned her head to see past the wings of her white training bonnet, so she could look at her mistress. "Your Eminence, perhaps it would be safer in the tower?"

The empress smoothed her hands over the velvety bodice of her dress and stretched her neck to ease the weight of her crown. "Our safety shouldn't be your primary concern."

Desmanda fixed her gaze forward. "The safety of the emperor must always come first." The girl's voice quivered when she spoke. When she walked, her steps were uneven and quick.

Cylene stopped mid-stride and turned. Desmanda averted her gaze to the ground, but Cylene lifted the girl's delicate chin with two fingers and smiled into those big, brown doe eyes. To every girl tending her body and her chambers, the empress was equal parts mother and mistress. She cared for her girls, but there was always one who needed firmer direction.

"Child, you needn't concern yourself with the safety of the emperor." She dropped the girl's chin and patted the pressure-sealed vial she wore around her neck. "Should the worst happen, a lady's only concern is preserving her dignity in death."

Desmanda paled.

"No worries, child. It won't happen with this rabble. I will make certain of it."

Ludus's personal guards stepped between them and the intricately carved throne room doors as they approached, hands straying toward their guns. Her ladies stiffened as the guards recited the emperor's orders not to be disturbed. Cylene parted the girls with a hand and stepped to the front. She had but to turn her gaze on these so-called war-hardened men before they averted their eyes and stepped aside. She waited until they opened the doors before stepping into the outer chamber and past the weapons scanners, waiting for the computer to clear them.

"Mistress," Desmanda started, her voice shaking. "The penalty for disobeying a direct order from the emperor is death."

"Do you fear for your safety, child?"

Desmanda averted her eyes once again. "Only yours, Mistress."

Ah, there was the source of her anxiety, the worthless urge for self-preservation. Cylene didn't understand why everyone was so afraid of Death. He was coming for them all. True power rested in having the ability to choose the time and place where one met Death. She couldn't explain it to these girls; they weren't ready.

"There are two sources of power in the empire, child. The first is the emperor's signet ring, the seal irrevocable and unmistakable. It commands the absolute loyalty of our people, sends men marching to their deaths, and burns cities on a whim."

The scanner buzzed and the inner chamber doors slid open with a hiss.

"And the second source, Mistress?"

"The loins of the empress," recited the other girl, Briar. Cylene almost smiled, but suppressed how impressed she was. There was hope for her yet.

The throne room was empty but for the emperor and his whores. There were six of them. Some danced barefoot on the marble floors; some sat at the foot of the throne, braiding each other's hair. One even sat on the emperor's lap, wearing nothing but a banner bearing the sigil of House Eflor. Cylene recognized one of her previous ladies-in-waiting.

As soon as the doors opened, their giggling ceased. Against the silence, Empress Cylene took a deep breath, put one foot forward and fell into an exaggerated curtsy.

Her girls mimicked her movements.

The emperor pushed the naked woman off his lap and unfolded himself to stand. The gold and crimson robes hung off his thin body like a funeral robe on a corpse. He straightened the crooked crown over his silver, receding hairline. "What do you want, woman? I'm busy."

"A crowd of protesters has gathered outside the palace, as I'm sure your Imperial Highness is well aware," Cylene said without rising. "They are demanding the release of Timothy Val."

Ludus motioned for the girls to go. They stopped only to collect their discarded bits of clothing. With the whores gone, Ludus ordered Cylene and her girls to stand. He descended the steps and put his hands behind his back. "What would you have me do?"

"Free him!"

Both the emperor and empress turned at the sound of Annon's voice. The emperor sighed as his son strode into the throne room. Cylene couldn't help but mimic her husband. Her youngest son was sweet and attractive, having inherited her high cheekbones and chestnut hair. Even if he had his father's eyes and ears, there was no mistaking Annon was his mother's son. He was dangerously naïve though. He let his feelings and relationships guide too many of his decisions. Annon and Timothy had been friends once and, even though it was long ago, she knew the captain held a dear place in Annon's heart.

"Annon," said the emperor, rubbing his mottled forehead. "It isn't that simple."

"You're the emperor. Issue an imperial edict ordering his release."

Cylene stepped between them. "Toria began with riots before the governor's mansion and well-intentioned but misguided leadership," she reminded Annon and then turned to her husband. "You must reassert your authority. This farce has gone on long enough. It's time for the law to silence Captain Val, before there's more blood on your hands."

"That blood is on Colonel Krail's hands," Annon said, turning to his mother, "and executing Timothy will anger the people more. He's a hero to them. They'll use his death as a rallying cry. Father, you'll lose control of more worlds in his death than just Toria. You know it's true."

Cylene reached out to her son and caressed his cheek. The poor boy had no grasp of the situation. How many riots had he seen? How many revolts? Annon couldn't see the reality of the impending riot. This mob would only be satisfied with blood. If they didn't execute Val, it might be royal blood they demanded next. "Annon, I know Timothy is your friend, but you can't let your feelings determine what's best for Senjele."

"Don't preach to me," Annon said, pulling away from her fingers. "People are dying of disease and starvation on Toria while we throw food away. They have every right to be upset."

"Enough!" Emperor Ludus's voice echoed off the dome ceiling, shaking Cylene's attention from her son. The emperor walked back to the throne with slow, shuffling steps and eased himself into it. Shaking his head, he said, "The empire must hold someone accountable. The crown cannot ignore blatant sedition and murder."

Annon knelt before the throne. "How is it seditious to object to the unlawful killing of women, children and invalids? There is a reason those people fought and died for Timothy Val on Toria, and during the Nautis Blitz. Kill him, and you create a martyr. You'll give them a symbol to stand behind All you will do is unite people under a banner against you."

Cylene wrinkled her nose and turned away. Annon was right. Alive, Val was far less dangerous, though she didn't think it would matter either way. Senjele was falling apart. Ludus's hesitation to respond to the matter only compounded the problem, planting seeds of doubt in people's mind. The people of Senjele needed better, more capable leadership. This old man, so disconnected from his people he couldn't even be bothered to calm a crisis … the time had come and gone for him to pass his mantle to Rebos.

Emperor Ludus leaned forward to touch his son on the shoulder. "It's barely been a week since there was an attempt on my life, Annon. You could be next. As hard as it is to accept, your friend may have had a part in it."

Annon shook his head and narrowed his eyes. "He didn't. I'm sure of it."

Ludus sighed. "I'll consider it and come to a decision before the end of the day." She heard his bones creak as he leaned back. "Cylene?"

She glided forward and gave an even lower curtsy. "Yes, Your Eminence?"

"Where is Rebos?"

"At the Senate meeting, as you commanded."

"The Senate closed hours ago," Ludus snapped. "If he is out drinking again—"

"There are worse vices a ruler can harbor than a little drink to wash the bitter taste of the Senate from his palate."

The emperor narrowed his eyes, hardening his face. "Where is my son?"

Annon stood and slunk backward, but even in his worst rages, Ludus never directed his fury at Annon. He saved it for his heir and his wife. Cylene put a comforting hand on Annon's shoulder but spoke to her husband. "I don't know. I'll send for him, but I suggest you do whatever it is you're going to do quickly. Those protesters are getting angrier every minute. Senator Clovis has them wrapped around his fat little finger." She turned to her son, guiding him away. "Come, Annon. Let's find your brother."

He glared at her, and at his father, and then wriggled free of her grasp. "Find him yourself," he snarled at her and stormed away.

Cylene moved to follow Annon, but stopped when Ludus called her name. "I've another task for you, Cylene. My council of advisors has assembled in the lower chamber. You will attend in my place since Rebos isn't available."

She flashed him a coy smile. "My emperor, I'm sure the council would delight in your direct words considering all that is happening."

"You speak with my voice," Ludus assured her. She watched his greedy eyes scan Desmanda's body. "I have other engagements."

Cylene gave her husband another exaggerated curtsy. "As you command," she said, and retreated to the door. "Chin up, Desmanda." She gathered her skirts and squared her jaw. "A lady must always carry herself with dignity."

The empress left her ladies in her suite to prepare it for the night, and traversed the stone staircase into the bowels of the keep to the council chambers. Here, the emperor's chair remained empty, rising like a great, black shadow.

Legend said the great Aldred Ambren had constructed

it in the ancient mountain forges of Helenia. The stories said the smoky, black steel drank in the sorcerer smith's miasma of blood and fire, giving the chair its strange, reflective surface. Some said the chair had the power to reveal a great man's true self in its reflection. The chair was as old as the Eflorian line, if not older, but Cylene didn't believe it had any power. When the emperor sat in it, the chair made him look even more shriveled. The emperor's long absence at the council meetings made it difficult to recall anyone aside from Senjele's heir sitting in the chair now. Rebos fit into it as if the seat were an extension of him. He was this council's voice of reason, their firm and unyielding leader, and yet even he had been absent too much of late.

The men at the table rose and offered her a courteous bow, one by one, some with much more embellishment than others. Cylene stiffened her back, took her customary seat beside the great, reflective chair, and called the meeting to order.

Caleres Utan, the rotund and aged Minister of Foreign Affairs, presented a report on their relations with the neighboring empire of Erolyia. Tensions were growing at the border. Erolyian scout ships dipped in and out of the far boundaries of the demilitarized zone around Yoris, testing the waters of their young treaty. Rebos would want to respond with a show of force, but their military was dealing with the aftermath of what had happened on Toria. The Erolyians knew this, and would take advantage of the empire's weakened state. They had agents in place, inciting civil unrest in many of the outer systems. Ludus would want to mass a force at the border and send an expensive caravan to aid Yoris and sway the people's opinion toward Senjele. It wouldn't work. Such caravans never did. Even all the way out there, the people saw the news. The people of Yoris would never trust an emperor willing to gun down his own citizens to hold onto his fleeting power.

Lord Utan drummed his fingers on the table. "Your Imperial Highness, this situation must be dealt with."

"I'm aware." She tried to sound firm and confident, but her voice came out shrill.

General Hallow, the Minister of Defense, tugged at the white whiskers on his chin. "Perhaps it would be best if we postponed this meeting until the emperor is available."

"I am here as his proxy," Cylene answered. "It is my right."

Reva Tzu, the short and pale man at the other end of the table, lowered the oxygen mask from over his face and nodded. "So it is, Your Highness. Perhaps this matter is best dealt with in the long term."

"Then let our first order of business be to know why you are here, sir," said the general, his cold, blue eyes fixed on Reva.

Reva opened his mouth, but the empress stilled him with her hand. "He is here because Rebos and I wish him to be. Or do you demand a more thorough explanation from your empress, General?"

"Your Highness …" Hallow's lower lip protruded, giving him a pouty look. "These are sensitive matters of the highest order. We discuss state secrets in this room. It's a matter of national security, not of any concern to a … public relations specialist."

Reva offered a smug grin. "Secrets are my only concern. My livelihood depends on ensuring the secrets of the imperial family remain secret. General, think of me as a loss prevention and damage control device. I can't protect a commodity if I don't have access to it."

Hallow's face contorted. "The imperial family is not a commodity, sir!"

"Their image is. If you don't believe me, read the news. Political campaigns are won and lost in the P.R. department, rebellions thwarted with a carefully omitted phrase—"

"Good advertising can crush a rebellion? That's the funniest thing I've heard all day." The general laughed, but no one joined him.

"Well," answered Reva, "military operations haven't dulled the roar of rebellion in the Torian system."

"Take your seat," Cylene ordered when the general rose in challenge to Reva. "Or I'll find another who will."

Hallow sank into the cushioned comfort of his chair, biting his lower lip.

Cylene continued. "Mr. Tzu makes a good point. I think Toria, and its aftermath, are on everyone's mind."

Lord Rais exchanged a careful glance with Lord Utan. They were old servants of Ludus', and unloved by Rebos. *As soon as my son is emperor, he will see this table filled with fresh and obedient minds.* Her gaze drifted to Reva, sipping his triple purified water from the wine goblet. *Loyal minds.*

The rest of the council turned their attention to the data pads in front of them. Lord Rais cleared his throat. "As I informed the imperial prince, we are facing a serious budgeting issue. The rerouting of our shipping corridors through the Lokurian gate has been a monumental expense. Our previous budget assumed normal operations would resume once control of the Torian system returned to imperial rule. We should have seen a dip in inflation in the outlying worlds as the economy stabilized and normalcy returned. Unfortunately, the blight makes this impossible. There are ways to combat it, but, without raising taxes or slashing other programs, we cannot bear the expense. Lokuria and Majoria have been working at double their standard rate to produce enough food for the empire, but the cost of importing necessities from the outlying worlds is higher than it would have been to import from Toria." He took a deep breath. "I'm predicting a shortfall in the imperial budget of no less than five billion credits, if nothing is done."

Cylene shifted on her cushion. "What do you propose, Lord Rais?"

"When the coffers fall short, there are only two possible solutions, Empress." Cylene could see tiny droplets of sweat forming on his brow. "Either we tighten our belts, or we pass the burden to the citizens of the empire."

"Neither of those will be popular options," Reva said.

The empress frowned, staring once again at the empty chair beside her. "Perhaps we could borrow the money."

Lord Rais raised his eyebrow. "Five billion credits? You will be hard pressed to find anyone with that kind of capital, short of the Erolyian crown."

"King Vyjorin would sooner swallow boiling oil than lend us a single gold coin," Lord Utan said, shaking his head. "We're one wrong word from a war with the Erolyians. They haven't forgotten Nautis."

Cylene pursed her lips. "Nor have we. We won't go begging to the Erolyians for their scraps. Who else is there?"

Lord Rais scrolled through his screens. "Private houses, perhaps, but the fees would be astronomical ..."

Reva cleared his throat again. "My lords, may I make a humble suggestion?" The room fell silent, all eyes heavy on Reva. "The houses are fickle and hoard money for their progeny. Perhaps they will lend us some but not in such a large amount. Why not seek finance from a private company instead?"

"Such as?" General Hallow asked.

"The IRMA Mining Company has more than enough revenue to cover those expenses. Given their longstanding and mutually beneficial agreement with the imperial crown, I'm sure they could be persuaded to do it with little interest."

Before he even spoke, Cylene understood his suggestion. From a political standpoint, it was sound advice, but to hear the name of the company spoken aloud made her taste bile. Illion had been her home not so long ago, and this IRMA Company had all but destroyed it, toppling ancient temples and rerouting rivers over priceless landmarks, all in the name of some elusive mineral resource.

"No!" she spat. "The crown will have no further dealings with thieves."

A heavy silence settled over the table. Cylene shook her head. "Lord Rais, speak with ambassadors from each of the houses. Re-evaluate your budget; see where we might tighten our belt. Let us see what we can pull together before we take any … drastic measures."

Lord Rais almost stammered when he spoke. "Y-Yes, Your Highness."

"Good. What else is there?"

General Hallow cleared his throat. "There is the matter of relief supplies for Toria."

Could these men speak of nothing else? Toria never should have happened. The first major task Ludus had entrusted to Rebos and it had ended in complete disaster, all because of a few weak links in the chain of command. The rest of the empire thought it was a sign her son would be a cruel and incompetent ruler. What did those half-naked peasants in the street know of ruling? What did they know of the pressures, the sacrifices she and her family faced every day so they could wallow in their own misery? Yet the common rabble held power, as Timothy Val was fast proving.

"I do not wish to discuss Toria. Ludus entrusted Toria to Prince Rebos. Is there nothing else?"

The emperor's advisors scrolled through their data pads, looking for less pertinent tasks for her to deal with. Lord Utan lifted his head, the folds in his chin quivering as he spoke. "Your Highness, there is the matter of Ionia Wicks."

"Ionia Wicks?" The empress rubbed her forehead. "Should I know that name, Lord Utan?"

Reva Tzu folded his hands one over the other and rested them on the table. "I know it. She was a former employee of yours, one of Prince Annon's tutors." He scrolled through his data pad screen. "She resigned her post a year ago, citing illness." He passed his data pad to Cylene. The picture in the profile might have been familiar, but so many women came and went it was impossible for Cylene to keep track of them all. She was an unattractive thing, round in the face with big, heavy breasts and frizzy red hair. Young, but not young enough to entice the interest of her sons.

"More than a tutor, if her claim is valid."

"Claim?" Cylene slid the data pad back to Reva. "What claim?"

"Ms. Wicks has petitioned the council for monetary support for her child in the amount befitting the upbringing of a bastard child of Eflorian blood."

Cylene clenched her fists in her lap. Ludus lusted after every woman in the empire but her. This wasn't the first bastard child nor was it likely to be the last. The casual tone these lords used when referring to the breach of what tiny shred of honor she had left … It was all she could do to put forward a calm and collected demeanor. "I assume Ms. Wicks has produced irrefutable proof of the child's ancestry?"

Utan shrugged. "The DNA sample appears to be in order."

"And what is the monthly support allocation for bastards?"

"Ten thousand credits, your highness, a mere pittance."

She gave a strained smile. "It's a pity we can't do more for these poor women. How many royal bastards are accounted for?"

"Eight, Your Highness," Utan reported. "The support payments are authorized only if the mother and child renounce all claim to legitimacy, swear an oath of fealty and agree to a life of seclusion … for the child's safety. Some might wish them harm."

The empress offered a dry smile. "I can't imagine it. Lord Rais, can the treasury bear this burden?"

Lord Rais's mouth fell open. "Your Highness, perhaps I was unclear. We are facing a shortfall of *five billion credits*. The treasury can bear no expenses. We risk defaulting on our current debts."

Empress Cylene rose from her seat and the emperor's advisors rose with her. "I will find the capital for Ms. Wicks personally. My apologies, my lords, for cutting our meeting short. I am not the bureaucrat my husband and son are. Please, see yourselves out." She turned her back to them, listening to their boots scrape and shuffle over the floor. "Mr. Tzu, you stay."

When they were alone, his footsteps echoed through the chamber, slow and heavy, the sound in all four corners at once. In a moment, he was beside her, sipping water from his crystalline goblet. She turned her head as his flowery scent filled her nose. "You are never to speak of the IRMA Company again in my presence. Ever. Am I clear?"

"My apologies. I did not realize the wound was so fresh." He took another sip, swirling the water first as if it were wine. "What will you do about the Wicks woman and the other bastards?"

Empress Cylene folded her hands in front of her and set her jaw squarely. "Do you still have contact with your Outer Rim mercenary troop?"

"Of course."

"Put me in contact. I have a job for them."

CHAPTER FIVE

Timothy

An eternity passed before the door to Timothy's cell opened again. He didn't recognize the guard at first. It was dark. His head was throbbing and his vision was shaky. Last time, he hadn't even gotten a good look at her. When she didn't beat him, he thought it might be the woman from before.

She came closer, placing a bucket on the floor. He heard water being wrung from a cloth and a moment later something cool and wet pressed against his forehead. He flinched, expecting her to change tactics and hit him again. "I'm not here to hurt you," she whispered and uncapped a water bottle. She held the top of it against his mouth.

Timothy hesitated and let the water pour down his

chin, even though he wanted nothing more than to gulp it down. The water could be poisoned or drugged. He didn't think Yolen was above those tactics to get a confession. But then, what did it matter? They would kill him anyway. He swallowed the first mouthful with caution and forgot she'd been beating him not so long ago.

"Not too fast," she warned. "You'll shock your system."

He took one more mouthful, savoring the cool water before swallowing. "Who are you?"

"A friend."

"I don't have friends, not here."

She screwed the lid back onto the bottle.

"Did Yolen send you?"

She shook her head. "Keep your voice down. He'll hang me upside down beside you if he finds me in here." She dabbed a cut on his forehead with the rag. "I'm sorry I had to strike you. If I didn't …"

"If the order given by a superior officer is unjust, it's a soldier's duty not to obey."

She paused in wiping the blood and dirt on his face. "Is that what happened with Krail?"

Timothy turned his head away.

"It's not so easy when your commanding officer is the High Executor. Yolen has the power to depose lords and topple the Senate if he chooses. He is the law given form and mind. He—"

"Save me the propaganda speech, guard."

She sighed and lowered her arm. "I'm not a guard. I'm an executor."

He narrowed his eyes at her. She wasn't as old as he'd first guessed, perhaps even younger than he. A fresh graduate, maybe, and clearly uncomfortable with how Yolen was handling the situation, but she wasn't a friend.

"I've been branded a traitor. A terrorist. I'm an enemy of the state," he said. "Why haven't I been executed? Why does Yolen want a confession so badly?"

Her lips parted and her eyes went wide, but a noise at the door gave her pause. She dropped the water bottle into her belt, grabbed the bucket and walked away from him, reaching the door as it opened. High Executor Yolen eyed her from the doorway, but stepped aside when he saw the bucket and a scrub brush in her hand. "Carry on, Executor Kaarsgard," he said, and she rushed away as soon as he stepped inside.

Timothy strained to pull himself upright in the chains. "Do you question all your prisoners personally, or are these visits just for me?"

Yolen didn't answer. He paced to the desk and opened the file, pretending to read. "I knew your father."

"My father was a senator and Lord Governor of Clevennia. Everyone knew him."

"I knew your mother, too. A beautiful woman, Risa Deyne. Proud, too, for a commoner. It's not surprising, though. You Vals were great once, but so was every noble family. Gods, there are so many! How do you blue bloods keep them all straight? If there is one family that has become insignificant and forgotten, it's the Val family. But not you. No. You made a name for yourself, despite being disowned. Amazing when you think about it."

"I don't."

"Do you never think about the people you killed to get where you are?" Yolen looked up. "I mean, you're a soldier. You've been to war, earned medals and commendations. You've killed people. How many orphans and widows have you made?" Yolen smiled when Timothy shifted in his chains. "All those men, following orders, doing their jobs while defending their homeland

and you walked away. Yet the one that gets you in trouble, the one death destroying you, is your own countryman. What's worse, he was from Clevennia, just like you. Are you asking yourself why this one matters when there were so many others? Why you? How it came to this?"

Timothy didn't answer.

Yolen came over to stand in front of him with his hands behind his back. "You're not special. You're not a hero. You're a common criminal."

Timothy leaned forward, straining against his chains. "Then take me down and kill me like one."

"Senjele needs a confession from you, Timothy Val. No one will rise up and save the people from the tyranny of the unjust and the apathy of the ruling class. That's not how life works. There are no heroes. There are only thieves and killers, and behind each one, propaganda and lies."

Timothy searched the High Executor's face and found it empty. "What happened to make you such a miserable bastard?"

"The world happened to me; now I happen to it."

The two men stared at each other for a good, long while in silence before Yolen took out his key and freed Timothy's hands. Still too weak to stand, Timothy sank to his knees.

For a moment, Timothy considered trying to choke the High Executor. Someone would discover him eventually, and Timothy would be taken to a firing squad. Death was his destination anyway. Why not take Yolen with him?

It wouldn't make any difference because killing this one man would change nothing. Someone else would rise through the ranks and take his place, and things would go on as they always had. The Senjelian judicial system was a well-oiled machine with decades of practice. The kinks had been worked out of the system, and the empire stood ready and able to make a carbon copy of the High Executor.

"I'll ask you one more time," Yolen said, his voice calm and even. "Will you confess to willfully and deliberately murdering Colonel Krail and to your involvement in the staging of a coup with the Torian rebels?"

"No."

Yolen squatted in front of Timothy and grabbed his hair. "Give me something." He hissed the last word. His face was so close Timothy could taste his aftershave in the air. "Don't make me kill you for nothing. If you won't do it to save yourself, do it to give this gods-forsaken empire some closure. You rebels have torn her apart. Do you know how many people will die because of what you've done?"

The executor pushed Timothy's head away and rose to pace. He walked to the far wall and rested his forehead against it.

Yolen had a point. Even if his execution were public, Timothy had thrown fuel onto the fire of rebellion. He hadn't meant to. All he'd wanted was to object to the unjust treatment of captured prisoners. If explaining what happened could help the empire heal, what was the harm in it? They would kill him anyway, so he had nothing to lose.

"I won't confess to it," Timothy said. "But if it means so much, I'll tell you the same thing I've been saying all along. I didn't plan for it to happen. I was on the ground, fighting for the gun with one of Krail's soldiers. It went off and burned a hole through his neck. I don't work with the Torian nationalists or for them. I'm not, nor will I ever be, aligned with the rebels. My loyalty is where it has always been—with Senjele. I've lived my life as a soldier. I'm prepared to die every day I wake up. If I have to die today, then so be it."

Yolen pushed away from the wall. He pulled his sidearm and stormed over to Timothy. Standing behind him, he pressed the barrel against Timothy's head, sleek and cool and welcome. "Tell me one thing before you die, Captain, just one thing. What you did on Toria, do you have any regrets? Knowing how this ends—you, a big, black stain on the Val family name after nine generations of loyalty—dead and buried in an unmarked traitor's grave. Would you have done the same thing? Would you have shot General Krail?"

A bubble burst in his chest, numbness spreading into his limbs. He wasn't sure if it was the drugs or the adrenaline, but for the first time since they'd strung him up in the Bloody Keep, Timothy felt free. His body shook as he swallowed the gathering dryness in his throat.

"If killing him meant saving everyone else, then, yes, I'd do it in a heartbeat." He squeezed his eyes tight as the gun buzzed to life with a high-pitched whirr. Yolen pulled the trigger.

Nothing happened.

Silence echoed through the room. Yolen lowered the weapon and tucked it into his belt before collecting his briefcase.

"I-I don't understand," Timothy stuttered.

"There's been an imperial edict ordering your release," the High Executor said.

Timothy shivered. "The gun …"

Yolen closed the clasps on the briefcase. "Was never loaded."

"But I-I confessed to sedition!"

"An inadmissible confession under coercion in the

course of an illegal trial." Two more shadows appeared in the doorway as Yolen made for the exit. "Clean him up," he ordered. "And call someone to collect him."

Timothy slumped forward, his forehead resting against his hands, shaking. If he'd had the water to waste, he would have wept, not for the joy of freedom or the pleasure of having his life spared by a timely imperial edict, but for letting Yolen win.

CHAPTER SIX

Vyjorin

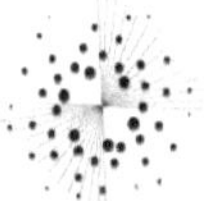

Summer in the Erolyian desert was stifling. The promise of rain hung in the air like a perfume, sweet, wet and dark. From atop his raised cushion, King Vyjorin Thagg sipped at bitter wine and wished it were water. He watched as two eunuchs rubbed crushed ice over his wife's bare back. The tiny, sparkling cubes melted almost as soon as they touched her, dampening the lower half of her dress. Water trickled over her shoulders and swollen breasts and onto the growing bump in her belly to pool in her lap. The new eunuch he had bought for her waved a feather fan in front of her face.

"You're sure?" he asked the informant who knelt with his face on the ground before them.

"Yes, Great One," the man said into the sand. "I verified the information thoroughly. The Senate on Senjele is launching a full investigation. They blame Erolyia for the uprising on Toria, saying the crown supplied Torian rebels with arms. This humble servant will recount what his lowborn eyes have seen in greater detail if it would please you."

"No." Vyjorin took another sip of the wine and sent it away. "It's too damn hot for stories."

"I want to hear." His wife, Kihran, leaned back on her hands and let the ice melt on her fine neck.

She's still such a girl, Vyjorin thought. Her eighteenth year was still a month away. Still, Kihran had won the honor of his bed in the temple rite, and if she bore him a son, he would make her his queen. He had no need of another wife. Of those, he had plenty, eight in all, each as barren as the sands that bore them.

"Please, love. Please?"

"What does it matter? The rabid empire tasted our blood at Nautis and are brazen in sending raiding parties into the demilitarized zone under the guise of peace to harass and disrupt our captains. They want their war. I am of a mind to give it to them."

Vyjorin shifted on his cushion and wished for the comfort of holding court in the shade of his garden. In the Sands, the region he and Kihran were touring, the sun was so wild and fierce that he had to keep someone on hand to rub oil into his skin, otherwise, it would dry and peel. He had given up wearing all but the lightest of clothing here, and often wore only the silken leggings the locals wore. Even in the most intense heat, however, he wore the great, brass eye that dangled over his sternum. The Eye of the King saw all.

He motioned for the informant to raise his head.

"Rise, sir."

The man rose but kept his eyes sealed tightly shut, as custom dictated. Kihran should have worn her veil but even Vyjorin admitted it was too hot. He didn't know how she could stand to leave her platinum hair trailing into the small of her back in this heat.

"You look to be born of sand and salt. How did you come to witness these things on Senjele?"

"Your Greatness ..." the man swallowed and his voice quivered. "This humble one went to take slaves from the Expanse into the Senjelian market."

Vyjorin frowned and leaned forward. "You are aware of the royal decree banning the sale of any goods or services from Erolyians to Senjelians without my express, written consent?"

The man nodded.

"Have I given you consent?"

The slaver shook his head, sending droplets of sweat flying.

"How many times have you broken the decree?" When the man was silent, Vyjorin rose, his hand wrapped around the heavy chain that hung from his neck. "Speak true and you will have nothing to fear. The king sees all."

The man fell flat on his face and answered in desperation. "Six, great one! Six times this unworthy fool has broken your laws!"

The king nodded to his eunuchs, who came forward to grab the man. "Then you will lose six toes for your treachery. Leave his big toes."

The eunuchs dragged the man away.

"You always ruin my fun, love." Kihran plunged her fingers into the ice bowl, brought out a large chunk and popped it into her mouth before continuing. "Why bother with the poor man's toes? Just take his head and be done with it."

"He can't learn from his mistakes if he's dead," Vyjorin reminded her. "And the uneducated dead have few uses to the living."

"But to live mutilated like that … it's such a shameful thing. Be merciful, my love. Kill the man."

Vyjorin winced at the crunching sound as she dug in the ice. He snatched the bowl of ice away from the pudgy-faced eunuch. "Away. Tell the others to move us. I want to be in Pearl Waters by dusk." He dismissed them all and took Kihran firmly by the wrists. "Come, wife."

She resisted him only until he let her grab the bowl of ice to take with them. Once she had it, he carried her up the steps and into the shaded silk tent behind his cushioned throne. As he ducked inside, the stones beneath them lurched forward and the great mobile palace of Erolyia began the slow journey west.

Somewhere below them, dozens of slaves slid along the narrow passageways, oiling the gears and mending the circuitry that made the palace mobile. It moved on a continuous track like the battle tanks of old. Dozens of tracks rolled along the desert, propelling them forward. There were faster means of travel, but none more luxurious. And part of the reason he and Kihran were touring now was to project his power, to remind the people of Erolyia that rebellions such as the one at Toria would not be tolerated. Nothing said power like a palace.

Their royal quarters were small but sufficient. The sheer fabric of the tent housed a circular mattress piled high with pillows and thin blankets, two ornate chests, and a mirror that doubled as a communication device, should he wish to speak to anyone. It was also home to two blind eunuchs. Even without their manhood, Vyjorin didn't like their eyes on his wife, and so he had ordered them to pluck out their own eyes. They didn't need their eyes to kill unannounced intruders. They were as deadly as any whole man with their blades, perhaps more so because they were full men no longer.

Vyjorin lowered his wife to the floor. He tossed the ice lazily onto the bed, spreading it gently with his hands. Kihran toyed with the braid in her hair and the silver rings she wore in it. "Why are you so interested in Senjelian politics," she asked as he undressed her.

"Because their policies decide many of mine."

"But you're a king, my love. A king should do as he likes."

"A king should do as he must." He checked to make sure his eunuchs were in their place, standing at the entrance with their backs to him.

"But—"

"Be silent. None of that matters right now." He fell onto the bed and pulled her down on top of him. There was no other way to do it now, since she was many months along. *The child will come soon*, Vyjorin thought. She was soft and widened already. The old women said it was good to pleasure a woman so close to her time. It would make the birth less difficult.

He could redirect her thoughts easily enough, but a fear lingered in him that even the warm wetness of her could not erase. It *did* matter. The prophecies spoke of a mad king who would bring about the eternal night, the end of all things. His priests spoke of the Great War, in which whole empires rose and fell at the whim of a dark prophet, the Shadeem Saleph.

If one could believe such a prophecy, it was the Thagg line that would produce the Mad King, but the Thagg line would also produce the only one who could stop him. Obsession with prophecy had swallowed his mother and driven his father to new depths of cruelty. In the end, Vyjorin had little choice but to kill his own father to end the madness.

Still, some called him kinslayer. Could they not see the dark path King Tyjor had set them on? No. They only saw the blood dripping slowly down the palace stairs and the broken, burning body of a king who made the realm prosperous and had nearly brought the Senjelians to their knees.

I was an untested boy when I killed him, Vyjorin remembered. His father sat on the thick, purple cushion with his belly shaking as he laughed. The white hair that crept between the old man's womanly tits made him look like an ape. Tyjor drank sweet wine, beat his slaves and fucked his wives out of boredom, if he could be bothered at all. Most of the time, the old king shamed his bed with unbloodied maidens who wailed and wept through the whole thing. Their cries kept everyone in the palace awake long into the night.

If Old King Tyjor was feeling particularly generous, he gave the used girls to Vyjorin. Vyjorin let his father believe he took them to his bed, but it wasn't so. Some of the girls were so distraught at the things his father had done to them that Vyjorin put them out of their misery. It was a kindness to kill someone so dead inside. King Tyjor's madness, it seemed, was catching. As he sank his fingers deep into his wife's hip flesh, Vyjorin wondered if he had not contracted some of it.

By the time they were done, the ice had melted into the pillows and dried in the heat. Through the circular window in the ceiling, Vyjorin spied two of Erolyia's three moons dancing in the late afternoon sky, each caught in the orbital pull of the other. Thousands of years from now, their orbits would cross and the two would trade glancing blows, sending a shower of hot stone into the atmosphere. Slowly, they would wear each other down until there was nothing left.

Kihran lifted his hand from his stomach and placed it on hers to feel the baby kick. "He is strong," she assured him. "We should name him *Ibel bal-Ammer*, Strength of the Gods."

Vyjorin hadn't bothered to learn Kihran's strange, native tongue, though he had heard her whisper to her handmaidens often in it. She was of the White Sands clan that hailed from deep in the Sands.

Luck had brought them together. His father had urged him to marry an off-world noble and gone so far as to enter her into the temple rite. Vyjorin had not noticed Kihran at first. She had been young, a child, really, when she bested ten other girls. Drawing blood there was a rite of passage reserved for the nobility, but it marked a transition too, a celebration. Fifteen or not, Kihran had become a woman in that arena.

Two years had passed since then. Vyjorin had refused to take a child to his bed, bloodied or not. At seventeen, she was of age and the years had been kind, turning her into a sun-kissed mirage of beauty. She had good blood, even if she still held the sense of a child. If she could produce an heir, he would let his father roll in his grave as he named a native girl his queen.

"No. He'll have an Erolyian name. A *princely* name. Wylan or Xaniath, maybe."

"Those are terrible names!" She made a gagging sound. "He should have a kingly name. Our son will be king after you." She giggled as he kissed the bump of her womb. Her smile faded when she saw the somber look in his eyes.

"He will be a young king, perhaps no more than a

boy." Vyjorin stroked her stomach.

Her fingertips brushed his cheek lightly. "No. You will live to be old and gray and a nuisance to us all."

Kihran's words did not move him. The galaxy was a pit of gaseous vipers, waiting for someone to light the flame of war. If the Senjelians had their war, his life span could shorten considerably. There were some things he did not wish Ki to hear, and even darker truths he would rather take to his grave. There were dark rumors on the west winds, whispers that the signs and wonders of the end of days were now upon them.

"Why are we going to Pearl Waters?" she asked him suddenly. "Why can't we return to Oasis?" Ki snuggled against him. "I want to go home."

"A king should look on his subjects, Ki, especially those who live practically in his backyard. I would go abroad, too, but it would mean leaving you, and your time draws nearer with each moon." It was only half-true. He had envoys across the empire, inspecting each city's defenses and making nightly reports that he reviewed while Ki slept. It was exhausting, but it was worth it not to see her face wrinkle with worry.

"You inspected an army at Sungate and ships at Glasswater. We're going to war, aren't we?"

"Perhaps. If it happens, I don't think it will last long. Their people are already revolting against their rulers. They've no stomach for a long war. We shall tread carefully and give them no reason to hate us further." *Would that I could get my hands on one of those princes*, he thought. *If one of them would be wise enough to listen to reason … we should not be fighting each other in such times.*

At dusk, Vyjorin and Kihran emerged from their tent and took their places on the stone stairway before the throne. The night ushered in cool winds and a ceiling of bright stars by which to conduct their business. The people of Pearl Waters pooled around the great fortress and piled gifts of polished gemstones and clean, cool water. The town elder, a stout old woman with sagging cheeks, bathed Kihran's feet in a sweet-smelling perfume and predicted she would bear a strong child, though she neglected to predict a gender. Kihran marveled at the steamed freshwater clams the townsfolk brought before them to feast on, offering the best of them to her husband. After they had eaten, a traveling singer entertained them with his deep and mournful voice, while his blind daughter plucked the strings of a zither.

All was beautiful and cool until the moon was high. It was then the screaming started. A few women in the back took up the wailing call and soon the crowd was mad with it. Women young and old beat their breasts and tore at their hair while the men gnashed their teeth and struck their chests. Kihran stiffened and reached for the comfort of her husband's foot as the crowd parted. A young woman passed in the opening, a pale, still child in her arms.

The dead girl could not have been more than three. She was dark of hair and skin, and swaddled in a thin, yellow blanket. The woman knelt and laid the child before her king. Kihran trembling so fiercely that Vyjorin thought she might faint. *I should have warned her this might happen,* he thought bitterly. *I should have known.* He passed out of Kihran's reach to stand before the woman and child.

"She is dead," the woman said through tears. "My only daughter, she is dead before her time. Please, my king, bring her back to me and I will pledge myself to you, body, mind and soul to do with as you wish. Only, return my Sana to me."

"Your faith," he whispered to the woman, "will be

rewarded." He lifted the heavy bronze Eye from his neck and held it high for all to see. "Behold the power of the gods, held by your king." He raised the pendant so the moonlight struck through the crystal eye in the center and fell on the dead child.

Vyjorin closed his eyes and waited as the moonlight lapped like water on the girl's face. The crowd fell silent. The wind remained still. There was only the sound of his breathing and the light turning through the crystal. When even that was beyond his hearing, he stretched one hand out and let the light swallow him.

It was everywhere and nowhere, palpable and yet beyond his grasp. The light was white and blue and red and green—all colors all at once, so vivid that he could taste them—spinning and twirling inside of him. The brilliance turned like a great water wheel, taking up a new prism of light and color with each rotation and setting down another, each one in its turn. The Wheel of Life, the place where all souls went to be sorted and reborn.

The Wheel sang the most peaceful song to him. Dark shapes danced around the river of light and called for him to join them. As welcoming as it was, it was not why he had come before the Wheel. He had come for the girl's soul. He reached for the Wheel. One of the dark shapes brushed against his arm and, suddenly, his thoughts were filled with empty nothingness. The peaceful bliss of death.

Vyjorin came back from the Wheel and sank to his knees, barely able to hold up the medallion he wore so proudly. There was pain in every inch of his body, exhaustion and an insatiable craving for food and drink. He was a mess of misery, but the girl was stirring and wailing in her mother's arms. "Bless you, Great King." The mother sobbed as she embraced her daughter. "Bless you!"

Vyjorin reached for a shadow in the corner of his vision. "Water."

Before he could draw his next breath, someone pressed sweet, cool ice into his mouth. It was even sweeter when he saw that it was Kihran, the dark makeup around her eyes streaked from tears. She helped him to his feet and he slid the heavy chain back over his neck.

"Woman," Vyjorin said weakly to the mother, "take your daughter to the temple. Make an offering of fire and water, and pledge your daughter to the service of the light. This is the payment required by the gods for your daughter's life." He observed the look of surprise on the woman's face and then let go of Ki to hobble back to the tent.

"Your king is tired," Kihran announced and waved both arms toward the exit. "Go home."

When she came to him a few minutes later, she was still shaking. "My love, what gods have blessed you with power over life and death?"

He placed a hand over the pendant resting heavily on his chest and felt it rise and fall with his breath. "Cruel gods," he answered, and fell into a dreamless sleep.

CHAPTER SEVEN

Clovis

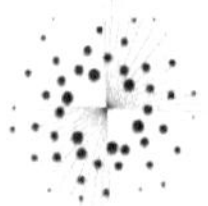

They kept Senator Clovis waiting forever in the receiving room of the citadel. With nothing but a few chairs, a desk, and a suitcase full of Timothy Val's personal effects to amuse him, Clovis resorted to rolling his chair from one end of the table to the other. He would have gone through the captain's suitcase if not for the cramp in his hand. There had been so much red tape around Val's release, Clovis didn't think he'd ever get through the mountain of paperwork. Then there were the phone calls. One to his office on Illion to transfer funds into Timothy's account; one to the ministry of travel and commerce to ensure the captain's passport was reinstated; one to his personal physician so the captain could be looked at.

He thanked his lucky stars he'd been able to convince the executors to release Val into his care. They didn't want him roaming around unsupervised. Clovis had enough sway and just enough credits to make sure Timothy went with him and not a military escort.

When Clovis grew bored with rolling around in the chair, he pulled out his data pad and queried Timothy's name. Most of the results were about his trial and impending freedom. There were three dozen or more live news feeds of reporters standing on the steps of the citadel, all promising exclusive first interviews with Captain Val on his release. He was the news story of the decade, thanks to the way Clovis had played his cards. The senator had to do everything in his power to keep Val the talk of the empire.

Clovis ignored the feeds and scrolled through old photographs of Captain Val instead. Most of them his commanding officers had submitted to the papers during the Nautis Blitz, featuring him as a clean-shaven and confident but handsome young man at the top of his career. Clovis didn't expect the same man to meet him, but he wasn't prepared for what walked through the door.

When the executor finally brought the captain to him, he was a shell of his former self. His face was pale and thin, his prison jumpsuit hanging loosely over his body. The guard was the only thing keeping him upright. The executors had done their best to cover the bruises on his face and had, at least, treated the glaring gash above his eye, but that hadn't done a thing for his mental state. Timothy's face was a blank slate. Even still, the senator recognized the rage boiling under the surface. The executor brought him in with chains around his wrists, ankles and waist, as if he were a rabid junkyard dog ready to charge at any moment.

Clovis rose from his seat. "What's this?"

The executor holding Timothy's leash stammered, "Captain Val, sir, as you requested."

"Gods, man, unchain him. He's a free man by the emperor's orders."

"Sorry, Senator," said the executor, fumbling with his keys. "High Executor Yolen's orders. They were still processing the paperwork when we pulled him out of recovery."

"Recovery," Clovis scoffed. Timothy flinched as the chains clinked and clanged to the floor. "You're blood-sucking monsters, and you can tell the High Executor I said so. And tell him he's got five minutes to finish processing those release forms before I make a call to the emperor to see what he has to say about it."

"Yes, Senator."

Clovis waited for the fool executor to move, but he didn't. He stood there as if he was a guard on duty. "Well? Get your chain and get out!"

The low-ranking executor did as Clovis ordered. They trained executors to be obedient little ticks.

Timothy leaned on the far end of the table, supporting himself on shaky arms, as Clovis debated what to do with him. He couldn't take him out of the Bloody Keep to face the reporters looking like that. He had to clean him up. But first, there were introductions due, some explaining. Some news.

Timothy didn't even let him speak before he offered a greeting in a weak voice. "Senator," he started and then sank into a chair, "what day is it?"

Clovis smiled. "What day *is* it? What *day* is it? Why, it's the first day of the rest of your life! What day is it, indeed!"

Timothy didn't respond.

Gods, what did they do to you, Val? This can't be the same man who stood up to Colonel Krail. Senator Clovis slipped into the seat next to Timothy. "I take it you know who I am, then?"

"Senator Waval Clovis. I've seen your campaign ads. No offense, Senator, but I never voted for you. Why are you here?"

"I knew your father when he was a senator. Lord Val was a pig-headed rebel to the end of his days, sadly lacking in the art of public speaking. We disagreed on policy most of the time, Lord Val and I, but I respected his candor."

For the first time, Timothy met Clovis's gaze. In his eyes, Clovis recognized Lord Talmon's stubbornness. "A thousand people on Senjele knew my father. One of them stabbed him to death. Most of the rest applauded his killer. You'll have to excuse me if I find it unlikely that you're here to help."

"Don't be daft, Val. I'm a senator, not a saint. I'm helping you because I'm hoping you'll return the favor." Clovis grabbed the suitcase and slid it toward Timothy. "But first, I've got to get you past an army of reporters on the front steps and see to it you're of sound body and mind."

When Timothy didn't move, Clovis opened the clasps and pulled out a small plastic bag with a sandwich inside. It wasn't much, Clovis knew, but food was an easy way to win a little trust. He didn't know what they'd been feeding him, if they'd been feeding him at all, but he hadn't meant to bring just a sandwich. There had been a whole meal, but the guards confiscated the rest.

Timothy eyed the sandwich. Clovis pushed it at him. "Go on, then. To get your strength back."

Timothy's eyes met Clovis's one more time before he snatched away the package and tore it open with his teeth.

He bit into the bread and cheese with all the ferocity of an animal, ripping it apart and stuffing his cheeks as if he might never eat again. He got through three bites before his face changed and he put the sandwich down. Too much too fast.

Clovis turned back to the suitcase and lifted out a fresh pair of polished shoes, a fine-toothed comb, a package of sanitary wipes, socks, and a green, pressed and folded, Senjelian officer's uniform. This, the senator held out to Timothy. "You'll want to put this on unless you like appearing in the papers as you are."

Timothy swallowed the last bite of sandwich and licked the crumbs from his fingers. He looked down at himself, inspected his clothes, and then back at the uniform. "They told me I'd been discharged."

"Honorably discharged."

Timothy looked up, disbelief etched in the sagging corners of his eyes. "I was a traitor and a terrorist this morning."

"Now you're a hero," Clovis said, patting him on the back. "I suppose word's finally gotten out about what happened on Toria. It was only a matter of time, my boy."

Timothy put his hand on the uniform, his eyes focusing on something far away. "Why should I trust you, Senator Clovis?"

"Why should you trust anyone, I suppose?" Clovis typed a search into his data pad and then handed it to Timothy with a show of headlines, the most recent of which read: *"SENATOR CLOVIS PUSHES FOR ACCUSED CAPTAIN'S RELEASE".*

"While Yolen was playing Olandan's Fifth Symphony on your ribcage, I was doing what I could to salvage your good name. I've invested a fortune in you, Val, a damned fortune; I've put my life and my career on the line to see this happen. Yes, I have ulterior motives. I won't sugarcoat it for you. But you're my most expensive investment to date, and I'm not about to let my money go to waste. Those reporters are waiting to drag you through the mud. If you want to have any chance of making it through their ranks and saving face, you'll need me. Unless you want to end up like your father?"

Timothy scowled and jerked the uniform away. He staggered when he stood, but refused any help from Clovis. "Tell me what it is you want in return, Senator," he asked as he pulled the prisoner jumpsuit off.

Clovis didn't answer. He was too busy sizing Timothy up, making plans for his image. The beard would have to go, but the security at the keep had confiscated the razor he brought. Timothy could use a haircut, a good rest and a hearty meal, but he'd recover. With image retouching and the right lighting, Clovis could sell him to the public as both a hero and a heartthrob.

Timothy finished wiping away days of sweat, dirt and dried blood, fixed his cuff sleeves and slid his unruly mop of auburn hair under the officer's cap Clovis had brought him. "Well," he said, trying to stand straight, "how do I look?"

"Better than you smell." Clovis rapped three times on the door and it slid open. "No worries. I have a transport waiting to take us to my villa on the other side of the city. I'll phone ahead and have the bath and sauna set up for you."

Timothy hobbled toward the door with one hand on the wall and said with awkward hesitation, "I appreciate your help, Senator."

"Don't thank me just yet."

They stepped into the hallway together and Clovis directed him to turn right. Ahead of them was a wide staircase with a set of double doors at the top. Although Timothy walked with a limp, he rejected Clovis's help when the senator offered it. Clovis hoped he'd at least take his advice about the reporters. "Answer none of their questions. Keep your eyes forward, your jaw set, and your ears closed. If they get too close, I'll push them back. Just remember: say nothing. Words have power only when used sparingly." Clovis stopped by the double doors. "Are you ready?"

Timothy took a deep breath and raised his head, trying to look more confident. To the untrained eye, the change in posture might work, but Clovis recognized fear and doubt when he saw it. Timothy nodded. Clovis returned the gesture and threw the doors open.

They stepped into unrelenting flashes of camera light, with Clovis guiding Timothy through a tide of microphones and voices. How did he feel about the imperial edict? What was his relationship with the senator? When did he expect to be returning home? Even if Timothy had wanted to, he couldn't have answered them. He leaned heavily on Clovis by the end, barely able to stand. It took almost all his effort to navigate the front steps of the Bloody Keep.

One insistent reporter, a bleached-blonde woman in an unflattering suit, pushed her way through the crowd to keep pace with them, shouting in a voice loud enough that neither he nor Timothy could ignore. "Captain Val!" She shoved two men aside and squeezed between two more with a camera bot hovering over her shoulder. "Captain Val, how are you dealing with your brother's death?"

Timothy stopped. The crowd closed in around them, silent but for the shuttering of lenses and the frantic movement of fingers across data pads. Clovis tightened his grip on Timothy when he almost collapsed, holding him up with both hands, sweat trickling into his good suit. There was no way he could haul him any further, not without help. Then, Timothy did the dumbest thing he could have done. He answered back. "What did you say?"

"Do you suspect foul play?" She shoved her microphone in his face and he staggered back only to find a wall of recording devices behind him.

"I ..."

Clovis summoned the strength to push Timothy the few steps forward to the waiting transport and shove him inside. Leaning against the open door, facing the flashing cameras, the senator threw a bone to the snarling dogs. "Captain Val is deeply saddened by the loss of his elder brother. He has offered his full cooperation with officials both local and abroad, investigating the death of Torbin Val."

"Is this a murder investigation, Senator?"

Clovis tried to look hesitant with his answer, even though he'd prepared it hours ago. "Since this is an ongoing investigation, I'm not at liberty to discuss any evidence the authorities may or may not have."

"Will he be petitioning the crown for control of his brother's assets?"

"I'm not prepared to comment at this time," Clovis said, glancing back at Timothy, who was lying against the opposite window inside the transport. "Neither is he." Clovis slid into the transport amidst even more questions and slammed the door shut. "Drive," he ordered the driver and adjusted himself in the seat. He turned to Timothy. "You're not hurt, are you? Damn paparazzi. They're vermin. Bloody scavengers."

Timothy fixed his eyes on the back of the driver's head. "Torbin's dead," he said. "My brother is dead ... and no one told me?" He shifted his attention to the senator, who averted his eyes to the street outside.

"I wanted to break it to you slowly. You've been through enough." Clovis did his best to sound genuine, but Val was smart enough to recognize the lie.

Rather than getting angry, Timothy fixed his gaze forward again.

"It had to be believable," Clovis explained. "They needed to see an honest reaction, or they never would have bought it. They might have even thought you were involved. You stand to gain much as your brother's sole surviving heir."

"I was stricken from my father's will and removed from the Val lines of succession, if you haven't heard."

Of course he had heard. Everyone had heard. When Timothy Val enlisted fifteen years ago, it had been the talk of the empire. Val wasn't the first noble-born boy to miss out on an inheritance for joining the army. But it was a rare man who threw his lot in with the enlisted men and work his way through the ranks.

"My brother's estate belongs to the empire now. As soon as I'm able, I'll go to Clevennia to oversee the transfer."

"Paperwork can change everything."

"I should have died on Toria," Timothy muttered.

"Why die when you have so much to live for? You're the hero of the hour, the selfless hero of Toria who stood up to an empire full of corruption at the risk of his own life. More than that, you're a breath away from becoming nobility again. Better you live and make your mark. You Vals were great once."

Timothy shook his head. "We're bankrupt, thanks to my brother, and disgraced, thanks to my father. It's better to let the line of Vals die with me than to go on under the pretext of greatness."

"Bankrupt?" Clovis leafed through his pockets and brought out the data pad to call up his transfer receipts. "You should be so lucky."

"Where did this come from?" Timothy stared at the nine-digit number sitting in his personal bank account.

Timothy was the poorest hero Senjele had ever known. Before his deployment, the captain had pushed his accounts into the red at a watering hole and brothel on the other side of Senjele. Making this man look like a saint instead of a soldier would be a tough, full-time job, but Clovis was up to the task. "I told you. I've made a significant investment in your future."

"Senator Clovis ..." Timothy held the data pad back out to him. "I can't accept this."

"Trust me," said the senator, as the transport slowed to a stop in front of a four-story, whitewashed villa with deep blue trim. A fountain in the shape of a leaping swordfish stood in the center of a row of evergreen hedges, pure, clean water spewing from between the fish's lips. "This money is clean. It's from my personal accounts, not my political ones. And I'll get a threefold return on my investment once you're well enough."

"But, Senator, what would I do with such a sum?"

Clovis grinned. Was he simple, or had the High Executor beat the sense out of him? If he were half the man Clovis believed him to be, Timothy must have guessed what his intentions were by now; still, being a thickheaded Val, he needed to hear it from the turkey's beak to be sure. "Serve as Lord Governor of Clevennia and restore Castle Valence and House Val to their former glory."

"Because a fat old senator who used to know my father told me to?"

"Because you've got nothing better to do. I'm not

going to let you fade into obscurity, Val. You're where you need to be." Clovis smiled and threw open the transport door. He walked around to open Timothy's door, too, but the fool had shoved it open and fallen out by the time he got there. Clovis picked him up, dusted him off and offered him a hand for stability. Timothy ignored it and walked stiffly to the front door.

CHAPTER EIGHT

Chaunstance

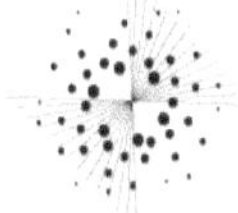

Timothy Val was not as tall as Senator Clovis made him sound, nor as young and heroic. From the front steps of Senator Clovis's villa, Chaunstance saw nothing worth the risk and fuss. With his wild, red beard and dark, sunken eyes, Timothy Val looked like no noble-born man she had ever seen the senator entertain. From the way he carried himself, the captain was a man used to giving orders rather than taking them, much like the senator. Having both Timothy and Clovis under one roof for any amount of time, no matter how short, would be stressful.

The maid standing next to Chaunstance fanned herself and leaned forward. Chaunstance shook her head, unimpressed. Half the women in the household had fallen in love with Timothy Val the first day they'd heard of his arrest on the news. Senjele was buzzing with the unremarkable choice he'd made to do the right thing.

"Lucenda."

The maid snapped back. "Yes, ma'am?"

"See to it the good towels and a fresh razor are ready in the guest washroom."

Lucenda gave an acknowledging bow of her head and scurried inside, stealing a backward glance at the captain as he and Clovis came up the walk.

Chaunstance moved to the side to block their entry. "Welcome home, Senator Clovis."

"Home indeed," huffed the senator as he fought to navigate the stairs while holding Timothy up. "You wear it like a prison, my dear. Smile a little. If not for me, do it for my company. Captain Val could use a warmer welcome."

Chaunstance turned, offered a stiff curtsy to Timothy, and returned her gaze to the senator. "Should I inform the kitchen to set another place?"

Timothy answered in Clovis's place. "No, but thank you."

"Nonsense," said Clovis. "You need to eat more than just a sandwich. Why, I can almost see your bones poking through. What did they feed you in there?"

"Nothing."

"Dr. Gwaren is waiting inside," Chaunstance informed the senator. "I'm sure he'll advise us what you can tolerate."

"Raw milk with the fat still in it," said Clovis, stepping past Timothy to put his hands on Chaunstance shoulders. "Val isn't the first half-starved stubborn fool I've nursed back to health."

Chaunstance averted her eyes. "As you wish." She

stepped aside and allowed them to pass.

Timothy paused in the foyer beyond and removed his cap. His eyes scanned the crystal chandelier, the square marble fountain with gold trim, and the spiraling split staircases leading into the east and west wings of the estate with unease. Chaunstance did not miss the way he wrung the fabric of his hat as he took in the tile mosaics on the floor and the silk tapestries on the wall. She cleared her throat and caught Clovis's attention. "Lady Bolin left another message, Senator."

"Blast and damn her." Clovis unpinned his cape and tossed it on the edge of the fountain. "What is it now?"

"She wouldn't say. She only demanded you make a swift reply yourself."

"Well, Val, it appears my work has followed me home. A civil servant is always on duty. Miss Chaunstance, will you see to it he's taken care of while I deal with this Bolin mess?" Clovis motioned to the wall as if it were to blame for his work and slipped around the fountain and into the back rooms of the estate.

Timothy's eyes followed the senator at first, but shifted back to Chaunstance, taking her in from head to toe.

Clovis had raved about this man's potential since he had come to Senjele. Timothy Val was a man who could make or break the empire. He was a symbol of integrity in the face of corruption, hope in Senjele's time of need, or so Clovis believed. When she looked at him, she saw none of these things. Timothy Val was flesh and bone, muscle and tendon, blood and sweat. *A soldier*, she reminded herself, and remembered how Clovis complained about the lack of decent women whenever soldiers put into port in the capital. Of course, Clovis's idea of a decent woman was a whore who would take checks. She met Timothy's gaze with one of her own, hers as sour as his was hungry.

"I didn't catch your name, my lady."

"Chaunstance," she said curtly, "and I'm not a lady. I'm a slave."

She started for the stairs. Like a lost, half-beaten dog, he followed. "Then the rumors are true. The senator is a man of no morals."

"All men have morals, sir. Yours are no better than his."

"I keep no slaves."

"Servitude is slavery under a different name."

"I don't have servants."

Chaunstance spun around to stand face to face and toe-to-toe with the captain. "No, but you are a killer just the same."

The muscles of his jaw flexed as he regarded her. In his eyes, she saw the familiar flicker of suppressed anger. "What have I done to offend you?"

"It is not your presence that offends, sir. It is your smell." Chaunstance turned, gathered her skirt and doubled her pace into the east wing. She threw open the double doors to the wide hallway and stopped next to the third door on the right. Timothy followed at a distance. "I've instructed the maid to make sure you have everything you need, sir. You have use of the guest quarters across the hall."

He paused mid-stride and leaned against the wall.

Chaunstance sighed. The idiot had exhausted himself trying to keep up with her. "Doctor Gwaren," she called, and the middle-aged physician stepped out from the guest quarters where she'd instructed him to wait.

The doctor looked at her before coming to Timothy's aid, half carrying him into the guest room and instructing him to lie on the bed.

Chaunstance followed and stood in the doorway, arms crossed. "Do you need anything, doctor?"

Doctor Gwaren helped Timothy out of his uniform jacket. He touched his hand to Timothy's forehead, checked the lymph nodes under his jaw, the elasticity of his skin. "What did they give you, Captain?"

Timothy rolled his head away. "Verifex."

The doctor's eyes widened. "This man needs a hospital!"

"The senator was clear. No hospitals. No public access."

Doctor Gwaren glared at her. "I don't think you understand—"

"I do understand. That's why I asked you if you needed anything. I've been instructed to get it for you."

The doctor's nostrils flared. He threw a hand up in disbelief. "I need a complete blood count and a full panel of drugs to treat this man. He's severely dehydrated and needs antibiotics—"

"No," Timothy said. "No medicines. No drugs."

The doctor scowled. "Captain, I can't help you if you won't let me."

"You heard the Captain," Chaunstance said firmly. "Treat him homeopathically or not at all, doctor."

Doctor Gwaren sighed and scratched his head before reciting a shopping list to her. "Milk. Purified water. Room temperature honey. Salt."

Chaunstance went to the kitchen to fetch everything, irritated that Timothy had said nothing to Clovis about the Verifex. If Clovis had known, he would have had the doctor meet them at the Bloody Keep. It was best to get those nanites out of his system as soon as possible, and the only way to do that was to flush them out.

That fool, she thought, putting the last of the items on a cart. *He could die and ruin everything.* Though she didn't know why she cared. Timothy Val was Clovis's investment, not hers, and if this scheme failed, Clovis would find another. Still, she would have to endure watching the senator sink into one of his depressions if the captain died. Worse, she would have to find a way to make his books balance. Clovis was a fool for investing millions in a man he didn't know. She hoped something came of it. Otherwise, Timothy Val might just be the ruin of Senator Clovis.

Chaunstance added bandages, antiseptic, rubbing alcohol, and a needle and thread to the cart as she went. She'd seen the gash on his forehead and assumed there were others. The last thing she wanted was another trip downstairs.

Doctor Gwaren didn't even bother to look up when she entered the room. He was too busy poking at various wounds on the captain's body. The man of the hour was dozing lightly with his mouth agape.

"Your supplies, doctor," she said and gave the cart a firm push into the room before she turned to leave.

"Just a minute. You need to learn to do this."

"I don't work for you."

"I'm leaving the captain in Clovis's care, which means I'm really leaving him in yours. The senator is a good man, but I wouldn't trust him to take care of a cat, let alone a man in this shape. I'd do it myself, but I have my practice."

Chaunstance frowned and wished the captain had gone to a proper hospital if he needed so much care. She wasn't in the habit of playing nursemaid to full-grown soldiers. She sighed and reminded herself this was for Clovis. The doctor gave her a long speech about how to measure ingredients and in what order to combine them for Timothy to drink. Chaunstance ignored everything he said. She could mix salt and honey in a glass of water with no problems. Keeping him on a liquid diet for the first twenty-four hours would not be a problem. He would likely sleep through most of it, judging by the yellow-and-purple bruising on him. The hardest part would be waking him to drink it. Sleep was what he needed. Enough sleep and time healed even the deepest wounds.

When the doctor finished showing her how to care for the more severe cuts and bruises, he packed up his bag and left her alone with him. The hero of Toria snored, which might have been cute if he were an infant instead of a ticking time bomb. Chaunstance touched his shoulder. When he didn't wake, she gave him a good, firm shake. He sat up, choking on one of his snores, and she thrust the glass of milk at him. "Drink it." The captain stared at her, confused until she added, "Or you can die of dehydration."

Timothy took the glass and swallowed it in a few loud gulps. He handed her the empty glass back. She offered him another, this one the honeyed salt water the doctor had mixed up.

He waved it away. "I can't."

"You're going to drink if I have to get a funnel."

He took it, albeit reluctantly, and sipped. He frowned at the taste and sat with it cradled in his lap. "Say the word and I'll find a way to free you," he offered.

His conviction almost made her smile. "Not every slave wants to be free." He looked up at her. "The senator isn't a bad man. High maintenance, but he is not a bad man. He invested a lot of money in you."

Timothy stared into the cup and swirled the water around. "So everyone keeps telling me. Where does a senator get so much money to begin with? It can't be legal."

"It is," she assured him. "I should know. I keep his books."

"What does he want from me?"

Chaunstance shrugged. "Clovis doesn't tell me everything. When he schemes like this, he rarely shares his wisdom with those wise enough to tell him he's a fool. Drink, Captain, and get some rest. Doctor's orders. When you're ready, you know where the shower is. If you need anything, you can ring for a maid."

"What about you?" he asked. "Can I ring directly for you?"

Chaunstance went to the door without looking back. "No," she said. "I'm not a maid. I don't work for you. I work for Clovis."

She closed the door behind her and leaned against it, one arm crossed over the other. *Timothy Val is a bold man to offer to free a slave while he is under her master's roof. If Clovis knew, he would be furious.*

She wrapped her fingers tightly around the cloth of her dress sleeves and wondered if it were true. Clovis would react but she wasn't sure the old senator would be furious. In the ten years she'd worked for him, Clovis had never struck her, never deprived her of anything she desired. Chaunstance was wise enough to know she enjoyed more luxuries as a wealthy senator's slave than she would have known as a free woman. There was stability in her situation, certainty. Clovis would never ask more of her than she was willing to give. He didn't expect her loyalty or love. He didn't ask her to service him beyond the needs of his household. Some masters ordered their slaves to perform disgusting sexual acts but Clovis was not that sort of man. He had been nothing but kind to her. Why should she want to leave him?

The doors to the west wing swung open and Clovis emerged, having come up the back stairs. Chaunstance straightened at the sight of him. "Chaunstance, my dear, are you well? You look even more unhappy than normal."

"Why did you bring him here, Senator? Nothing good will come of him."

Senator Clovis crossed the balcony overlooking the foyer but stopped short of her. "Emperor Ludus will not live forever, child. One day, Rebos will inherit the throne and destroy everything his father worked so hard to protect, everything men like Timothy Val have worked hard to protect. We will live in dangerous times then, Chaunstance. We must form our alliances now. If we wait, it may be too late." He stepped forward to place his hands gently on her shoulders. "I won't ask you to like him, only that you trust me. We need Timothy Val—and he must be made to realize how much he needs us."

Chaunstance shook her head. "We can survive without him."

"But Senjele cannot." He nodded as if his answer should have satisfied her. "Now, put those thoughts behind you. There's work to be done."

Chaunstance stole a glance at the closed doors behind her and moved to follow the senator. *Oh, Clovis, what kind of mess have you gotten yourself into this time.*

CHAPTER NINE

Timothy

Timothy sat bolt upright, choking on a gasp. *A nightmare,* he realized looking around the unfamiliar room. He touched his cheeks, his arms and the tender spots on his chest. How long had he been recovering at Clovis's villa? Long enough that even the deepest bruises were fading. He'd spent most of his time asleep. All he remembered of his waking hours was the terrible mixture Clovis's slave made him drink. He wanted real food. Timothy pushed aside the blankets and put his feet on the floor. His nose wrinkled when he smelled his own stink. First, he needed a shower.

His legs were a little shaky and his body sore, but he forced himself to walk out of the room without holding onto anything. The blue light of pre-dawn bathed the hallway through the large window at the far end. Timothy stumbled across the hall and into the bathroom. He stripped down and found his way into the shower with minimal difficulty, despite the stiffness in his limbs.

The shower was heaven. The first ones at home always were. On deployment, the best they had was lukewarm, recycled water on the ships and dry showers at base camp. He tried to determine how long it had been since he'd had an actual, hot shower.

Must've been shore leave, he realized, *a few days before the jump to Toria.* He met up with a platoon of Deynes from Clevennia on the far side of Senjele. They were shipping out for the stronghold of Olarin the next day, expecting heavy resistance. Timothy had bought them drinks and whores. As much as he had wanted a woman for himself, all he could think of was Nareen. The wound was too fresh, so he'd drunk himself into his usual stupor.

That bitch. His hands clenched into fists. He hated her for manipulating him, twisting his heart and body until he could think of nothing else. He'd almost given up his career for her. She had made him love her with all the fierceness of a madman, promising him the world. Then he came calling one day and found he wasn't the only man to have taken an interest in Nareen. He was a side project, someone to warm her bed while she fought and clawed her way up the social ladder to Prince Rebos. She'd drawn Timothy along as a plaything until she no longer had a use for him.

He realized his hand was red from how tightly he squeezed his fist, and let it go with a long, loud sigh.

When he stepped out of the shower, someone had already swapped out the dirty uniform for a clean outfit and a towel. He put his hand on the towel to discover it was warm. *Chaunstance.* A chill went through him as he realized she'd come and gone and he hadn't even heard her. He recognized the clothes she left him as the civvies he kept in his personal locker on the ship and wondered how she'd gotten them. When he slipped them on, they were looser than he remembered.

Timothy forced himself to look in the mirror. The face staring back was not his own. It was ancient and haggard, too thin and too pale, belonging to a man five years his senior. *My brother's face,* he realized as he dared to touch the glass. *A dead man's face.* Only as he moved his fingers along the cold, smooth surface of the mirror did he remember Torbin was a thicker man with higher cheekbones and their father's brown eyes. *If only I looked more like you, father, and less like my mother. I've always been too much of one thing and not enough of another. Are we all such mongrels in the eyes of our parents?*

After he dressed and trimmed his beard, he exited to find Chaunstance waiting for him in the hallway, her face as grim as always. "Good morning," he offered.

"Is it? I hadn't noticed." She held out her hand, retracting it only when he surrendered his used towel. "The senator wishes you to join him for breakfast on the terrace."

"Breakfast, yes. With the senator." He didn't want to be rude, but he did not intend to accept Clovis's offer. He was sure Clovis would talk about his plans for Timothy's future. Still, he couldn't say no to breakfast, not as hungry as he was. "Why not?"

"This way, Captain."

Chaunstance took off in long, determined strides and

Timothy followed. "You don't have to call me captain. I don't have that title anymore."

"As far as I'm aware, the paperwork is still processing." She pushed through the double doors. He had to rush to keep pace with her down the stairs.

"How long was I asleep?"

"Four days the first time. You woke up screaming, so I had the doctor prescribe you something to help you relax. Homeopathic, as you requested, but it worked better than I expected. You've been asleep for six days, waking just long enough to take a piss and swallow your medicine."

"Ten days?" He shook his head as she led him out the rear exit and onto the terrace where Clovis was waiting.

The senator rose from his seat at the table where he was enjoying a breakfast of sausage, egg and toast with wine. "Val! So glad to see you're awake. How do you feel?"

Clovis extended his hand and Timothy took it out of instinct. "Like hell, to be honest."

"You look much better." He motioned to the seat across from him and Timothy sat.

Chaunstance left and returned with a hot cup of black coffee, filled to the brim, exactly the way he drank it. She also placed his breakfast in front of him: a fruit salad and two eggs over easy, with a single slice of untoasted bread, the same breakfast he always ate on leave. He stared at the plate, the coffee, and then looked to the senator.

"She's amazing, isn't she?" said Clovis with a wink and a smile.

Timothy watched her standing by the doorway with a blank look on her face. *No, not blank.* He sipped his coffee and chewed his breakfast. She was difficult to read, but not impossible. There was a glint in her eye. Pleased. She looked pleased. *Yes, I suppose you would be, knowing so much about me, especially when I know nothing about you. You must think you have the upper hand, but we'll see.*

"You're friends with Prince Annon, are you not?"

Timothy almost choked on his coffee. "I suppose so."

Clovis turned off his data pad and placed it on the table in front of him. "You suppose? Val, I'm a politician. I can spot a lie from sixty feet away."

"It wasn't a lie, Senator. The last time we spoke, it was via official military channels. I haven't made a social call to the palace in a very long time. I've no idea what terms we're on after what happened."

"But?"

Timothy sighed. "But I suspect Annon had something to do with the edict ordering my release." Timothy stared into his half-empty cup. "Ludus would have been more than happy to let me rot and Yolen ..." He trailed off and put the cup down harder than he meant to. "Why?"

"Just making conversation."

Timothy frowned. "Listen, Senator Clovis. About Torbin, was it because of me?"

"I've no idea. You'll have to go to Clevennia to find out."

Timothy pushed his plate away, half-finished. "I'll admit you've got my attention, Senator, but you won't convince me to take over Castle Valence to solve my brother's murder. In case you haven't heard, my brother and I weren't on the best of terms. I mourned him once already. My father, too. If you want to convince me to go back and serve as a lord, you'll have to do better than that."

Clovis lifted his cup, swirled the wine in it and swallowed it in two gulps. "Do you consider yourself a patriot, Captain Val?"

"A patriot?" Timothy shot back. "What kind of a question is that?"

"A loaded one, but I must ask. Are you a patriot, Timothy Val?"

"I am a man loyal to Senjele."

"Ah, but to the crown and its retainers, or to the people?"

The point made Timothy squirm. Clovis was splitting hairs, though Timothy saw a clear difference. The divide between Senjele's nobility and the average man on the street had grown in recent years. Some argued the ruling class was so disconnected from what was going on a revolution was in order. That kind of talk led to the revolts on Toria and Illion. Timothy had opinions on the topic, but they were not rooted in politics. He was a soldier. He saw things from the ground, not balconies and castle walls.

"Have you no answer, Captain?"

Timothy stared at his eggs, drawing a hard line in his expression and flexing his throat and jaw muscles as if preparing to vomit rather than speak. "Are they not one and the same, Senator?"

"You know damn well they are not." Clovis gave a signal to Chaunstance, who acknowledged him with a nod and stepped forward to remove their dishes. "You and a large percentage of the population of the voters of Nebarius. If the people had faith in their government, Toria would not have happened." Clovis leaned toward Timothy. "I represent a faction of individuals who believe the current lines of succession in Senjele must be redrawn."

Timothy searched Clovis's face. "You're with the rebellion?"

Clovis smiled and leaned back in his chair. "The revolution, Captain."

"Call it what you will. Plotting against the emperor is treason. I've only just pulled my neck from the noose. I'm not so eager to put it back in."

"It is the emperor's eldest son we're concerned with, not the emperor himself." Clovis shook his head. "You've got it all wrong. Those rebels on Toria were wrong. We can achieve our goals bloodlessly—with a vote of no confidence in the Senate. Unfortunately, a vote of no confidence must be ratified by two-thirds of the noble houses and I must put an alternate forward."

"Gods," Timothy said, feeling a little sick. "You mean to put Annon forward."

"With your support."

"I am no lord."

"You will be. I've already financed the restoration of your estate and put my funds at your disposal, should you need them. I'll see to it you have more than enough to raise suitable troops to defend Clevennia should the need arise—interest-free, of course. In the meantime, I will drum up support among the other houses and in the Senate. All you need to do is sign a document when the time comes. It should be a simple matter."

Timothy pushed himself away from the table and stood, eyeing the exit across the table from his seat. "You still don't understand, do you, Senator Clovis? I have no desire to be a lord. I'm as fit for a title as a fish is for walking. I'm a soldier in service to the crown. No amount of money will ever change that."

"Your brother's murder means nothing to you, then?"

"My brother was dead to me six years ago." Timothy made a curt bow to the senator. "I thank you for the hospitality you've shown me, Senator, but I'm afraid I've lost my appetite." He marched to the door only to have Chaunstance block his exit. Timothy glared at her and she at him. He bowed to her. "My lady," he acknowledged before pushing past her and through the doors. Chaunstance moved to follow.

"Let him go," Clovis said, and called after Timothy. "There's too much Deyne in you to walk away from a good fight and too much Val in you to let a guilty man go free! Consider it, Val. What have you got to lose?"

My honor, he thought with distaste. *Or what's left of it.* As he marched through the hallway even he knew it wasn't true. He would accept Clovis's offer and likely support the rebellion, too, gods help him. The best thing he could do for Senjele was to swallow his distaste for nobility and titles and become everything he had ever hated.

Timothy wandered through the house for most of the rest of the morning, trying to decide what he would do. Near noon, he found himself back in the main hall, staring at the front door, wondering what would happen if he walked through it and caught the first flight to Clevennia. I could be gone and settle everything before the senator even knew I'd left. Why am I even hesitating?

"If you're waiting for the senator, I wouldn't expect him until a quarter past three. The Senate is in session today."

Timothy turned at the sound of Chaunstance's voice.

She bent over a table, wiping it clean, a feather duster tucked into her back pocket. When she looked up, she tucked a stray strand of hair behind her ear. "Or should I be expecting someone else?"

"I was just thinking."

She gave him a distrustful look before pulling out the feather duster and moving it over the recesses in the wall.

"Doesn't he have a maid or a housekeeper?"

"Of course he does. If I waited for her to get to every nook and cranny, I'd be waiting all day. She has her tasks, and I have mine. Now you're up and about and I don't have to babysit you all day, I have time to clean the place properly."

Timothy cleared his throat. "I suppose I should thank

you." She shrugged and went on cleaning. "Can I ask you a personal question, my lady?"

"Chaunstance," she reminded him. "Ask what you like, and I'll answer as I please."

"How did you come to be in the senator's service?"

She moved to the opposite corner before answering. "The senator purchased me and found a use for me."

"Before that. I mean, where are you from? Who took you and why? Why didn't you run away as soon as he bought you? You could have sought asylum almost anywhere. Foreign slaves do it all the time."

"Foreign," she scoffed. "What makes you think I'm so exotic? Perhaps I'm just some unlucky Erolyian girl or a Yoris debtor's daughter."

"No. You're not Erolyian. Your skin's too light; your hair's the wrong color. And no slaving ship would ever leave the Yoris system unchallenged. Yoris used to be Erolyian, and the Erolyians are very much against slavers trading their people outside of the empire. Besides, do you know what kind of scrutiny the senator would be under for harboring Erolyians under his roof, slave or not? You're from the Expanse, aren't you?"

She let out a bitter laugh and collected her supplies. "What does it matter? I can't go back. My place is here now," she said, moving into the adjoining room. He stood in the doorway, watching her wipe down a bar and straighten the glasses behind it. "I don't know why you're so fascinated with me, Captain. I promise you, I'm not so interesting."

"You interest me because you're a paradox." She stopped wiping down the wood and looked up at him. "I've never met a woman so content at being reduced to another man's property."

"And I've never met a dog who enjoyed being kicked

as much as you." He opened his mouth to reply, but she interrupted. "You disobey an order and your life hangs in the balance whereas, if I do so, the worst I can expect is to be moved to kitchen duty for a day." She stepped away from the bar toward him, and the whole room shrank. "Women on the street can be bought for half a day's wages, and they risk sleeping in the cold with empty bellies. If that is freedom, you can keep it. I am worth more than some bread vendor's spare change."

"How much did the senator pay for you?"

A dark smile played on her lips. "Do you plan to buy me out from under the senator, Captain? Do you think I would be of greater value under you?"

"I think nothing of the sort, my lady."

"Do you not find me an attractive woman, Captain?"

"I …" What answer was there to satisfy this woman? No matter what he said now, she would take offense. *She thinks she can trap me with her words, just like the senator.* Timothy took a half-step toward her and smiled. "Are you flirting with me, my lady?"

Her smile faded and her face reddened. "Of course not. The senator told me to be more personable—which is impossible so long as you're undressing me with your eyes, sir."

"There's a fine line, my lady, between being personable and being disturbingly forward. It makes me wonder if you're not acting on Clovis's behalf."

"Then let us clear the air of that suspicion, Captain. If I offered you sex in exchange for your cooperation with the senator's plans, would you accept?"

"No," Timothy answered. "If Clovis thinks me that sort of man—"

"I assure you he does not." She went back to ignoring him.

Timothy knew if he pushed the conversation further, it would do little more than anger her. He sighed and wandered out of the room, deciding a short run would clear his mind and pass the time before the senator's return. He was much more comfortable outside, even if the air in Nebarius never sat well with him. The air always felt too thin. He missed the cold, damp sea air of the grounds at Castle Valence, the sound of gulls screaming at the waves, the uneven layer of white salt against black stone. Everything here was too neat, too organized and too predictable. For the first time in six years, Timothy missed Clevennia.

When he jogged back onto the villa's grounds, Senator Clovis was waiting for him on the front steps, a large, official-looking envelope in his hands. Timothy stopped just short of the step Clovis stood on and bent over to catch his breath, his hands resting on his knees.

"Looks like they've finally processed your paperwork," Clovis said holding the envelope out to him. "Congratulations. You've officially received an honorable discharge from the Senjelian armed forces." Clovis said it as if Timothy should be happy about it.

Timothy took the envelope, opened it and scanned through the first few pages. Everything looked like it was in order, but he felt sick looking at the official blue and black inks dictating an end to his military career. He'd planned on never leaving the service. It had always been his intention to die defending Senjele on foreign soil, not cooped up in some castle signing papers and issuing tax orders. *But,* he reminded himself, closing the envelope, *service to the empire can come in many forms.* "I've been thinking about what you said, Senator."

"Oh?" The old man raised an eyebrow.

"About petitioning the crown for control of my

brother's assets."

"And?"

"And …" He sucked in a deep breath before continuing. Once he said it out loud, he could never change his mind. "I'll do it. On one condition."

Clovis smiled and extended his arm to pat Timothy on the back. "My boy, you need but only name it!"

Timothy leaned in close and whispered it to him. Then, he leaned back and watched Clovis pale.

"You're certain you need *that*?"

Timothy crossed his arms and nodded.

"I—I'll see to it," said the senator, and stumbled into his villa.

CHAPTER TEN

Rebos

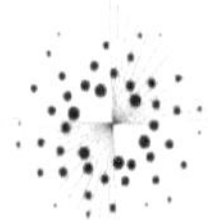

Rebos turned away from the screen and rubbed his dry, aching eyes. If he had to spend one more minute staring at reports about Toria and how things had gone so badly, he would punch someone. Toria should have been a simple matter. The law was clear on how to handle traitors who took up arms against the empire. Yes, the law said they were entitled to a trial but those were a farce. They would face a firing squad anyway.

The prince rose and went to the window of his office, looking at the courtyard below. A groundskeeper sprayed a hose over the colorful bricks on the path while another scrubbed them. He wondered if the two of them had been in the crowd of protesters gathered there only days before, demanding Timothy Val's release. Did they care that they had cheered for a guilty man? Val had shot his commanding officer. He should have been stripped of his command, dishonorably discharged and publicly executed for his treason and insubordination. Instead, Ludus had pardoned him and intended to make him Lord Governor of Clevennia. Did those simple groundskeepers know their emperor was a weak old fool?

The door to his office slid open with a hiss, and Rebos turned away from the window to regard his mother as she offered him a formal curtsey. "Afternoon, Mother," he said with a hint of a growl. "What do you want?"

"Your father is asking for you."

Rebos scowled at her, but not because of anything she had done. "Since when is it the empress's job to fetch a prince for the emperor? You shouldn't be running errands for him." He sank back into the comfortable office chair and turned off the screen. "Why do you let him treat you this way?"

She smiled, but it was frigid. "Because he is my emperor."

"If I were emperor, you wouldn't have to. One of the first things I'll do is execute every one of those whores for humiliating you."

Rebos opened the top drawer of his desk and brought out an unopened bottle of brandy. He opened the bottle and took a swig.

His mother frowned. "Your father will be angry if he smells alcohol on your breath again, Rebos."

"Father can kiss my royal ass," he said, taking another drink.

His mother took a few more steps into the room and lowered her voice. "Be careful saying such things, Rebos. You know what he'll do if word gets back to him."

"Order you to belt me?" Rebos laughed and shook his head. "Why should I be afraid of a brittle old man? He didn't have the stones to execute Timothy Val or any of the other traitors on Toria. He won't raise a hand against me and, if he does, I will kill him."

"That's sedition," she hissed.

"Haven't you heard? Sedition and treason are all the rage right now." Rebos went to take another drink, but she snatched the bottle out of his hand. He glared at her as she placed it on the corner of his desk. "I didn't come here just because your father sent me. I came with news. Your father has another bastard, this time with Ionia Vale." Rebos cursed his father, but his mother cut him off. "I have set up a meeting with a pair of mercenaries to deal with them."

"Deal with them?" Rebos wrinkled his brow and leaned forward. "Why? Those whores and their offspring are an embarrassment, but not worth your time to kill."

"They are a threat to your rule." She knelt in front of him and grabbed his fingers. Her hands felt cold in his. "With the empire in chaos, what's to stop these rebels from finding one of these bastards and throwing their support behind him?"

"They've relinquished their claims of legitimacy. They are not a threat."

"Any of those bastards could be propped up with nothing more than a vote from the Senate."

The Senate. Rebos remembered how Senator Clovis had derailed the meeting. The consequences of giving Clovis the Senate floor even for a few minutes had resulted in a decisive shift in public opinion toward Timothy Val. Clovis had opposed Rebos's measure in the Senate, too, delaying it because the senator didn't like him. While Rebos had gained the loyalty of the executors, several governors and others in key positions, the Senate proved difficult. They would never love him.

He pulled his hands away from hers and rose, again going to the window. The groundskeepers were gone, and the bricks glistened from the cleaning. "Some of them are infants," he whispered. "And the women aren't to blame. They didn't choose to go to Ludus's bed. He ordered it."

"Sometimes. But how will you decide which ones are innocent and which are guilty?" She put her hand on his shoulder. "It's not a decision I came to lightly, my son—but Ludus's bastards must be buried. These mercenaries can do it without exposing our involvement. It's what they do."

Rebos closed his eyes, knowing she was right. There was no guarantee he would rule, not so long as there was anyone alive to challenge him. Even then, the Senate didn't have to ratify him as the new emperor. After the way he had failed the empire on Toria, handpicking Krail to oversee the prisoners, they would foam at the mouth to find a scapegoat. He would have to act quickly.

"What about Annon?" he asked his mother, turning to her. "They might prop him up just as easily. Would you kill my brother, too?"

His mother took his chin in her hands and smiled. "Annon has no ambitions for your throne."

"Perhaps these children don't either."

"Don't worry about Annon. I will make arrangements so he is close to you but never a threat."

Rebos frowned. As his mother, she had been doting, giving him everything he wanted. But she had been overprotective. Every time he was interested in a woman, she bullied them away. Every time he took an interest in a hobby or something other than his future as heir, she kept him away from it. Cylene Herrin-Eflor was a scheming, bitter woman, but she was right: he was born to be the Emperor of Senjele. Every part of him, blood, muscle and bone, had to belong to the empire. Killing Ludus's bastard children was good for Senjele, even if it left a bitter taste in his mouth.

"If you judge it best, then I will make it so," he said, and kissed her on the cheek. "Be careful. Mercenaries are only as loyal as you pay them to be."

"I am the Empress of Senjele," she said with a sly smile. "I know the worth of words as well as gold, my son."

Rebos took his leave of her and went to find his father.

The emperor was alone in his chambers when Rebos arrived. The old man didn't look up from his book. "I trust you've read the reports from Toria by now?"

"I have."

"And what conclusion did you draw?"

Rebos stepped forward, hands folded behind his back. "It was a mistake to send Colonel Krail."

Ludus lowered the book and raised an eyebrow. "A mistake?"

"I chose Krail because of his unique experience. He was from Clevennia, a planet fiercely loyal to the empire, but he also lived on Toria for a time. His record as a soldier was exemplary, and he understood the difficulty of the situation in both credits and human costs. Based on the information I had, I believed he was the best choice. I did not think he would incite such hatred from the men under him."

"He didn't," said Ludus, standing. "And Krail wasn't your mistake. Your mistake was thinking in terms of credits at all."

Rebos lowered his gaze. "Our coffers are empty. As it is, the empire is considering taking a loan from the noble houses to pay its expenses. We are in debt. The cost of dozens of trials, of medical treatment for the people who rebelled against the empire—"

The first strike came as a surprise. It hit Rebos across the mouth and was just strong enough to snap Rebos's head to the right when Ludus's knuckles connected with his jaw. The emperor was old and weak, but his fists still hurt. Another punch struck Rebos in the gut, and he fell. Ludus kicked him twice. The emperor was feeble, so no bones broke this time, but it didn't remove the sting of being struck by his father again.

"Do not think for a moment, Rebos, that I don't know what you're thinking, what you've been thinking all this time." Ludus reached up with shaky fingers and removed the crown from his head. "Do you really think you will do better than me?"

"Yes," Rebos hissed, clutching the ache in his stomach. He fought to get to his knees, and glared at his father. "I will be twice the emperor you ever were."

Ludus long fingers closed around the crown. "Since you want it so badly …"

And then the real beating began. Ludus swung the crown at him, connecting with Rebos's chin. When Rebos doubled over and curled into a ball, he beat him on the back until the metal crown bent and the jewels flew out.

All the while, Rebos lay on the floor, fists clenched, and counted the blows.

Rebos winced as Nareen Ambren laid another cold compress on his back. He would have much rather had her warm, naked body pressed against his, but she insisted that he let her try and do something for the bruises.

Nothing was broken. The crown had given way before his body. Still, he didn't like for her to see him this way. It made him feel weak. But he couldn't trust anyone else.

Nareen was his beautiful, most closely guarded secret. Even his mother didn't know about her. Yes, everyone knew she was spending the summer in the palace, but a lot of noble men and women were. They came every year to spend months in the empire's bosom, learning the inner workings of the empire so, one day, they might become competent governors and statesmen on their own.

Nareen didn't need to learn. She was already as fierce and sharp as a hawk. She was beautiful; so beautiful she had to dress down at formal occasions to keep from outshining the empress. How could Rebos ever have hoped to ignore her? There were some—his mother included—who would argue that she only came to his bed because she was a ladder-climbing, title-seeking whore. Few women in the empire weren't. Rebos respected her all the more because she had told him immediately she would not have paid him any attention if he weren't the heir apparent. She was a woman who knew what she wanted, and nothing would stand in her way, but she wasn't heartless like his mother. Even if it was only one-sided, Rebos loved her.

Nareen paused in rubbing the largest bruise on his back and slid a strand of long, black hair behind her head. "Why do you let him do this to you?"

"Because he has the power of the throne," Rebos said bitterly. He turned over and sat up in his bed. Surrounded by all the finery, given anything he wanted—even the company of a beauty like Nareen Ambren—he should have been happy. "If I strike him back, I can be executed."

Nareen's arm snaked up and over his shoulder and she pressed her breasts against his back, kissing the nape of his neck. "Let me help you take your mind off it."

Rebos pushed her hand away. "I don't want to stop thinking about it," he said, rising and going to the window. "He doesn't deserve the throne. He's weak. He's broken, and the empire is crumbling underneath him. If I stand and wait for him to die, there will be nothing left for me to claim."

"You're worried about Timothy Val."

He looked back at her, and his anger faltered. She had that effect, her beauty overriding every thought and emotion at the most inopportune times.

Nareen may have been the daughter of C-list nobility from a mining world, but she was a beauty with her raven hair, creamy skin and perfectly proportioned face. She had been wasted on Timothy Val. The moment Rebos saw her at the palace, he knew he had to have her. His mother would send her back to Helenia if she found out. As it was, she would leave him when the summer drew to a close in a few weeks. He didn't want her to go.

He turned away from her and stared back out the window at the gardens below, afraid if he looked at her too long, she might vanish. "Ludus intends to name Val the next governor of Clevennia, as if freeing the man and pinning a medal to his chest wasn't enough. Now he's to be made a lord."

"A lord who will owe you his fealty," she reminded him.

"The nobility owes me nothing so long as Ludus lives, least of all Timothy Val. He's not stupid. He knows Yolen is my man. I pushed for his confession. If he'd given it, Toria might have been an isolated incident instead of a festering, spreading wound. He'll blame me for it, if he doesn't already, and if Senator Clovis moves the rest of the Senate and they refuse to ratify me as emperor ..."

Rebos shook his head. "From Castle Valence, he can hole up like a rat, hiding behind stone walls and anti-aircraft guns. Clevennia's planetary defense grid is second only to our own in firepower. When Ludus dies, should Captain Val and his banner men decide my brother or any of my father's bastards are preferable to me, Toria will be a pleasant memory compared to what I must do to take Clevennia."

"What madman would think Annon the better ruler?" She rose from the bed and went to put her arms around him. "He's got no experience. He's not a leader."

"But he'd be an excellent puppet for the Senate. All they would need to float a vote of no confidence would be two-thirds of the houses. With Val's popularity and Clovis's scheming, it could happen."

Nareen tugged on his shoulder, turning him around before taking his face in her hands. He looked into those flame-blue eyes and almost lost interest in anything but taking her back to bed. "Then you must win him. Win Val and you will control everything. Not even Senator Clovis will be a threat to you."

He shook his head. "I would sooner win the confidence of the Erolyians after the way Yolen handled him at the Bloody Keep."

"Then let me win him for you." She smiled and walked back to the bed, searching for the robe she'd discarded.

"No," Rebos snapped, his voice more panicked than he intended. "I won't let you go to him. I couldn't stand it, knowing you were with him again."

"Val would never have me back. Not now. Not ever. Never again."

"Because of what happened in the Bloody Keep?"

Nareen slipped on her robe, crossing one side over the other. She neglected to tie it, but held it closed as she turned to him, a hesitant smile in her eyes. "Because I'm carrying your child."

A chill went through Rebos, starting at the back of his neck and his skin prickled. Silence reigned in the room as he processed the announcement and what to do about it. Once it sank in, everything else mattered less. He went to her, kissing her lips with a renewed fever, trying to hide his shaking hands. She pulled him back to the bed, letting the robe fall away again, and he loved her until neither could move.

When the sun came up, the pink hues of dawn bathed the white carpet and the soft sigh of a breeze swept through the chambers. Rebos held Nareen against him, a hand over her stomach. He would give their child everything, he vowed, all the glory and greatness he had been denied. He wouldn't be like Ludus, going to bed with whores, turning his back on the empire and beating his children.

The people on Toria rebelled because they believed they'd get away with it. And why not? What was the price for their treason? Ludus hadn't so much as sanctioned them, and the few rebels the executors had arrested died too quickly. Senjele needed to be ruled with an iron fist inside of a velvet glove, not from behind closed doors. The people would have no desire to love and obey a man they couldn't know or see. Rebos would not make those same mistakes.

First, he would have to get control of the situation with Val and Toria. He would have to know everything.

Rebos shifted and put his lips next to Nareen's ear. "Who else knows?"

"No one," she said in a dreamy tone. "Except the doctor, and I paid him for his silence."

"Tell no one." Rebos kissed her ear.

She turned onto her back to look up at him. "I won't be able to hide this forever."

He stroked her hair. "You won't have to. Marry me, Nareen. Be my empress. Help me fix the damage my father has done to Senjele."

Nareen smiled.

For the first time since the incident on Toria, Rebos felt at peace.

CHAPTER ELEVEN

Cylene

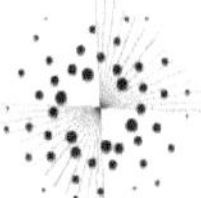

When asked, the servants said the empress's chambers were the warmest in the palace. She'd complained often enough that maintenance workers had installed extra fans last summer, but the noise was so loud she couldn't hear herself think. And so, Empress Cylene resigned to make the best of the late summer heat and dressed down while in her chambers.

The gown she wore to meet the mercenary captains was sheer, the likes of which even Ludus might find distracting, but it had no effect on Reva, as the sly minister of secrets had no interest in her. He was content to sit by the open window, his oxygen machine humming quietly under his seat as he lifted the mask to his face for a puff every now and again. Senjele's summer air was too thick, he complained, but he would manage. Reva always did.

Cylene sat in a velvet chair, her long hair pulled up and away from her neck, allowing her priceless jewelry to shimmer in the moonlight. They kept the lights off to avoid drawing the whispers of others in the palace. Reva had suggested it. The staff would already be talking about the two fit but rough-looking men the empress had invited to her chambers. Let them talk. If Ludus could have his whores out in the open, then she could invite strange men to her room.

They were big men with good, strong arms and callouses on their hands. Both were foreigners with no loyalty to Senjele or Erolyia. Reva's background check said both had come from the Expanse, which accounted for their exotic eye coloring and strange tattoos. She bid them sit in the comfortable chairs her ladies had brought in, and they did, sweeping their eyes side to side, absentmindedly checking the room for threats the way soldiers often did. The one on the right, a well-built man with amber eyes and dark skin, gave her a hungry look before even sitting down. She smiled at him and crossed one leg over the other.

"Is there anything I can get for you gentlemen?" she offered. "Some wine or something to eat perhaps? I know you've been waiting all day to see me. I'm sorry business kept me so long."

"No, Highness," said the mercenary on the left. He had a distinguishable accent but spoke with a deep, velvety voice that made her heart flutter. "Kind of you to ask but we'd rather get down to business."

Cylene offered another smile. "Of course, Captain …?"

"Katz," said the man on the left. "Brek Katz. But you

knew that already, Your Majesty, especially if your friend here's done his homework." He gave Reva a stern glare.

"You must be Shen," she said addressing the one with the amber eyes.

"I am."

"Well, Shen and Brek, the two of you come highly recommended."

"We ought to," Brek grunted. "Between the two of us, we've seen more combat than most of your soldiers ever will. But private work is where the money is. You can think of us as problem solvers. We can jump through the hoops bigger, more regulated military groups can't, go places they might not want to go, do things they don't want to."

"We don't usually deal with royalty behind closed doors," Shen said. "Our contracts tend toward military executives or bounties from the executors on Senjele, things a lady might not want to hear about."

Cylene leaned forward, pleased when she saw Shen's eyes travel south of her face. "Your resumés were never in question. I've seen enough to know you're the men I want to handle this for me."

A bead of sweat trickled down the side of Brek's face. "What can we do for you, Your Highness?"

Cylene stood and went to the window, letting the breeze cool her. If she hadn't had company, she would have climbed into a bath with some ice to cool down. She might do it still, once their business was complete. Maybe one or both would join her.

Reva pulled the oxygen mask away from his face. "First, the empress has asked me to inquire about the terms of your standard contract. The work we would like to hire you for is highly delicate. It must be handled with discretion and care of the highest order. All names, addresses or funds exchanged, and their source, must never be revealed. It must never be known you met with the empress to discuss these matters. Since this concerns national security, she wishes to swear you to secrecy with a contract." He produced a data pad from his pocket and held it out to them.

Brek took it and looked it over, swiping his finger up and down the screen.

"Seems kind of stupid to sign a contract saying you won't leave a paper trail," Shen said.

A wolfish smile spread over Reva's face. "Now here is a man who understands discretion is the better part of valor."

"I don't do valor," Shen said as Brek handed the data pad back to Reva—unsigned. "Valor is for soldiers. You want me to work for you, give me credits. We can keep our mouths shut."

"Silence is expensive," added Brek.

"The crown is prepared to pay for it."

Brek and Shen exchanged quick glances. "Then you've got it," said Brek after a moment. "So, what's the job, Majesty? Sooner we get to it, the sooner we can get it done."

"It's no secret my husband is drilling every woman in the empire but me." Cylene turned and leaned against the railing. With the moon behind her and her skin damp with sweat, she was sure the men were getting an eyeful. "My husband has eight bastards from eight different women. Each receives a stipend of ten thousand credits per month, a cost our overburdened treasury would have to support until each one reaches their twenty-first birthday. Aside from the astronomical cost of paying for them—and however many he begets in the future—there is the issue of my son's ascension. Each of these children could stake a claim. Whores are nothing but ambitious. They'd have to be to find an emperor's cock." She turned her head aside. "I want them to go away."

"Forgive me, Highness," said Brek, folding his hands. "You'll have to be more specific."

She turned her head back. "I want you to kill them, all eight bastards and all eight mothers. Is that specific enough?"

Shen turned to Brek who shrugged. Neither of them looked shocked.

"How do you want it done?" Brek asked when Shen turned his head away. "You want it to be public? You want witnesses gone too? How do you want the bodies found?"

"I don't care! Throw them in a fucking sun if you want. It makes no difference, so long as they are dead!"

Reva turned his head away and put his oxygen mask back on. The two mercenaries sat up in their chairs. Cylene composed herself, smoothing her hands over her body.

"It doesn't matter," the empress repeated, "but I'll need proof."

"Proof without leaving evidence will be difficult," Shen said. "I'm not sure this is something we can help with."

"Of course we can," Brek insisted, giving Shen a slap on the back. "What kind of proof? Hearts? Heads? Pictures for your dresser?"

Reva chuckled, and Cylene shot him a warning glare he paid no mind to.

"Pictures and transmissions can be intercepted. I'm not so gruesome and unreasonable I'd want a collection of body parts turning up at my door either."

Reva lowered his mask and shifted to one side of the chair. "Here is what I propose. As much as her majesty would like to see those women dead, such a punishment is far too kind. Instead, put the women in chains. Take them as slaves and sell them to the whore houses on Amasia, where they will fetch a good price. Let the masses fill them with seed and disease until they burst."

"What of the children?" Shen asked, his voice on edge.

"The children must die," Reva answered. "There is no way around it. Perhaps they are innocents now, but if ambition ever sets their hearts aflame, they will be as divisive to Senjele as Toria and Illion have been. Yes, they must die, but they need not suffer." Reva reached into a fold of his robe and brought out a vial of clear liquid, holding it between two fingers. "One drop blocks the pain messages in the brain. Two brings a long, pleasant sleep. Three slows the heart to a stop. They will die peacefully, dreaming of better things."

He offered the vial of poison to Brek, who took it and held it in a stream of moonlight.

"As for proof," continued Cylene. "Each time you complete an assignment you will travel back here and relate the story of how you accomplished your task to Reva and I."

"How is that proof?" scoffed Brek as he pocketed the vial. "I could concoct some elaborate story and you'd be none the wiser. It's not a very good plan."

"You scratch your eye when you lie," Reva announced to Brek. "When you're unsure of something, you shift your weight forward. Your eyes tick to the left when you've omitted information and the right when you think you've given too much."

Brek scowled. "How'd you know that?"

"And you," said Reva as he turned to Shen. "There is a delicate shift in your eyes when you're uncomfortable. Your respiration rate increases when you omit a truth and, when you outright lie, you look at your hands or lean to one side."

Shen frowned. "You've paid this man well, Highness."

"He is the best at what he does." Cylene offered a sanguine grin. "He's worth every copper coin. It is impossible to lie to Reva and, therefore, impossible to lie to me." She sauntered back over and took her seat, again making a show of crossing one leg over the other. "So? Will you take the job, or won't you?"

Brek leaned into Shen and the two spoke in whispers of a foreign tongue. To Cylene, it sounded like Shen had some objection Brek was trying to field, and she smirked as she listened to the argument heat up. A mercenary with morals. How quaint. Selling women into slavery didn't bother him, but murdering children, even in this humane way, unsettled him.

She stood and walked over to them, interrupting their conversation. "Perhaps I can sweeten the deal for you, gentlemen," she said and swung her hands between their legs, groping until she felt them harden. Cylene leaned against Shen and put her lips next to his ear. "I promise you, I have enough appetite for both of you."

He raised his head and she shivered when he put his mouth against her ear. "Sorry. Not interested," he said, and grasped her wrist so tight it hurt.

She let him go and took half a step back, giving him a wary look. No one had ever turned her away. Not even Ludus could have resisted this play, even if he couldn't satisfy her.

Shen relaxed in his chair and jerked his head to the side, indicating Brek. "You'll have to make do with Brek today, Majesty. I'm afraid you and I wouldn't get on."

Brek laughed at him and pulled her into his lap as if she were a common whore. "That's where your mistake is, Shen. It's not about getting on. It's about getting off."

Brek dared to give her a sloppy kiss.

As much as Cylene wished to, she didn't push the mercenary away. She needed his loyalty—more loyalty than money could buy. She needed him to keep coming back. She only wished she could have the other one, since he was more attractive and better built than Brek. She might have laid under him all night instead of this scarred-up ruffian. But if it secured her place in the empire after Ludus's passing, it was worth a few moments of misery.

She stood and pulled Brek up, luring him toward the bed. As she passed, Reva put away his oxygen and rose, smoothing his soft hands over his robe. "I believe that is our cue to step out."

"Oh, you're not taking part?" asked Brek as she helped him out of his clothes.

Reva laughed. "Master Brek, I'm happily married to a very jealous man."

"Let him stay," Cylene said, smiling as Brek's hand probed between her legs. "You too, Reva. Everything is more fun with an audience."

Reva wasn't bothered. He never was when she had male company. A hundred times he must have stood by and watched, ever the faithful guardian, making sure no man took more than she was willing to give. He'd grown up the youngest nephew of an Amasian lord and Amasia was well known for its whore houses. Reva's family owned half a dozen. Sex was just another thing to him. Best of all, Reva had no illusions about ever being invited to partake, though it excited her when he watched.

The other mercenary, though, he would squirm and try to look away. She would make certain he could hear what he was missing. Next time, he would jump at the chance.

CHAPTER TWELVE

Shen

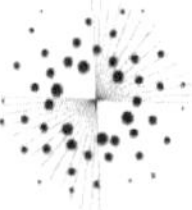

Shen smoked his pipe, eying the man who sat across from him. On the other side of the room, Brek had his fun. It was background noise. The woman thought she was sealing the deal. It wasn't the first time some tart had offered to exchange sex for murder and it wouldn't be the last. Brek always handled it. He was a people person, even if he wasn't very smart. Both mercenaries knew Shen carried the pair when it came to fighting, just as both knew the core of the job they'd just taken had almost nothing to do with the woman.

The strange man had brokered it, even if the empire's money financed it. And Shen didn't like Reva Tzu from Amasia. He was trying too hard to peddle his act. The oxygen, the slight hands and frail build made more obvious by wearing clothes two sizes too big. Reva might have the Senjelians fooled but Shen didn't buy it.

"Where did you serve?" Shen asked him casually, tapping on the bowl of his pipe.

"Serve?" answered Reva, raising an eyebrow. "I'm not sure what you mean."

"You were military. Or you've had military training. Hard to see you on the front lines somewhere but behind a desk with an earpiece or reading documents isn't too far-fetched."

"I have always been and always shall be a servant of the royal family of Senjele."

"Hmm," Shen huffed and puffed on the pipe. "Always in this capacity?"

A sly grin touched the corners of Reva's thin lips. "For most of my adult life."

"You didn't like Amasia, then?"

"I like it just fine."

"Yet you are here." There was a long silence between them, filled in by moans from the other side of the room. "I assume we'll get the names and locations of the bastards from you?"

"I will arrange for you to receive the first ones on your way out." He looked across the room. "Once they are finished."

"It won't be long."

"No," Reva agreed. "It's never as long as you'd like to think."

Shen removed the pipe from between his lips. "Do you have a medical condition?"

"Pardon?" Reva raised an eyebrow.

Shen gestured to the oxygen. "The thing you wear on your face. I met another fellow who had something like it once. I cut out one of his lungs and the poor bastard still managed to survive. He was breathing from a tube for the rest of his life. Two years later, he hired me to finish him. Said it was a damn shameful way to live, eating and breathing and shitting into tubes and pans."

Reva gave a lighthearted chuckle. "Sorry to disappoint you, but nothing so exciting has ever happened to me." He pulled down the collar of his robe, revealing a chest full of gnarled, pink and twisted skin. It looked as if his body were made of raw beef, hardened with clay. "I was in an accident when I was younger, an industrial chemical spill. The vapors were caustic, and my lungs badly damaged."

"What luck you survived."

"Indeed," said Reva, pulling his collar back up, "but not my luck. Someone pulled me from the spill, a passerby."

"Hmm," Shen grunted. "Why wasn't he burned?"

Reva's mouth twitched. "I believe he wasn't human."

Shen laughed so hard his eyes teared. "That's a new one. Are you one of those alien theorists?" He flashed his hands and made a face. "We're not alone in the stars?"

"It's egocentric believing humans alone have evolved in the galaxy. Where did we come from? How did we spread so far across the stars? Who built the massive jump gates we use for interstellar travel? We don't know how they came to be any more than we know how to maintain them. When one stops functioning, whole systems are abandoned because we lack the knowledge to make even the most basic repairs. Something was here before us."

"You think one of them pulled you from a chemical spill?" Shen rolled his eyes.

"Is it so difficult to believe the beings some call gods are just another race? Perhaps we are a great social experiment, the result of generations of uncontrolled tests and observations."

There was a loud noise on the other side of the room. Shen smirked, realizing things were already drawing to a close.

"I believe human evolution is driven by more than the need to reproduce," Reva said.

"I thought natural selection and selective breeding were generally accepted nowadays."

"Then explain why you would reject the advances of the empress." Shen's eyes snapped back to Reva, whose tone had changed. "She is powerful, beautiful. Every man she meets desires her."

"You don't."

Reva chuckled. "You miss the point. If reproduction is the ultimate aim of our species, is it not in your best interest to spread your seed far and wide as often as possible? Is it not genetic suicide to reject the chance to do so? What of those men who prefer the company of other men, or women who love only women? Are these social constructs? No. They appear in nature also. I posit once more that if the production of offspring is our reason for existence, why is the phallus not the largest organ?"

"According to your argument, you think humans are just large filters, since the liver is the largest organ," Shen answered with a grunt.

"Wrong," Reva said, leaning forward. "Skin is the largest organ on a human. Yet, even skin ceases to function without access to the brain. The brain is the most important part of a man, Shen. Not the heart, not the phallus. The brain. Why would we develop such large brains if not to question things? Your brain allowed you to see there was more advantage, more power, in refusing to sleep with Cylene than there ever will be in giving her what she wants. By denying her, you give yourself power over her. You make her want you even more."

Shen put the pipe back in his mouth. He hadn't thought about it in those terms. It just didn't sit right, the way she threw herself at them, eager to offer her body as currency. Sex for pleasure and to pass the time was one thing, but it served no use as a bargaining chip. Brek wouldn't value her more because of it. It wouldn't hurt the emperor any, since he didn't care who came to his empress's chambers, and it wouldn't do anything to ease the bitterness slowly strangling the woman's heart. But she used it to gain power anyway. She just couldn't help herself.

Shen lit his pipe again. "So, you believe human evolution is driven by aliens who favor big brains and who rescued you from a potentially fatal accident. What a strange little man you are, Reva."

Reva leaned even further forward, lowering his voice below a whisper. If Shen's hearing had not been so good, he would not have heard him. "Do you think I don't know what you are?" he said.

Shen shook out the match and puffed on the pipe until he had a good burn going. "What am I?"

Reva's only answer was a smile.

CHAPTER THIRTEEN

Vyjorin

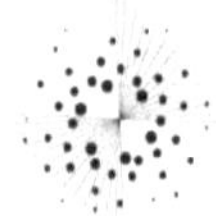

Twenty maidens and twenty crones in red silk swayed back and forth in rows like waves in a bloody sea. In unison, they raised their hands to the sky and joined them. They whipped their heads around so violently as they entered the trance, Vyjorin thought their veils might fly off. He frowned as sweat trickled between his eyes and turned to the eunuch standing next to him. "She's not coming, is she?" The eunuch didn't answer. He just kept waving his feathered fan. "Curse that woman. I told her to be here. This is important."

"Would you like some ice?"

At least now he knew the eunuch wasn't mute. "No." He shifted his weight on the pillow and wished he could move the palace faster. The slaves had moved it into high gear hours ago, and they were still only halfway to the Bitter Caves. He had forced them to work through the night and now through their breakfast and they still wouldn't make it before sundown. The child would be here before then, judging by Ki's anguished moans behind him. It was a bad omen for a prince to be born in the desert. It meant a dry reign.

There was little he could do about omens and superstitions, but he would certainly do something about that older sister of his. He'd gotten word two nights ago that she had brought the *Freyja* into dock in the Bitter Caves region, and he'd sent an urgent summons to her ship. Vyjorin expected her to be late—not for her not to ignore him altogether. He couldn't let such a blatant insult go unpunished.

She was probably still sore about the oath of fealty he'd made her swear. The king sipped his wine through clenched teeth as he remembered how she had laughed at him when he insisted on it. "I relinquish my claim," she teased, throwing her hands up, "And the claims of my heirs. Rule your kingdom, brother. Wear the eye. But this is my ship, and here I am queen." As a joke, she had raised a new banner on her ship, the Eye of the King, white on black, and called her pirate flag the Black Eye. Vyjorin did not think it was funny in the least.

Thank the light, he had one sister who knew her place. He looked down at the empty pillow where Kihran usually sat and then walked his eyes across the step to where Princess Shireen waited patiently. She was a maiden girl of fifteen, and yet Vyjorin saw the flowering of womanhood in his sister as she gently swayed to the singing. She had a slew of suitors, most of whom hadn't even seen her. The gods blessed Shireen with her mother's beauty and an early flowering, making her look at least four years older. Kihran's personal physician examined her on her arrival and found her fit and ready for bearing children of her own. How Shireen's eyes had beamed at the thought of entering the temple rites herself! As the head of his house, the decision fell to Vyjorin on who and when she would wed. If she knew what he was considering, she might have been less pleased.

"How long does this blasted ceremony last?" he asked of her. Vyjorin had insisted that the priestesses raise Shireen without taking vows. The Red Sisters studied the gods, the stars, and were renowned anatomists. The sisters cut his eunuchs and would soon birth his son, but that was not the reason for Shireen's placement. The Red Sisters also believed in enlightenment through pleasure and taught the secrets of their practices to their initiates. Shireen's training would make her considerably more valuable and her groom infinitely more pliable to Vyjorin's wishes. He sighed and leaned on one arm. "Does it actually *do* anything?"

"It will make the birthing easier," Shireen said. When she turned her head back to look at him, Vyjorin could see the sparkle of a smile in her brown eyes. "Have you thought of a name yet?"

"I shall call him Slowest Child Ever Born. Even you did not take this long to crawl out of mother's womb."

"I was a third child. The old women say it takes less time after the first."

The thought didn't comfort Vyjorin any. He wondered just how far in her training she had advanced, and quickly dismissed the thought of asking. They were blood. He did not need to know details. "Must they sway? It's making me sick."

"I think it's beautiful." She watched them sway. "Can

I hold the baby when it comes?"

"After the midwife looks at him, yes. After I've had a look. And Ki, too."

She scooted up one tier closer to his throne. It was her right to sit closer, he supposed. She was his sister. What was he to do, cut off her feet?

"Vyjorin?" She leaned closer.

Behind him, the birthing crones commanded his wife to push. Ki let out a cry of protest. He wanted to be there with her, holding her hand and kissing the sweat from her brow. As king, he should have decreed that they accept his presence, but the midwives would have none of it. It was a woman's pain to bear. Not his.

"Vyjorin!" Shireen tugged at the bell on his shoe and made it jingle.

"What is it, Shireen?"

"Have you given any thought to who my match will be?"

"Now is not the time. You're still young. I would rather see you grow into womanhood and complete your training. The timing is less urgent, now that I have an heir."

"But I'm taller than Kihran. Priestess Tiysha says I'm ready to enter the temple rites. All I need is your blessing!"

"I won't give it! Gods, no, Shireen. Height has nothing to do with it! Don't they educate you in that temple? I swear, I'll call you home and get you a proper tutor."

Her forehead flushed. "I know that. I was only pointing out that it isn't fair for you to call me a child when the woman you sleep with is practically a dwarf."

He drew his hand back to strike her.

She fell to her face before he could follow through. "Forgive my words, my king!"

With a sigh, he dropped his hand back down. "All is

forgiven, Shireen. Go."

"I'm sure you know best, Brother," she said before retreating down to her pillow.

The chanting had started inside the tent now, and it was driving him mad. Vyjorin could sit no longer. He found his feet and paced. The king looked up to the moons and fingered the eye around his neck. *A boy*, he prayed. *It must be a healthy boy.*

The mobile palace suddenly lurched to a stop, the great wheels screeching and the gears grinding. Vyjorin nearly fell from the platform. "Why have they stopped?" he shouted as he regained his balance. His head slave, a eunuch with gauged ears that hung near to his shoulders, crawled onto the palace steps and fell on his face to whisper to the freed men. A report quickly came up that one of the careless slaves had fallen into the gears, tangling his entrails into the mechanism in a mangled, bloody mess. They could go nowhere until the other workers attempted repairs. Vyjorin threw his hands into the air. They would never make Bitter Caves in time now. There was nothing to do but retire from the heat while the slaves cleaned up their mess.

Vyjorin retreated into the antechambers of the mobile palace and seized the use of Shireen's quarters and a flagon of sweet wine. He swallowed the flagon, listening to the distant cries of pain, the chanting and the overseer's whip at work, growing drowsy and irritable at even the slightest noise. The bed was soft and scented so heavily that he fell into a lucid dream.

Vyjorin turned in the darkness and saw a tall, slender form shift on the bed next to him. In his drugged sleep, he reached for the form, believing it to be Kihran. When he felt the distinct flicker of a reptile's tongue against his fingers, he recoiled with a cry of terror. The creature laughed. "You are your father's son." When she spoke, it was with a legion of voices, all deep, twisted, and dark.

"Who's there?" Vyjorin tried to growl but his voice cracked with fear. "Show yourself!"

A light flashed in the darkness and Vyjorin saw a woman's face wearing skin the color of death, made whiter by her ruby lips and blood red eyes. The scream was too thick in his throat to find its way out. He kicked away the blankets and tumbled to the floor, only to hear a low growl next to his ear. Foul, sulfurous breath snorted in his face as a lipless mouth opened into a hiss. "Heed me, King," said the female creature. "My pets will not harm you."

"What do you want?" The king shivered, even though it was mid-afternoon and at least a hundred degrees outside. "Who are you?"

A forked tongue darted out from between her lips. "A servant of the Nameless God."

Vyjorin's heart thumped so hard, he thought it might jump out of his chest. The Nameless God? There were no servants of Him remaining. They'd been wiped out in the great purge generations ago. "Lies," he croaked. "That cannot be."

"That thing you wear around your neck—you have no idea what it is, do you, fool king?" Vyjorin's hand instinctively closed around the chain. "If you did, you would not use it so lightly. Tell me, when you touch the power you hold, do you see the light or the pit?"

He didn't want to answer her, didn't even know if he could. Yet she compelled his lips, even against his heart. "The light."

"That will change soon enough. You may call me Lillith." She reached through the darkness to caress his jaw. "I have the gift of foresight, King, and I come to you with a proposition. Your wife is in the throes of a difficult birth that will claim her life."

"No," Vyjorin croaked. "She is strong."

"Your midwives have turned the child." She spoke as if she hadn't heard him. "And they have doomed it. There is nothing I can do for the child. He is already blue and cold. But your wife, she still bleeds." Her fingers floated against his chest. "And she will continue to bleed until she dies. It is an unpleasant death. She will live to see you hold the bloated babe, and curse her and the gods that brought her to you. Then she will pass … unless you heed my words."

Vyjorin's chest ached as he entertained the image. He could never curse Kihran. Even if she bore a still child, he couldn't. Gods forgive him, he loved her. He would not curse her, and he would not turn from his gods. If she died, he held the answer around his neck. "Your words are empty." He let go of the chain and let the eye fall heavy to his chest. "I do not fear death."

A smirk curled her lips on one side. "It is not death you need to fear, Your Highness. My master descends upon this world. Now is the time to choose whether you will kneel or die. My offer is simple. Give me the dead child. I will carry it off and you need not worry about a burial. In return, you will be spared from His wrath."

"No!" Vyjorin shouted so loudly someone should have heard him, but the darkness devoured the sound.

Her form faded, shifted somehow, and reappeared beside him. "This is foolish. I have made an offer to save her and to save you." She plucked a hair from her head and held the strand between two fingers. "Her life is a thread and it is shortening. The scissors of fate have closed their teeth around her."

Vyjorin clenched his eyes shut. "Be gone, demon! I will not strike a bargain with you! Not even if your lies ring true."

Lillith snapped her fingers and the darkness came up again, concealing all but her face. "When you change your mind, make an offering of blood and fire in the Black Temple. We will strike our deal then." She vanished in a flash of light. Her pet, however, remained. It turned on Vyjorin in a furious flash of gnashing teeth and claws, ripping and tearing mercilessly into his chest, cleaving the Eye in two.

Vyjorin sat up in the strange bed with a scream caught in his throat. The room was black, but did not hold the same oppressive, soundless darkness as it had in his dream. His fingers ran over his body and the Eye. Only when he found it whole did he shakily throw the covers aside and wander into the brightness of the sun. He shielded his eyes from the blinding light as Shireen came up to meet him.

"Brother," she started and then stopped. "Are you sick? You look pale."

His eyes finally adjusted to the light. He was relieved to see the forty red women still chanting and swaying. Vyjorin waved her concern away. "You burn too many herbs in your bedchamber, sister."

"It helps me sleep."

It was then that he noted the oddity of her coming to him unsummoned. "Why are you here?"

"The crones sent me. Your wife calls for you."

Vyjorin shoved Shireen aside and made for his chambers with her on his heels. When he reached the tent, he did not wait for an invitation, but threw aside the flap and peered in. There was no chanting inside, no singing and no coos of praise. There was only the gentle sound of water lapping at skin. The three midwives knelt in a circle with their backs to him, sprinkling a small form with water. Kihran lay, pale, weak and damp on their marriage bed. When his wife saw him, she reached for him and said weakly, "A boy, my love. They say it was a boy."

Was? Could Kihran have uttered a more terrible word? Perhaps she was in the grip of the sleep wine for her birthing pains. His legs shook with every step as he crossed the threshold and came to the midwives. I don't want to see. I don't. But I must.

What he saw was not a child. It was a swollen, blue, lump of flesh, twisted and deformed, with lidless eyes and the tail of a beast. There was a hollow where the suckling mouth should have been. Vyjorin felt his stomach lurch.

He turned on his wife and lifted the blanket covering her legs. The sheets and the mattress beneath it were soaked in blood. They had packed her full of cotton and gauze and still the flow came forth, black and foul. He threw the covers down in disgust.

"Will you not hold your son?" Kihran said weakly.

In a rage, Vyjorin pushed the midwives aside. "Cease! Give no rites to this thing!" He took it up using the blanket they had wrapped it in and spun so she could see the monstrous thing she had borne him. "This is no child of mine!" He tossed the corpse back to the midwives with a soggy thud and tried to keep from gagging. "And you are no wife of mine." He stormed from the tent and back out onto the deck. Those miserable women were still at their chant. "Quiet, you gargling whores!" He took up the royal cushion and threw it into their ranks. "Be gone from my sight! I renounce your gods for their cruelty! I curse the very sands you walk upon! May your feet burn and blister with every step!"

Vyjorin ran forward to take Kihran's pillow and throw it at them as they filed out, but he stumbled and fell to his knees, his chest aching and his hands trembling.

Shireen rested a hand on his shoulder. "My king," she

said tenderly, sinking to her knees beside him. She was crying. "Brother, Kihran's spirit is gone from her body."

"It's that she-demon," he said as he crawled up the stairs. "She did this."

"Who?" Shireen insisted and followed. "Who did this?"

Vyjorin burst into the tent, ignoring the midwives, and crawled on his knees to Kihran's bedside. He pulled the medallion from his chest and lifted it into the tiny shaft of moonlight that broke through the tent walls. Holding back tears, he managed, "Behold the power of the gods, held by your king."

He waited, held his breath and prayed but nothing happened. He shook the pendant as he held it higher and repeated the words, screaming them into her cooling flesh. "Behold the power of the gods, held by your king!" But the power did not come.

Vyjorin buried his face in Kihran's breasts. He shook and wept furiously. "I will kill her," he said, as he flung the pendant away. "I *will* kill her!"

"Who?" Shireen insisted. "Tell us, brother, and we'll bring her to you."

Vyjorin spun with his mouth open to scream at them. What was there to say? A dream? A vision? Whatever it was, he was the only witness. The voices in the darkness had whispered to him and him alone.

I am mad, Vyjorin realized as he caressed his corpse bride. *As my father before me. The light save me, I am mad!* He rose slowly and walked to retrieve the amulet he had discarded, dropping it with heavy hands over his head. "Clean the body," he ordered. "But do not embalm her. Bring all the ice that can be made and craft a bed for her to rest on. And tell the slaves they are to change course."

"Yes, your Royal Majesty," a eunuch offered with a

bow. "Where is our new destination?"

Vyjorin turned to look at the gnarled and twisted body of the son Kihran had grown inside her. He would have to preserve it, too, though he would craft a holding for it that did not require him to look at it. "The Black Temple," he said confidently. "Tell them I will personally punish any slave that slows us down. If another body falls into the gears, they are to pull it out immediately to keep it from clogging them." The eunuch bowed even lower and took his leave. "Shireen." She jumped as he said her name. "You will reside at the temple no longer. I will arrange a teacher for you here."

CHAPTER FOURTEEN

Timothy

Timothy took another over-sized swallow of his wine and watched as Senator Clovis drummed his fingers on the far end of the house's longest table. Through two courses, the senator hadn't lifted his eyes from the plate. The air in the dining hall was more volatile than rocket fuel. Clovis was not happy with the condition Timothy had set forward.

However, if the old senator was to get what he wanted, he would have to give something up, too. *There isn't enough wine in the house to ease the tension in here.* Timothy emptied his cup a third time. Chaunstance came forward to fill it. Clovis gnawed on a chicken bone. *I can't take this anymore.* He looked up at Chaunstance as she stepped away. "Thank you, my lady." Timothy lifted the cup and took a drink before addressing her. "You should join us."

Chaunstance glanced at Clovis, and turned her attention back to Timothy. "I eat with the kitchen staff."

"Nonsense, Chaunstance. Val's right. You should sit. Don't be so damn serious all the time." Chaunstance had filled Clovis's cup twice as often as Timothy's. He should have been at least tipsy, but he sounded as clear-headed as always. "Sit."

Chaunstance did as he bid her, calling in one of the serving girls to bring her a plate of food and fill her cup, all in silence. Chaunstance ignored the silence and turned to Timothy. "When will you be leaving us, Captain?"

"Chaunstance," Clovis said, "don't be so rude. Val is an honored guest. He can stay as long as he likes."

Spoken like a true politician, Timothy thought. Clovis was an excellent liar. "I'm a captain no longer. Just Timothy will do. To answer your question, though, I'll be leaving soon."

"You'll be returning to Clevennia, then?"

"Us too, it seems," Clovis grumbled. "Val's been kind enough to invite us to be his guests. What we'll do in a drafty old castle is beyond me."

"Castle Valence may be made of stone, Senator, and Clevennia is less temperate, but I wouldn't call it drafty. To be honest, Senjele is too damn hot most of the time and Toria was even worse." Timothy stared into the thick, red drink. The bitter tasting wine was making his tongue loose. He could hear each of his words slipping into the next. He knew he was drunk, but couldn't stop himself. "I keep thinking about it … about how I almost let it happen. There was a moment when I might have turned my head and pretended not to notice."

Chaunstance stood, her plate untouched. "I'll excuse myself unless—"

"Yes, you should." Timothy twisted sideways in his chair. "Leave the talk of war and death to the men. Rebos will shove a rifle in your hands soon enough when he runs out of boys to throw at the Erolyian fleet."

She sat back down. "Perhaps I'll stay and learn how to salute the high and mighty Captain Val."

"Chaunstance!" Clovis gave her a scolding glare and she lowered her head. Clovis shook his head and raised a forkful of food to his mouth. "The army ought to conscript women as well, Timothy, if their aim is as sharp as their tongues."

"I didn't mean it as it came, milady," he said. "It's the wine talking. I think I've had enough." He pushed his cup away. "I only meant—" *Tread carefully, Timothy.* "Tensions with Erolyia are on the rise again. There've been so many border skirmishes in the last decade, there's been talk of a blockade. We'll have a war soon enough, such as this galaxy has never seen. A damned bloody war where ships and coin will only count for so much. Bodies in uniforms win wars. Whoever runs out of them first loses. I don't like walking away from a fight, but I have a duty to the people. You and I, Senator, we're not so different after all, are we? We're both servants of the people. Chaunstance, you're a lucky woman to only have one man to care for. It's much more difficult to have the weight of an entire world on your shoulders."

He lifted his eyes from the table to Clovis. The senator's face was blank and unreadable, but least he wasn't angry. There was a long silence as Clovis chewed his bread. Chaunstance stared at her plate. Timothy sipped his wine.

The double doors to the dining room burst open and a heavyset, red-faced servant rushed forward to whisper into Chaunstance's ear. "I'll deal with it," Chaunstance whispered, and sent the woman away. "Excuse me, Senator," Chaunstance said, rising, and then acknowledged Timothy with a bow of her head. "Something's come up. Enjoy your meal. I'll return shortly."

"Well, at least she's being more personable," Clovis said. "She seems to have taken a liking to you, Val, though I can't see why. You're an ass, a complete and total ass."

"I suppose even a zebra knows his own stripes when he sees them on another."

Clovis stiffened at the insult and then smiled. "Touché," he said, raising his glass. "To being an ass!" Timothy raised his own glass and they toasted one another, the tension finally easing between them.

By the time Chaunstance returned with an envelope in her hands, Clovis and Timothy were both drunk. The senator recited a bawdy limerick in tune. Timothy was laughing so hard he didn't notice her until she interrupted Clovis's chuckling. "A messenger from the palace, Senator," she announced before handing the envelope to Clovis.

Clovis grumbled as he fumbled with the clasp. He pulled out an official-looking document on thick, expensive paper and held it away from his face. As his eyes trailed down the page, the senator's brow wrinkled, and he sobered.

"Well?" demanded Timothy as he pulled himself back up. "What does it say?"

"It's for you," the senator said in an irritated tone, and handed it back to Chaunstance.

The room shifted and shrank as Chaunstance held the letter out to him. Timothy shook his head. "Sorry, milady. I'm too drunk. Best you read it, or it won't make sense."

Clovis snickered, then snorted and chortled. In no

time at all, both were howling with laughter again. Chaunstance had to raise her voice to be heard. "To Timothy Val: His Imperial Highness, Ludus Eflor, commands your presence at an award ceremony in your honor at which time you shall receive commendation for your heroic actions during the Torian rebellion."

Timothy choked on his own laughter. He had expected to receive some kind of commendation, especially since the executors were kind enough not to execute him. The crown had to either acknowledge him or make an apology and reparations, the latter of which was far more difficult to keep out of the tabloids. Even so, he hadn't expected this.

"His Imperial Highness and all his retainers also wish to formally recognize you as heir to the Val lines of succession, awarding you governorship of the planet of Clevennia, all her moons and satellites, and the surrounding space to the nearest gate, not to exceed three hundred thousand kilometers except where expressly stated on the legally drawn boundaries of Clevennia."

"Gods," Timothy breathed. It was really happening. There was no backing out now.

"You will appear before His Imperial Highness and his court promptly at four o'clock tomorrow afternoon in formal attire for the gracious acceptance of both the gold star for valor and governorship of Clevennia. Signed, His Imperial Majesty Ludus Eflor."

"Is this your idea of a joke, Senator," Timothy asked as he took the letter from Chaunstance to examine the authenticity of it. Clovis had to have something to do with it. It had only been days since he began the paperwork. Government never worked this fast.

"Say what you want about me, sir," Clovis slurred. "But I'm a terrible forger. Even if I were decent at it, I'm not stupid enough to forge the emperor's signature and his seal. That's a death by beheading. I've become attached to my head over the years."

Timothy turned the letter in all directions, trying to find some discrepancy, some proof it was false. It didn't matter, he supposed. He would take the position anyway. Since it was an imperial edict, he couldn't back out of it. He just didn't want the fuss of a ceremony. He lowered the paper, feeling hot and sick. His thoughts were too slow, too disjointed to deal with this now. Worse, words kept falling out of his mouth, even before he realized he was talking. "I have nothing to wear," he was saying. "I'm not going."

"You're going, Val, if I have to drag you there myself."

Timothy shook his head and pushed his plate away. "I don't have a date and I can't dance. These things always have dancing."

"You can take Chaunstance."

Color crept into Chaunstance's cheeks. "Absolutely not!"

Clovis ignored her. "She's an excellent dancer, has to be to make me look good when I dance at these affairs."

"You're drunk," Chaunstance said, and snatched away the senator's cup. "I've sent for Mistress Danayla. Get yourself to bed and sleep off this nonsense. We'll talk about it in the morning."

"So we will," the senator said, and excused himself from the table.

"Well, milady," Timothy said. "That's my cue to retire." He stood, but the room spun, and he wound up leaning over the table instead.

"You men talk nonsense when you drink," she said. "You don't hold your liquor well, Lord Captain." There was amusement in her voice, but she wasn't smiling.

"Clovis is an alcoholic trying to pickle his liver. You shouldn't try to keep up."

She stood with all the grace of the lady of the house, walked the length of the table and grabbed him by his cuffs. "Come on, let's get you to bed so you can sleep it off before you say something else."

She half-dragged, half-pushed him up the stairs. His legs were under him well enough, but she wanted to go faster than he did. "Slow down." She didn't listen. Before he knew it, she'd stuffed him into his tiny guest room.

"This is backward." He lifted his hands away from her. "I should walk you to your room instead of you to mine. The servants will talk."

"You don't even know where my room is. You'd stumble in on Clovis. He'd be cross with you for interrupting."

By the way she helped him unbutton his jacket, he knew she'd helped Clovis to bed many a time. He didn't want her help. He swatted her hands away and almost fell. She kept him upright.

"I'm not so drunk I don't know how to undress," Timothy insisted.

"You're a terrible drunk. It makes me wonder how you did any of the things they say you did. Are they true? The stories they tell?"

"I don't want to think about that now," he said and took her by the shoulders. "I want …" He trailed off as the words disappeared into the haze in his head. He didn't have the gift for words, not like Clovis, nor was he good at being a drunk, but maybe he could be good to her. He placed a hand behind her head and pulled her lips to his without giving her time to protest.

She shoved him away and gave him a sobering slap. "You should be ashamed of yourself."

"You need honor to have shame," Timothy said.

But she was right, Chaunstance wasn't some barmaid or the younger sister of cadet so-and-so. This woman didn't want a drunken soldier like him. She deserved a better man, a sober man.

But the dance had started, even if he'd missed a few steps. "Does it matter? You want me. I felt it just now on your lips. And I want you."

She shook her head. "You don't even know me." She gathered her skirts and left him staggering.

He collapsed into the bed, still half-undressed. "Damn you, Senator Clovis. Damn you and your wine … and you, woman … and you, Timothy. Especially me."

Timothy closed his eyes and fell into a deep, drunken sleep. He dreamed of the battle, the explosions, Private Malor's helmet filled with brain soup. When he woke, it was dark, and his head was screaming. He cursed the wine once more and tried to roll over. Even the soft mattress did little to quiet the protests of his stomach.

He was almost asleep again when he heard a faint and unfamiliar sound in the room. The captain's eyes snapped open and he stared into the darkness. There was a feeling in his gut, not from the rich food or rejection or wine. The night was too dark, the shadows too deep and the bed too comfortable. It was *that* feeling. Unfamiliar, malicious eyes latched onto the back of his head. *Someone else is in this room*, he thought, and tried to control his breathing. *Someone I don't know.*

Timothy's eyes trailed along the floor, searching for his jacket. He always kept a sidearm with him, even when he wasn't on duty. Since his discharge from the Keep, he hadn't replaced the one he'd lost on Toria. There hadn't been time. Now he was cursing himself for being so careless. He glanced at the end table beside the bed. Nothing there but an alarm clock and a lamp.

A shadow shifted in front of him. Timothy lunged and grabbed for the lamp, but he wasn't fast enough. Lightning flashed as a gun went off, the super-heated plasma barely missing his outstretched arm. The shot struck the wall behind him, leaving a charred circle behind. The light was brief, only a strobe, but it was enough for Timothy to see his attacker was a large, dark-skinned male. Timothy swung his legs over the bed and struck something fleshy. A gun clattered to the floor. Timothy jumped out of bed and tackled the man, landing three hard blows to his head. Blood oozed out of the man's nose and lip, but even that didn't gather Val's attention. What he saw was the cold, black metal alloy of the man's gun and the blood on his hands. He saw his commanding officer on Toria, the High Executor as he poured the water onto the floor. He saw his father.

Timothy reached for the gun, still trying to hold the man down. When his fingers finally found it, he brought it up and pressed it hard against the man's temple, the heat of the barrel burning an indentation into the man's skin. Timothy thought he would be sick at the scent of burning flesh.

The man sneered at the pain. "Kill me while you can," he said, voice thick with an Erolyian accent. "I see a man who has killed a thousand of me in his mind. I smell blood on you."

Another shape shifted in Timothy's peripheral vision. He swung the gun toward the movement. Chaunstance stood, pale and stiff in the doorway, her fingers on the dimmer switch. Something struck the back of Timothy's head, and the gun skittered across the floor toward the door. Before he could react, the intruder was on top of him, swinging a twisted, serrated blade. Timothy grabbed for a wrist and caught an elbow. The knife bit into his side and came away dark and bloody. He shifted, twisted his hands around the man's arm as the knife bit into him again. There was the crack of bone and cartilage twisting and snapping as the assailant's wrist gave out under the pressure. The knife, though, was lodged in Timothy's side, and his attacker used his forearm to push it deeper. Only the discharge of a gun drowned out Timothy's gasp of pain.

The plasma hit the intruder in the shoulder. He fell away from Timothy and against the wall. Timothy jerked the knife free and tossed it out of reach before taking the man's throat in his hands. The shot had only stunned him as it bored a small hole through his shoulder. Crooked yellow teeth smiled as Timothy's hands tightened around his trachea.

"That it?" the other man managed as Timothy strained to cut off the air. The smile lasted until he lost consciousness and first twinges of blue crept into his face, still taunting Val.

Round, heavy fingers gripped Timothy's shoulders and jerked him back. "You'll kill him before we've had the chance to interrogate him, fool," said Clovis as he pulled Timothy away.

When he struck the floor, Timothy's side burned. In the heat of the moment, he'd barely felt the knife. Now the adrenaline was wearing off, he felt nothing else. Chaunstance pulled the fabric of his shirt free to have a look at the wound. She still held the gun tightly in one hand. "It's nothing," he told her, and pulled the shirt back down. He nodded at the unconscious man on the floor. "You shoot well, my lady." He winced as he took the gun from her and sat up. He'd sustained worse wounds a half-dozen times or more. All he needed was a bandage, antiseptic and maybe a few stitches after he got the bleeding stopped. He looked over to where the knife rested. The thin, jagged teeth glistened in the dim light.

"Senator," Timothy said as he pulled himself up. Clovis was using a belt to tie the assassin up. "I trust you have a cellar?"

The senator caught his intention. "There's a cold room below."

Timothy nodded and lifted his shirt again to look at the wound. He wadded up a fistful of sheet from the bed and pressed it to the wound to try and stifle the bleeding.

"Chaunstance, my dear, go to your room. Lock your door and stay there until I come for you."

"What are you going to do to him?"

Timothy and Clovis exchanged a knowing look as Timothy hobbled over to pick up the knife. Clovis put it to her as delicately as he was able. "Things a lady should never see."

Clovis dragged the man below while Timothy did his best to treat his wounds. By the time he arrived in the lower chamber, Clovis had the assassin stripped naked and dropped a pig carcass from one of the meat hooks.

"Help me string him up," Timothy said, as he stuck the Erolyian knife through the top of a wooden table. Timothy wrapped his belt tight around the man's wrists and they used it to hoist him onto the hook. They tied his ankles with Clovis's belt.

"Did you see the tattoo?" Timothy asked as they stepped back to examine their handiwork.

Clovis nodded. "Erolyian conscript."

"No, he's more than that. He's a Sandman."

"Sandman?"

From his tone, Timothy knew Clovis had never heard of them. He wasn't surprised. Even in the ranks, it was rare to hear them mentioned. Timothy hadn't been sure they'd existed until now. There were scouts who claimed to have seen their insignia carved into the sides of black ships or, occasionally, into bodies. The stories said the Erolyians bred the Sandmen in pits and made them fight for every grain of sustenance their Saleph fed them. Murder was their religion, brutality their prayer. They were killers of the highest caliber and torturers in the employ of the Erolyian crown. When a Sandman came of age, they made him cut the heart out of a giant sandworm and eat it raw. Only then did they receive the brand of the Erolyian king on the thigh: the great, ever-seeing eye.

"Assassins. Expensive assassins from Erolyia. They know killing and little else. Get the water."

The Sandman woke with a start when they poured water over him, and fought his restraints. When he found no way to free himself, he smiled. "I like this room. I can smell the fear."

"Tell us who hired you and why," Timothy demanded.

Clouds of breath erupted from his mouth as the Sandman chuckled. "Or what? You'll torture me? Break me and make me tell you? You can't break what's already broken. You ought to know that, lap dog."

Timothy struck him hard in the face and bloodied his nose again.

The assassin spat blood at him and laughed. "I pay bitches to hit me. You a bitch, Captain? Lift your ass up here and we'll see."

Timothy punched him in the stomach. It knocked the air out of him but not the insolence.

He lifted his head and smiled at Clovis. "You too, piggy. I want you to squeal."

"I'm honored," Clovis said. "Tell me whose name I should squeal?"

"Your mother's."

Timothy walked over to the table and pried the knife free. He returned and wedged it under the edge of one of the Sandman's big toenails. The prisoner growled when the edge drew blood. "I believe the senator asked your name."

"Fuck you, and fuck your whore mother, too."

Val dug the knife deep and pried the nail free, the Sandman grinding his teeth and cursing the whole time. "Your name?"

"Jane bloody Smith."

Timothy pried three more toenails off and twisted the joint on the Eroylian's little finger with a pair of pliers. Each time, he saw the executors' faces as they beat him. He could withstand the physical punishment as well as the man he was tormenting. It was the mental anguish that had ruined him. *They broke me*, Timothy thought as he wiped blood from his hands. *Everyone can be broken.*

"Your name!" Timothy shouted as he went for a fingernail.

"Ethern, you son of a bitch. Pleased as hell to meet you."

"Who hired you to kill me?"

Ethern laughed like a wild man, even as Timothy worked his fingernail free.

"We're not getting anywhere," Clovis said, watching the blood trickle to the floor.

"Spare me your speeches, old man," Ethern spat. "You should be honored. I would have given you a good death, a clean and quiet death. You'll not get that now. No, it'll be slow and messy for all the empire to see."

Timothy stole a glance at Clovis, who shrugged. "Who

hired you?" When he didn't answer fast enough, Timothy seized his other hand and put the knife to his middle finger at the base of the digit. "Answer me!"

The Sandman spat on Timothy and hissed in agony as Timothy sawed through the flesh with the knife. There was resistance when he struck the bone, but he sawed through it. Then, he took hold of Ethern's manhood with a pair of pliers and put the point of the blade to it.

"Who hired you? Was it the executors? The Erolyians? Tell me, Ethern, or I'll slice through and send it to your master as a token of my esteem."

"Timothy …" Clovis was turning white.

"Tell me!"

The Sandman gritted his teeth until they cracked. Then he roared, "Some black-haired bitch in the castle!"

"Her name!"

"Ambren!" the assassin screamed. "Her name's Ambren."

Timothy almost lost his grip on the knife as blood pounded in his forehead. He swallowed. "Nareen Ambren?"

A smile twisted the Sandman's face.

Timothy steeled his expression, but it was too late. Ethern knew he'd struck a nerve.

"Aye. A bitch with good tits and a good, firm ass and a mouth fit for—"

Timothy punched him hard in the face. Ethern slumped over, blood dripping into a growing pool on the floor.

Clovis's hand came down on Timothy's shoulder and the senator led him back to the doorway. "Timothy, before this goes any further—"

"That stupid bitch tried to kill me! Could have killed you and Chaunstance!" He shook his head and leaned against the doorway, trying to find a position to ease the ache in his side. "Why? After all this time, why would she lash out like this? How did she get in contact with a Sandman?"

"I know you're angry," Clovis said. "I know the history between you two is rocky. But think. She didn't send a Sandman to kill you because she's a spurned lover."

Timothy drew a deep breath. The senator was right. Tomorrow night, he would become the lord governor of Clevennia. She wanted to prevent that from happening. But why would she even care what happened to him?

"There are whispers she's Prince Rebos's newest bed warmer," Clovis said.

Timothy glared at the senator, the rage rising in him again. Once, he would have believed murder for advancement beyond her. Nareen might have spread her legs to climb the social ladder, but murder was new. She must have seen him as an obstacle to Rebos. The prince was onto what they were planning. He had to be. That was the only explanation that fit.

He glanced back at Ethern. Their captive shivered and bled over the cellar floor. "We have to kill him." Timothy looked at his hands. They itched where the blood was drying. "This is your house, Senator. Where I come from, that right is yours if you want it."

Clovis shifted, uneasy. *So easy to talk of rebellion and war when the blood's not on your hands, isn't it, Senator?* But that was his role, to decide from the rear, to vote and send men to their deaths with nothing but a yea or nay. A role that would soon be Timothy's.

"I'll do it," Timothy said. He drew his pistol and aimed from the doorway. His side ached, but not so much as the hole in his chest. This man was not even loyal to his own empire. He was no man and did not deserve to die like one. Instead of firing, Timothy walked over and sawed through the belt with his knife.

Ethern crumpled to the floor and stirred awake. He grinned at Timothy. "Do you know how many of your kind I killed, lord captain? Dozens. In the warmth of their bed, their necks bent over desks or some whore. I got one taking a piss once. Gutted him ass to ear. I've flayed men. Burned them, drowned them, beat them and cut them. But what I've done is a kindness compared to what my master will do when he gets his claws in you."

Timothy jerked Ethern to his knees by his greasy hair and pressed the pistol into the back of his head. "I'll send him your regards when I kill him."

"Kill him?" Ethern sneered and laughed. "Kill the Nameless God? Can you poison a whisper? Boil a shadow? Can you—"

The hot plasma burned through flesh and bone, turning Ethern's brain to the consistency of hot wax. Even still, the bastard died with a smile on his lips.

CHAPTER FIFTEEN

Chaunstance

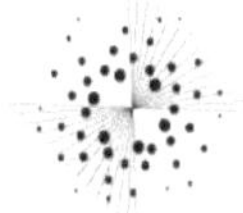

Chaunstance stood in the doorway with her fingers on the dimming switch, staring at the pool of blood in Timothy's room, just as she had done an hour ago. She'd done as Clovis instructed at first, retreating to her room and locking the door behind her. Sitting on the end of her bed, staring at the doorknob and waiting for it to turn, only increased her anxiety.

Chaunstance knew what they were doing to the would-be assassin below: buying answers with blood. That didn't bother her as much as the implications of the assassination attempt itself. The event replayed itself in her head, second by second, the details more vivid in memory than they had been in the moment. *What if I hadn't been there to pick up that gun? What if I hadn't fired?* She knew the answer. Timothy would be dead. All Clovis's planning, all the risks the senator had taken, would be for nothing. The senator had gambled everything on the fragile life of Timothy Val, never imagining he'd have to protect the lord captain. This assassination attempt made it clear they had to be more careful.

The thoughts were too much for her to take sitting alone in her room. She had to do something, even if it meant cleaning up blood. Chaunstance took a bucket of soapy water and hauled it deeper into the bedroom. With a heavy heart, she wrung out the sponge and placed it in the pool of blood. The sponge turned red and, when she dipped it back into the water, all the water in the bucket did too. The stain on the floor remained.

She sighed, squeezed out the sponge, and put it back into the carpet. As she did, a sharp pain shot through her head. Panic rose in her throat as she fought the onslaught of images and visions, pictures of a life not her own. She stood in someone else's skin, lightly tanned and stretched taut over a thick, muscle-bound form. A fire burned in the hearth of an ancient, stone castle while she leaned, fuming, against the cool, gray stone walls. Behind her, a thick man, fat with age and thin of honor, flung a glass of whiskey into the fire. The flames leapt and devoured the alcohol hungrily.

"I told you, no! Damn you, boy, and damn your mother for dying squeezing you out. You're a Val, not some common man in the street. We don't dirty our hands in other people's fights. Not anymore. Wasn't it enough to kill your mother? What does it take to quench your thirst for blood?"

She watched Timothy's unfamiliar fists—her fists— clench and release. Guilt and anger rushed through her.

"I'm going," Timothy's voice said through her mouth. "With or without your blessing, I'm enlisting."

"Then you're no son of mine."

She had the overwhelming urge to punch something, to drive those hot wedges of glass into his throat. "So be it."

A flash. Something struck her hard in the face. No, not her face—Timothy's. Something soft and scented like lilac and lilies. A hand. Here, a woman stood before him: dark and tall, slender and naked, ice-blue eyes heavy with the sleep his sneaking in had interrupted. Tears welled in those eyes now and it stung worse than the slap. The woman wrapped her arms around his neck and opened her mouth to Timothy's. Desire stirred, accompanied by pangs of regret as hands groped to undo his belt. The tears didn't fall until he was already in her and she turned her lips to his ear and whispered, "Don't you ever leave me again, you bastard. Don't—" He clasped her hands and kissed her on the mouth. It was strangely, sickeningly sweet.

Another flash brought her back to the same room, this time fully clothed in pressed military garb. Lady Ambren wept again, but these were the hot, disbelieving tears of rage. Chaunstance's—no, Timothy's hands folded around the bill of his hat. Time had passed. The lady was no longer an unseasoned girl of twenty cycles. She was a woman grown, responsible for her own actions and decisions.

A cool rage burned inside Timothy, an icy fireball spinning counterclockwise at breakneck speed. Betrayal. Chaunstance knew the feeling well.

"Did you ever love me?" Timothy spat at her as she wept. "Or was I just another rung on your ladder?"

Flash. The streets smelled like rotting, burning

garbage, with a sickening corpse-rot undertone. Nautis. The Blitz. A liberation from Erolyian oppression, they'd called it. But the people of Nautis hadn't been starving or ill-treated, not before Senjelian forces arrived. The blockade had left them starving, and forced power outages left them burning garbage in the streets for warmth. This wasn't how it was supposed to be.

Flash. Chaunstance was in his body, in his mind, as Timothy's lips came down against hers. She felt the flush of the wine, tasted the sweetness of her own lips and felt the fire of desire making him hard. Even through the cloud of drunken lust, she saw the pain, felt it sitting like a rock in his chest. A sharp bitterness gnawed inside him, knowing that whoever he loved would just use him. Not a man. A tool. An instrument of war, of political power, of pleasure. Even inside the vision, Chaunstance knew the ache of being so used up.

The last flash struck her hard. The intruder hung by a leather belt in Clovis's cold room, the point of a knife digging into his manhood, a pair of pliers stretching the soft flesh thin. It was cruel, bloody torture, but the bastard deserved it. Rapist, Timothy was thinking as he tugged harder. Killer. This death is too good for you. I should cut it off and feed it to you. See who the bitch is then. You deserve no less for all the lives you've taken. You're not even a man.

As the bound man hissed and spat at him, she heard Timothy wonder what difference there was between himself and this Ethern. The lines were blurry, so very blurry. *I am not a man. I am as guilty as the others. I promised they'd be safe. I did this.* Pity and guilt made him put a spray of hot plasma into Ethern's brain, not malice and anger.

With a gasp, she fell out of the vision and back into reality. There were hands on her, firm hands, one against the small of her back and the other against her head. She pushed them away and scrambled forward. She was blind. Everything was white and dark at the same time and her insides burned.

"Chaunstance!" The voice was familiar, but she couldn't place it. "Breathe!"

Hot tears seared her cheeks as she groped for the wall, then vomited. She clenched her eyes closed and, when she opened them, she was back in Clovis's estate with the stench of blood in her nose.

"Clovis," she called and spun, but it wasn't him she found. She fell weeping and gasping for air into Timothy's arms. "Help me," she pleaded.

His hands moved over her hair, patting her. "Don't look." He tried to shield her eyes from the blood. His voice and touch were gentle, but she knew better. He was a killer. A cold-blooded killer. The world passed beneath her, distant and untouchable. He smelled like wine, sweat and blood and it made her want to vomit again. "Clovis told you to stay here. Don't you listen, even to him?"

She lifted her head and realized she was in her own room. Everything was as it should be. Her books were in their places, her desk neat and tidy, and the dress she had chosen to wear the next day hung on the rack. Dawn was breaking through the window in shades of crimson and pink. She stared at it dully as he lowered her into bed. "You killed him, didn't you?" He pulled the blankets over her without answering. She grabbed his face and turned him toward her. "Didn't you?"

He refused to meet her eyes.

"I saw ..." How could she tell him? Where would she begin? It sounded like madness to her. Chaunstance couldn't even imagine what it might sound like to him. Yet he waited patiently, kneeling at her bedside. "Where is Clovis?"

"He's dealing with the body," he said, lowering her hands from his face. She wasn't sure whether to be relieved or disgusted by his candor. "Stay here,

Chaunstance. Please, listen this time."

Timothy moved to go. A part of her was glad he was leaving her alone. Chaunstance closed her eyes and pressed two fingertips to her lips, remembering the taste of him … the taste of her. Even drunk, he had not been *so* unpleasant. He was a killer, yes, but there was a hesitant gentleness about him, too.

What he had seen on Toria … after Nareen rejected him, he had no one left. Used and alone. They had that much in common, at least.

She sat up in bed, even though the world was spinning. "Wait!"

The turn was painful. She saw the hesitation in his step and the instinctive grab at the wound in his side. "Yes, my lady?" He sounded as if she could say the right words and make the world a better place.

"Your wound …"

"I saw to it."

"I saw the knife. You need more than a bandage. Let me see."

With a sigh, he sat on the side of the bed with his back to her. She tugged the shirt up to look at it. He'd done a poor job of bandaging it, which wasn't surprising, considering where the assassin had stabbed him. The blood had already soaked through the dressing. Any healing that had happened was undone when he picked her up. With careful fingers, she peeled away the tape and wet gauze. One hole was a small slice that would close itself in time but the other was open, jagged, and weeping blood.

"Is it bad?" His tone was hopeful.

"You're no medic. That much is obvious. You need stitches."

Timothy turned his head. "Do this often, do you?"

"Let's just say this isn't the first time a stubborn man has come to me with a hole in a place it shouldn't be, though Clovis whines more and curses a lot."

He laughed and then winced. "Come on. We'll do it in the upstairs washroom. I've got a kit there."

Chaunstance threw the covers off before she could change her mind and went to the guest bathroom across the hall from Timothy's room. While she got everything out and sterilized a needle with alcohol, he stood in front of the mirror, pulling up his shirt, trying to get a look at it.

"Take your shirt off," she ordered, as she finished cleaning her supplies. "And tug your pants down a little."

"Yes, ma'am." Timothy gave her a playful salute.

"Be still," she said, and took out the needle and thread. "I have to sew you back up." Chaunstance threaded the needle. "This won't be pleasant."

"I've been through it before. Just do it."

He turned his head away as she worked, never saying a word. Once, he made a slight grunt when her needle missed its mark and she drew the thread too tight but, otherwise, he was silent. When the wound was closed, she doused it with peroxide and slathered it with antibiotic ointment before giving him a proper bandage.

He rubbed the edges of the bandage and gave an awkward nod. "Thank you, my lady."

"I told you to stop calling me that." She helped him ease into a chair and went about, collecting the bloody bandages.

"Sorry, my la—" he started but when she turned back around he finished with a sheepish grin. "Chaunstance it is, then." She nodded.

Chaunstance didn't like the way he watched her while she worked. His mind was filled with thoughts many men had for her before she knew Clovis. When she was a girl, she was property. The men who took her from her home hadn't been as kind as Clovis. They, too, had lustful thoughts in their heads.

"Dance with me," Timothy blurted.

She frowned at him, not pausing in her work. "What?"

"Tomorrow night at the palace. I want you to dance with me."

"I'm sure you can find a noble-born lady to dance with you."

"I don't want a noble lady. I want you."

She dropped the rag into the sink. "Why are you so fascinated with me? I am no one. I am nothing. A slave. Tomorrow, you will be a lord and have every fine-looking woman in the empire clamoring to stand at your side."

"That's the point." He shifted in the chair. "You're not interested in titles. You won't dance with me because there's something to gain, or stand and flirt with me because you think I'm your ticket to something better. I am not a rung on some ladder you're climbing. You're honest. You hate politics, maybe even more than I do, but, unlike me, you know how they work. The senator wouldn't be so hesitant to dismiss you if you didn't."

Chaunstance leaned in closer. "What makes you so certain I'm the least bit interested in you?"

"If there's one thing I've learned since Toria, it's that nothing in life is certain. You don't trust me, but I don't trust myself either. If I do something foolish, I need someone to tell me."

She shook her head. "You don't know me."

When she rose and turned to go, Timothy grabbed her by the wrist. "I know enough to know I want to know more."

She looked down. It was his blood painting her hands,

staining her dress. Why had she jumped in to save him?

"You don't think it will reflect poorly on your reputation to dance with a slave girl?"

"What slave?" He smiled. "I've negotiated with Clovis to free you. It's part of our agreement."

Chaunstance felt cold. She jerked her hand away. "I told you I didn't want to be free! Do you know what you've done?"

"You won't be put out," he promised. "You'll have work, the same as you do now, and a monthly stipend. Everything you want and need will be taken care of."

She shook her head and turned on the sink to wash her hands, watching the bloody water swirl down the drain. Freedom … For so long, she had said she didn't want it. With freedom came uncertainty. She would lose Clovis's protection, but she would gain autonomy. She could leave Senjele if she chose.

Leave, she mused. *And go where? Senjele is not your home, but neither is anywhere else.* Home had no meaning. Home belonged to other people. If she was free, she had nothing. She didn't even have Clovis anymore. The thought brought tears to her eyes. What good was it to be free if she was alone?

Why had Timothy Val made her freedom part of his agreement with Clovis? She had nothing to do with him! Did he expect her to be grateful and throw herself at him? Is that what he wanted? She didn't feel grateful. She felt numb.

"I'm sorry," Timothy said. "I thought you'd be happy."

She stopped scrubbing her hands and looked up at him. He looked tired. "Why are you so transfixed by my situation? Have you never met a slave before?"

"I believe everyone should choose their path in life," he answered. "A slave does not get a choice. You don't get to choose to come or go, to work or sleep."

"Freedom is an idea. Ideas only live in the hearts and minds of men. They have little bearing in reality."

"It has bearing now." Timothy shifted forward, wincing as he changed positions. "Tell me you don't want to dance with me and I won't ask again. I'll be sad, and a little put out, but I won't bother you again. You and I will go our own ways in life and not think much about it. But, if you agree to dance with me, and forgive me for being a drunken idiot earlier, I will ask you to dance with me again someday. Being close to you will be the closest thing to happiness I've known in a long time, no matter what anyone says tomorrow. Maybe you and I will find common ground and, in doing so, find the universe a little more bearable."

"Do you expect me to love you for convincing Clovis to free me?"

Timothy smiled and shook his head. "Why are you making this so complicated? I see you're a beautiful woman. Clovis says you can dance. Is it so terrible of me to want to dance with you?"

She hesitated. She'd danced with Clovis at functions like this, despite the whispering lords and ladies did behind their backs. She liked to dance, even if it meant people would look at her. Most of the time, she would have preferred to sink into the background and go unnoticed. No one cared who a fat old senator danced with, but Timothy ... Timothy would be the hero of the hour. Everyone would care who he danced with and every fine, eligible lady would try their chance with him. They would be jealous of her. She might make enemies if she danced with him.

Was she afraid of making enemies? She might be more afraid of getting to know him. She had tried so hard to dislike him. He was a soldier, a killer. She knew all too well what soldiers were like. But Timothy wouldn't be unlikable. Even when he had kissed her earlier it wasn't so unpleasant. It hadn't been filled with malice or anger. He hadn't wanted to hurt her, only to find comfort as he struggled through the situation he'd been thrust into.

They had a lot in common, she and Timothy. Neither of them wanted to be at the forefront of this, whatever this was, and neither of them wanted to be alone. Wasn't it worth taking a chance at being happy? It was only for one night and it was only a dance.

"Who else will you dance with?"

"No one," he promised. "I give you my word."

"If I still say no?"

"Then I will stand by my promise and dance with no one tomorrow night."

She laughed but he didn't smile. "You're almost as stubborn as Clovis."

"Thank you. I take it as a compliment."

She dried her hands on a towel and then turned to leave the bathroom.

"Chaunstance," he called, and she hesitated in the doorway without looking back. "You will dance with me?"

"Yes," she said after a pause. "So long as it's a slow dance. I don't want to undo the hard work I just did. You should get out of those bloody clothes. Put them by your door and I'll collect them in the morning. In the meantime, I'll get fresh sheets for you. I suggest you shut the window and lock it. We don't want any more unexpected visitors."

CHAPTER SIXTEEN

Clovis

Clovis grunted and lowered his mug of cheap ale as a greasy-looking man slid into the booth across from him. Captain Jovi Null, wore a pistol at each hip and a cutoff shirt tucked into a faded pair of fatigues. If they had been a particular color once, they retained it no longer. Jovi could have used a shave and a shower but, in the presence of all the other smells, Clovis barely noticed Jovi's stench.

"Howdy," offered Jovi.

"Did you take care of it?" By *it*, Clovis meant the body he'd paid Jovi to move. Moving Ethern into his transport had been a feat in itself. Clovis didn't want to deal with dumping him in the river—or whatever other method of disposal Jovi had thought of.

"Course I did. That's what you paid me for, isn't it?"

Clovis gestured to the closest waitress and ordered Jovi a drink. There was no use in specifying what kind because such a place only carried one thing on tap: cheap, watered-down ale.

Jovi leaned back in his seat. "You know, I hadn't heard from you in so long, I thought you'd forgotten about me."

"Forget about you, Jovi? I think not?"

The captain extended a thick, grimy hand to Clovis, who shook it. When Clovis took his hand away, he wiped his fingers clean on his shirt. "I trust you've made your repairs?"

"The *Andraste* is better than ever and at your disposal, Senator, provided you've got the credits."

"Quiet," Clovis hissed. "I'd prefer not to draw attention."

"Of course."

The waitress came back and gave Jovi his ale and a bowl of stale peanuts.

Jovi leaned forward. "Your call couldn't have come at a better time. King Vyjorin just upped the bounty on my head. Seems he wasn't too appreciative of the supplies I liberated from a merchant ship. He's been manning the gates with patrols, so it'll be harder to tag goods. If that's what you're wanting. I'll have to charge extra."

"What I've got in mind is more smuggling than pirating. But first ..." Clovis leaned into the table and lowered his voice. "What else have you heard out of Erolyia?"

The captain cracked open a peanut and chewed for a long minute before answering. "I heard he knocked some broad up."

"About time. Which wife?"

"None of the ones I know. Must be a new one."

"Gods above. This makes what now … nine?"

"Eight," Jovi answered. "One died. Heard she was as mad as a mockingbird anyway."

"So there's to be an Erolyian heir," Clovis mused. "Now that Vyjorin is more confident in his position in the empire, I wonder if we'll see more raids on the border."

"Maybe," Jovi said with a shrug. "All I know is people suddenly can't get enough of him. They say he's got magic powers. They say he's a god king, touched by the gods or something. What a crock of shit." He slurped at his ale.

The senator snickered. "*They* say I'm a fat slob and you know how true it is."

"It isn't what *they* say that I'm worried about." He tugged a small, oblong message crystal from his pocket and held it toward Clovis. The senator hadn't seen one in years, let alone held one. The crystals were old tech, beautiful to look at, expensive to craft and undetectable to modern scanners. "I *entertained* a royal envoy some weeks ago. She was carrying coded information about King Vyjorin's little sister. Seems she's older than everyone was guessing."

"I'm not surprised, with how paranoid everyone says the Erolyian crown is. We all knew there was a younger sister, but no one knew where to look. Amazing he could hide her away so well all these years." Clovis reached for the crystal but Jovi closed his hand.

"Five thousand credits."

"Five thousand!" Clovis made a choking sound. "For information soon to be common knowledge?"

"Yep. By then, to you, it'll be old news and you'll have plotted your next move." He leaned back in the booth and spread his arms wide. "How about it, Clovis? Five grand is a deal to keep one step ahead, I think."

"You're a dog."

"Woof, woof."

"Fine," Clovis grumbled and pulled out a wad of bills. These days, it was rare to make cash transactions, but if he paid Jovi electronically, someone could trace the source. He slid several bills over the table to Jovi who took them and tossed the crystal on the table. Clovis took it and held it to the light. "Can I assume you've already seen the contents?"

"More than seen," Jovi said with a smirk. "Aside from the boring biographicals, there's a photo. She's a looker. Shireen Thagg. No age in the file but, from the look, I'd guess at sixteen, maybe seventeen. Has a nice rack and an ass you could ride all night."

"She's a child." Clovis frowned.

"Not on Erolyia. Age of majority is fifteen, which is probably why Vyjorin brought her out of hiding. With his heir on the way, he'll be looking to marry off the little princess."

A wide grin spread across Clovis's face. He closed his hand around the crystal before pocketing it. "Perfect."

"So," said Jovi, leaning forward again and clearing his throat. "About this job you were offering me."

Clovis didn't answer. Instead, he counted out a few more bills under Jovi's fierce stare. "Have the access codes I've given you worked well? You've had no problems docking anywhere?"

"I haven't *been* anywhere asides from here lately. Yeah, they worked fine enough the last time."

"You're certain no one can best your ship in speed?"

"She's the fastest ship in the galaxy. Why?"

"How much warning would you require to launch?"

"Well," Jovi counted on his fingers. "If the engines were already warm, I could do it in twenty minutes. Course, it takes a while for the engines to warm. Maybe an hour if the cargo is light. What are you thinking, senator?"

"I will soon have a package I need delivered to Erolyia."

"Erolyia?" Jovi said, choking on his ale. "You've got to be shitting me! Do you know the price on my head in Erolyia? They'll shoot me down before I get halfway there."

"Not with the access codes I've given you. You'll be well compensated for your time."

Jovi frowned until Clovis passed him the entire wad of bills. He tried to take the money, but Clovis didn't let it go until Jovi met his eyes. "This is a retainer in good faith. Don't leave Senjele, and I'm paying you to be ready at a moment's notice, Jovi."

"I get it. This'll cover docking fees for four days but, if you need me longer, I'll need more."

"I'll arrange it."

"I'll need food, supplies, entertainment …"

"It's no problem," said the senator. "I'll take care of it. You'll have everything you need aboard the *Andraste*."

"Don't call me; I'll call you. I get it," Jovi said with another sly smirk. "Just don't keep me waiting too long! I have needs."

"I'm sure you do."

"So, while I've got you here, I heard you've fallen in with the hero of Toria. Is it true? He's under your roof?"

"True enough for now, though he'll soon be taking governorship of Clevennia."

"How did you work that?"

Clovis took up his drink and sipped at it, looking up at the bare rafters in the ceiling. "I had nothing to do with it."

"Aw, come on now, Senator. You don't expect me to believe that? Nothing goes on around here without you having your hand in it somewhere. I'm a foreigner, but even I know what a sly bastard you are. If you can afford to grease my palms, then you can afford a hell of a lot. I'm not cheap, even for a crook."

Clovis didn't tell Jovi he could afford him at twice the price. There were plenty of rascals with fast ships who could carry cargo and information around the galaxy, but none of them were like Jovi. Jovi occupied a unique position and knew all the right people. Jovi was a known quantity. With a little money, a drink and a few women, Clovis could get Jovi to do almost anything. Best of all, Jovi would keep his mouth shut. The information flowed only one way with Jovi, which was more than Clovis could say for many of his sources. Since Jovi had no interest in politics, either on Senjele or elsewhere, he was pleasant enough to talk to—even if it meant drinking watered-down ale and sitting in the disgusting little alehouse on the edge of Nebarius.

"You think too much of me, Jovi," Clovis said. "I'm just a humble politician, a servant of the people."

"That's a load of bork drool," said the captain, and then erupted into laughter. "Ah, but that's what I'd expect to hear from you. Always a smug, quiet and conniving bastard, you. It's a wonder you keep getting yourself elected. The people here must love you."

"The politicians hate me." He sighed. "If they have their way, we'll have a war before the year's end, if something isn't done about you know who." He was careful to lower his voice as he spoke. Rebos had spies and informants everywhere. The only person in the galaxy Clovis could be sure would never work for Rebos was sitting before him. Still, Jovi didn't understand the meaning of delicate.

"I say, put a knife in his back before he puts it in yours."

"Treason and murder win no votes, as I understand it."

Jovi shrugged. "No one gave a damn about votes on Erolyia. You did what the mad king said or you got crushed in the gears of war. Vyjorin's not so different, 'cept he'd feed you, fuck you, and then crush you. You—now you—Senator, I like. You pay me. Maybe you'll fuck me later, but at least I know your coin is good."

Clovis flipped open his pocket watch and glanced down at it. In a little under twelve hours, he would sip sweet wine with the most powerful people in the empire. Before then, he had to find proper attire, select an appropriate gift for Timothy, and practice bowing. He sighed as he realized there would be no time for sleep. Jovi Null did not know just how good he had it.

"I must be on my way," Clovis said to Jovi.

"Already?" Jovi raised an eyebrow. "What should I do if I don't hear from you, and the cash runs out?"

"Whatever you want," Clovis said, standing and adjusting his shirt. "If the cash stops flowing and you don't hear from me, assume I'm dead."

Jovi raised his mug. "I'll drink a pint in your memory, then."

"Let's hope it doesn't come to that."

Jovi nodded. "Then we drink to long lives full of trouble and worry. May we both die on our backs in our beds with a fat whore between our legs."

"Now that I can drink to." Clovis lifted the mug of ale and swallowed a mouthful before putting it back on the table. "Goodbye, Jovi."

"'Till next time, Senator," answered the pirate and then polished off his ale.

CHAPTER SEVENTEEN

Vyjorin

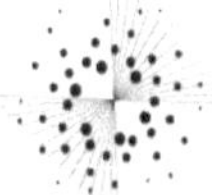

The Black Temple was massive, the land surrounding it lifeless and desolate. Even the sand shunned this place. The ground beneath his feet was dead obsidian that sloped into seven great, pointed claws, sharp enough to impale a man. Wind and sun should have weathered the ancient spikes, but this was an unnatural place. Neither sun nor time held sway here.

Shireen shivered as she stepped into the temple's shadow. "I dislike this place, brother. The stone ... see how it drinks the light?"

"I see it." Obsidian, he had seen before. It was black glass, smooth and silky, with edges sharp enough to cut men in half, sharper than any of his guards' *ikhiri*. The inert rock did not stir his caution as much as the lack of a greeting. Erolyia had more temples than gods, all with a thousand priests and half as many priestesses. The grounds should have been crawling with people, yet they did not even see scorpions or sand snakes. Dead. He marveled at the finality of the word, and the uncertainty of its opposite. "Bring them."

The crack of a whip echoed through the valley as twenty slaves grunted and heaved Kihran's heavy bed of ice up onto their backs. A female slave came behind, bearing Kihran's malformed offspring in a chest filled with ice.

The preservation effort had gone well. Kihran was pale and bluish, but not swollen or overtaken by decay. Her distended womb would shrink with time and effort once she came back to him. Everything would be as it was.

Vyjorin studied Shireen as the procession passed, wondering if she knew what he intended. The temple of the Nameless God is not a place of internment or rest for the dead. "You will stay," he told her flatly, and turned to the pair of eunuchs he'd set to guarding her. "Keep her here."

The obsidian arms passed over his head, a shimmering blackness to usher in a welcome relief from the desert heat. Vyjorin's fingers wrapped tightly around the Eye hanging against his chest as the darkness swallowed him, the memory of Lillith's voice echoing in his ears. Tell me, when you touch the power you hold, do you see the light or the pit?

Light, he thought as he waited fruitlessly for his eyes to adjust. The light has power over darkness. "Bring me a lantern." They brought one, the pale, artificial light nearly powerless in all the dark. The obsidian lapped at it hungrily. He lifted it higher.

They were in a long tunnel, stretching deep into the valley. Black, ionic columns ribbed the rounded space, each bearing a giant stone initiate in various stages of torture or execution. The sculptor had carved the crucified, the hanged, the burning, all with distant, euphoric gazes. The headless carving at the end of the hall slumped against his column, pointing them down another hallway with a crooked finger.

Vyjorin, Kihran's body and his slaves went in silence, but he saw the fear reflecting in the slaves' eyes. The stories about the Black Temple put naughty children to bed at night and warned folk away from this entire region. Scholars wrote that the rites once held here made the sands red with blood, and if the crown hadn't put down the practitioners, all Erolyia would be as cold and dead as this place. It was the Nameless God who rained down curses of infertility, deformity and madness, the Nameless God who had touched the Thaggs a generation ago and passed their poison into Vyjorin's genetic material. If he could purge that with a little blood and fire, it was a small price to pay.

The hallway ended abruptly in an elaborate pair of ebony doors, the panel carvings depicting an army of winged men spearing a bleeding moon. Droplets of blood formed horrific creatures with twisted legs and bony blades for arms. These creatures battled the winged men, sending them tumbling into a set of fiery teeth when they fell. An empty recess shaped like the great, all-seeing Eye, rested on the other panel.

"The door is barred," said one of the eunuchs as he grunted, pulling on the carved handles.

Vyjorin pushed him aside and tried the door, to no avail. His fist wrapped around the Eye on his chest and he yanked it free of the chain. You have no idea what it is, do you, fool king? If you did, you would not use it so lightly.

The Eye slid perfectly into the depression. The room shook, and dust flowed freely from the frame as the doors parted, moving the Eye behind the blackness of the temple walls. Vyjorin didn't try to retrieve it, but led the procession through.

The next room was even more massive than the first, the sculptures standing sentry in scraps of leather and iron, a curved cane in one hand and a stalk of wilted wheat in the other. Wings of tattered black feathers traced with gold sprouted from their shoulders, and the curved beak of a raptor replaced the mouth. Benches of frosted obsidian faced a center aisle, where a deep trench ran through the room, parted at the altar and ran into bowl shaped kneeling places. It was here the faithful made their prayers.

Vyjorin pointed at the altar. "Put her there." The ice left a trail of water as they lifted it and pushed forward with a grunt. The female slave carrying the icebox waited beneath one of the winged men. Was she shivering with cold or trembling in fear? "You. Slave girl." She jerked into a posture of submission, nose against the ground, when he addressed her. "Tell me your name and how you came to be in my service."

"A slave is not worthy to address you, master," she said hesitantly.

"I command it. Answer me."

"As you command. I am Assherinai among the slaves, but when I was free, I was Dulan of Decarion. Slavers beset my village and carried me away. The eunuchs bought me, Great One, to serve as bed slave to your father."

"Did you service my father?"

"As I was commanded, Great One."

Vyjorin scowled. "I murdered my father, slave, for his madness. Did you know that? For taking foreigners and the unbloodied to his bed, for cutting the throats of men and boys alike, and tossing babes into the flame for his twisted rituals. Yet my father never stood here, never contemplated what I must. He was a cruel man, was he not?"

"If my king says it, it must be so."

"Don't just agree with me." Vyjorin snapped. "Speak the truth. Did he treat you cruelly?"

She shifted her nose against the temple floor. "Yes, Great King. His tastes were dark and dreadful. He hurt for spite, but it must not always have been so. A man does not turn so evil on his own. Something makes him that way."

Or someone. Vyjorin shifted his eyes around the parameter of the room, searching for any movement that did not belong to his slaves. He saw nothing.

"Do you ever wish for death, for the sweet release from the madness that he put in you? Do you wake in the night, sweaty and weeping, cries of anguish and loss stifled in the desert heat? Is it too much to ask, to sleep the dreamless sleep when one's mind is no longer calm, even in the grasp of dreams? Or is what I mistake for a mad man's murders truly only the bitter, biting blade of mercy?"

She lifted her head, more in curiosity than in defiance. "My king?"

He waved a hand through the air to dismiss his doubt. "Take the box to the front. Kneel and pray to your god."

"Will the Lord of Light hear me in this dark place?" Her voice quivered as she spoke.

"He will hear you," he lied as she rose. "Stone walls, no matter how dark, hold no gods, only their shades."

She went to pray, kneeling in one of the depressions beside the altar. Vyjorin placed a hand on the head eunuch's shoulder as he went forward to join the corpse of his wife and child, sliding one of the ikhiri from the cut man's belt. "The girl slave stays. The rest must go."

"As you command, my king." Their bare feet shuffled across the floor and out the open door twice as fast as they'd come in.

Vyjorin knelt in front of the other depression, tugging a skin of bitter wine from his waist. He gave the libation, holding the memory of Kihran's embrace at the forefront of his mind. When he struck the fire, it caught quickly, and he looked over to Assherinai, her head bowed against two fingers, eyes closed deep in a prayer. He stood and went to her, straddling her calves and holding the ikhiri tightly in one hand.

The words he spoke were a whisper, swallowed like the light by the obsidian around them. "Assherinai, I free you in the name of my forefathers and in the sight of gods and men." Vyjorin grasped her tightly by the hair and firmly pulled her head back. Tears fell from her eyes, but she made no sound, not even a whimper. "Go from here a free woman and turn from the dark practices your cruel masters have taught you."

When he opened her throat with the blade, she didn't fight him, but her eyes were full of panic and fearful desperation. In them, he saw his own reflection, black and cold as night. The crimson blood fell thick and warm over his fingers while he watched her die, the droplets shimmering in the firelight as they fell into the depression.

He let her fall and the *ikhiri* clanked against the floor. The blood and fire poured from their indentations on the floor, mixing in the trench. Vyjorin turned to watch the flow of flame.

"So, you have come," said a voice, high and mournful. Vyjorin's head whipped around to see a face in the shadows that was not Lillith: white as milk, with bright, glowing blue eyes. Long tendrils of black hair crawled from her scalp in uneven tusks, lost in the heavy, tattered burial robes she wore. She had the voice of a child, the body of a woman. When she spoke again, Vyjorin saw rows of jagged, pointed teeth in her mouth. "Did you bring the child?"

"Where is the she-demon?"

A set of cold fingers caressed his cheek from behind. "Here." Lillith laughed, and she floated effortlessly over to join the other woman. "You look less since we met last."

"Less? Less what?"

Lillith's mouth parted into a smile. "Less."

Vyjorin pointed to the icebox just beyond the offering of blood, the lid still tightly closed. "I brought what you asked for. Now, restore my wife to me."

Lillith's eyes flashed bright red as she turned to the other creature and motioned to the box. "After you, Fayte."

Fayte drifted to the box as if she had no feet, though Vyjorin could clearly see white, speckled ankles moving beneath the heavy shroud. She moved the lid with a single finger and peered inside. "This is the spawn?" She looked to Lillith.

Lillith shrugged. "Dead is dead."

Fayte turned her cold gaze back on Vyjorin. *She hasn't blinked*, he realized, and the room suddenly felt colder. "Where is the Eye?"

Vyjorin opened his mouth to tell her he'd left it in the door, but Lillith produced the amulet and dangled it tauntingly over Kihran's body. The ice was melting quickly. She tossed it to Fayte who caught it in her unnaturally long fingers. "He's been using it to bring spirits over, but it's sealed now."

"How many times have you used it?"

Vyjorin swallowed a cold breath and tried to count. "Three."

"Enough," Lillith assured Fayte. "Look at what it cost him."

Fayte looked back into the box.

"What will you do with it?" Vyjorin wasn't sure he wanted to know but the question needed to come all the same. Kihran would want to know.

"Turn it." Fayte lifted the chain of the Eye over her neck and let it drop. The crystal iris looked a pale red in place of the white.

"Turn it?" Vyjorin's blood felt cold, even though he had no understanding of what the creature could mean. If she could turn that thing, what about the others he had brought back? He had told their mothers to take them to the temples that served the light. These dark servants of the Nameless One could not touch them.

Fayte ignored his question and lifted the Eye; a pale, red light reflected into the box of ice. "Behold," she said, "the power of Drelè. I pledge myself a servant to the dark in body, mind and spirit. Let him who holds dominion over this form release it into my hands."

A terrible scream shot up from the box, so loud that Vyjorin's hands on his ears could not shut it out. It was so painful that he could not think. The box rocked as the dead child fought to be free. Fayte dropped the Eye back to her breasts and reached in to take up the creature. "There, there. All is well."

The babe curled its tail and claws around Fayte's breast, ripped at the funerary shroud until Lillith took it away, placing it at her own breast. It dug thick claws into her until tiny pinpricks of blood surfaced. The creature drank desperately.

"What—what is that?" He didn't even try to keep his voice from trembling.

Lillith smiled and tickled under the thing's hollow mouth. "An old soul, unable to survive in the world without a little help. You may have loved your wife, King, but you could not have sired him without my help. It is you who is barren, not your wives. You have the spawn you wanted so badly. This is the price. Your seed will bear only these macabre infants. Macabre. Yes, that will do nicely." The word rolled pleasantly off her tongue.

Vyjorin backed away, shaking. "No ... that *thing* is no blood of mine."

"It will be your only blood if you fail to heed me again."

Shireen ... She means Shireen. He couldn't care less if they dealt with his older sister but, now that he had no heir, Shireen must survive. "Leave my sister be. She is innocent." He fell to his knees, weak and exhausted from trying to make sense of it all. What if Shireen ... what if her children were dark and twisted like this? He must not let them have her. She must bear *normal* children. "Please, whatever you want. Keep your curses from my sister. I-I will listen."

"Good." Lillith shifted the Macabre noisily from one breast to the other. "You will march your palace back to Oasis and give the news of your inability to produce heirs to your other wives. You will dismiss them. I will return your queen to you if you wish but you will lie with her no longer. I needed you to sire only one spawn to gain the loyalty of my people. Once the other queens have seen the child, once I've shown them their salvation, they will bend the knee. That matters nothing to you. What matters is that you will rule. You will obey. Do as I say, and Erolyia will stand while Senjele falls into chaos. The empire of your sister's children will be great." She caressed the Macabre, folding her fingers gently over its tail. "Now bend the knee and pledge yourself to us."

Vyjorin had no choice. He could endure their torture if only they would give Kihran back to him, beautiful and loving as she was. Surely, it was an even trade.

His knees and back ached as he lowered his body into the unfamiliar position of submission. "I pledge myself to you, Lillith and you, Fayte, and swear to do as you bid. So long as you and your kind do no harm to my sister, I will obey."

Lillith smiled and nodded to Fayte who glided back to Kihran's body and pledged herself once again to the god he could not name. The red light flickered over his wife and her eyelids fluttered open. "Rise," Fayte commanded, and Kihran's stiff form rose, turning bright, burning blue and empty eyes on him, eyes that were Fayte's and not hers.

No ..." Vyjorin backed away as Kihran's stiff fingers reached for him. She crawled down from the melting altar of ice, twisting and writhing, unnaturally stiff as she went.

Hot tears crawled down Vyjorin's cheeks. *This isn't how it should be ... This isn't what I want!* "No!"

His bladder let go as she wrapped her fingers around his throat, and they tumbled backward together, splashing in the trench of blood and fire. The flames leapt onto his clothes, curling over his arm, up the side of his face and onto Kihran. She let out a screech as the fire overtook her, and fell back, flailing. Vyjorin fought the fire but it had caught too well. He felt the flesh on his face melting. When he fell against the coolness of the stone, the last thing he saw was Kihran's flaming form, clawing at the ice, the beautiful skin on her fingertips slipping away with each new grasp. Lillith smiled. The child fed. The darkness swallowed all of them whole.

CHAPTER EIGHTEEN

Timothy

The pomp and circumstance of an award ceremony made Timothy feel more like a fool than an honored guest. He wore his parade uniform with all the stripes he had earned and even dusted off the old pin that bore the symbol of House Val: a sword beneath a crest of five stars, in crimson and blue. He used it to pin his ceremonial cloak to his shoulder. He had trimmed his beard and wished it had grown in dark and thin rather than red and thick. Even though Clovis had advised him against it, he wore his sword at his hip. It meant nothing here, but on Clevennia, a man was judged by the weapon he wore. Timothy had spent all morning sharpening and polishing the sword until he could see his reflection in the blade.

When he had dressed, he paused in front of the full-length mirror in his room and made a few small adjustments. Then he scratched his beard and remembered something Yolen had said. *You can dye wool any color you like. That doesn't change the fact it itches.* He stopped scratching at the sound of knocking at his door.

He walked with only a slight pain in his side from where the stitches pulled, but one or two pain pills would dull it to nothing by the time he arrived at the ceremony. It didn't stop him from wincing as he opened the door. Chaunstance waited on the other side in a strapless floor-length gown the color of the sea after a heavy rain, a steely sort of gray-green. On anyone else, the color might have looked sickly, but Chaunstance glowed in it. She wore her hair in a tight pile on top of her head. In a word, he would have described her as stunning.

She frowned at him. "Is it bad?"

"What? No. It's the pain in my side, my lady."

"Quit calling me that," she said and stepped into the room, though this time her objection was a little less. "At least we won't clash. I wanted to make sure your bandages would hold up."

"The stitching is fine. I changed the bandages earlier." He leaned into the hall and looked up and down. Rain tapped on the window pane at the end of the hall. It would be muggy and miserable outside. "Where is Clovis?"

"Arranging for a car. He wants to make a show of your arrival."

Timothy shook his head. "He wants to make a show of me in general. It's getting on my last nerve. My only hope is he settles down a little when we get to Clevennia."

"Will you wear that when you give your oath to the emperor?" she asked, pointing at the sword. "Won't they disarm you before you enter? You know they don't allow weapons within thirty feet of the throne."

He patted the hilt. "It's largely ceremonial. I'm not going without it, though. If they want to make a fuss, they'll make a concession. I go where the sword goes."

"I'm amazed anyone still carries a sword." She reached out and ran her fingers over the simple cross guard. "Is it a tradition where you're from?"

"Very much so. My people claim to be made of salt and iron."

Chaunstance smiled. "Salt and iron. What a strange thing to say."

"Perhaps you'll understand it a little better when you get to Clevennia."

"Oh, I won't be going," she said, shaking her head. "There will be too much to do here. Someone will have to look after his estate while he's tending to yours. Besides, what would I do there?"

"You might find it preferable to all the formalities here. My people are much more … relaxed."

She straightened his collar and dusted something off the front of him. "I like structure. If you don't know what's going to happen, how can you make plans?"

"That's the beauty of life, my lady. The surprise." He reached over and took a box from the top of the dresser. It had taken him most of the afternoon to find what he wanted and more money than he'd wanted to spend, but the look of suspicion on Chaunstance's face was well worth the price. He held the box out to her. "For you, my lady."

She didn't take it. "Clovis should have told you I don't accept gifts."

"At least open it before you turn it down."

Cautiously, Chaunstance took the box and slid off the lid, her eyes going to Timothy's when she saw the contents. "It's moonstone," he explained. "The jeweler recommended diamonds, but they didn't seem right for you. You'd never wear diamonds. But moonstones … moonstones are only semi-precious. Beautiful, yet unassuming, and these are a very special kind." He removed the necklace from the box and placed it around her neck, clasping it with care.

"What is so special about them?" Chaunstance asked.

"They're yours."

Chaunstance put a hand over the line of small, opalescent and blue-sheened stones around her neck. She opened her mouth but, for once, had nothing to say.

"There you are." Both turned to see Clovis standing in the doorway. The senator waddled in, wearing a feathered cap and a fine, silk suit. The chain of a golden pocket watch dangled from the suit pocket. "I've drafted a special car to take us to the palace."

"I won't be going in your hired car," Timothy announced, then smiled at how flustered Clovis became. "We'll go in your private car, and to a side entrance, or I'll book my own transportation."

"Now see here, Val," said Clovis, wagging his finger, his face growing red. "Why are you so bullheaded after all I've done for you?"

Chaunstance put a hand on Clovis's shoulder and he calmed, though he was still fuming. "Remember your blood pressure, Senator. It doesn't matter which car we take, does it, so long as we arrive?"

Clovis puffed out his cheeks and looked from Timothy to Chaunstance. "Fine," he conceded. "I'll cancel the car."

The three of them piled into the back of Clovis's private car, and his driver took them across town to the palace. Timothy sat across from Clovis and Chaunstance.

As much as he wanted to pay attention to everything the senator was saying, he couldn't help but stare at Chaunstance. She barely looked at him, preferring to stare out the window, lips held in a straight line.

Clovis snapped his fingers in front of Timothy. "Are you listening to me, boy?"

"I'm trying."

"Good," Clovis grunted. "Because this is important. It's what I do. You've got no political sense, Timothy Val, so I thought I'd squash any fool notions you might have gotten into your head. There are protocols to follow, traditions. Be sure to bow before you reach the throne; never look the emperor in the face."

Clovis droned on, but Timothy quickly lost interest. He'd learned the proper protocol for addressing royalty as a boy. Even as he practiced bowing to his brother, all he could ever think about as a child was running off to go fishing or catch sand crabs. Protocol was boring. Tradition was for stuffy lords in high palaces. All he wanted was for it to be over.

"… and never forget, all eyes will be on you." Clovis glanced at Timothy's sword and frowned. "I thought you weren't going to wear that."

"I can't swear an oath without it."

"They'll disarm you. You know that, don't you?"

Again, Timothy looked to Chaunstance. She turned away from the window and offered him a smile.

"So I'm told. They can have it when they pry it from my stiff, dead fingers. If they want my oath, they'll allow me my sword."

"Stubborn ass," Clovis muttered.

"I take it as a compliment."

Clovis turned to Chaunstance, who was still smiling, and frowned when he saw the necklace. "Where did you get such a thing?"

Chaunstance swatted the senator's fingers away when he tried to touch them. "From a man who wouldn't take no for an answer."

Clovis narrowed his eyes at Timothy, who could only beam.

Clovis's car pulled to a side entrance, and Timothy was glad for it. The front of the palace was bustling with reporters and lesser lords and ladies, all of them dying to get a look at him.

The driver came and opened the doors and Timothy stepped out into the stifling summer air and adjusted his jacket.

Clovis climbed out behind him with all the grace of a duck. "Well, Chaunstance and I will have to go around to the front to hand in our invitations. I'm sure you can find your way from here?"

One of the palace servants opened the side door for Timothy. "I believe so," he said, and turned to address Chaunstance. "I'll see you after. Keep the senator out of trouble until then."

Inside, he paced outside the throne room, waiting for them to signal his grand entrance. Timothy lifted his cap to his head and pulled it down again, checked the buttons on his jacket, and made sure he'd laced his boots tightly enough. Gods on high, why did it take so damn long for politicians to get anything done?

Timothy thought of Clovis and felt sick. He couldn't imagine things had gotten so bad on Senjele he could serve the empire better as a lord than a soldier. *I'll have an army at my back*, Timothy thought. The Val banner men were some of the fiercest soldiers he'd ever had the honor of fighting alongside. He hoped he would never have need of them.

If Clovis has his way, the transition will be mostly bloodless. True, Rebos would retain some of his supporters, but there wouldn't be enough for him to think about starting a civil war.

Why am I thinking of this? He checked his pin again. *Ludus is still healthy. If luck is with us, I won't have to make good on my promise to help Clovis win his vote until I'm old and gray myself.*

The side entrance opened, and Timothy started, thinking he was about to be summoned. When he saw who it was, he stiffened. Prince Annon stepped into the hallway. Gods, how long had it been since the two of them had stood face-to-face?

Annon was fifteen years Timothy's junior. The first time they had met, Annon was barely a head above a fencepost in height. He'd been a rotten kid with a squeaky voice and scrawny arms. A late bloomer, too.

"Gods, look at you," Timothy said. He'd grown into those long arms and legs and put on a little muscle. There was even the scrap of a beard on his chin. In his surprise, Timothy almost forgot he was addressing a prince. His recovery was clumsy. "I'm sorry, Highness. It's been so long." He lowered his head in a bow.

"No!" Annon exclaimed, and made a quick move to keep Timothy from bowing any lower. When Timothy looked up, Annon was beaming. "You promised you'd never bow to me again."

A wide grin spread across Timothy's face as he straightened. "I made a boy that promise, and I've come back and found a man. What happened to you? Did you take up some kind of sport? You look like you've been lifting whole transports!"

"I've taken up sword fighting," Annon answered. "I hired a tutor and everything. I've gotten better at shooting, too."

Timothy couldn't help but feel proud. Between deployments, he'd spent a year on Senjele at the behest of the royal family, a tutor for Prince Annon. His directive had been vague: take a scrawny, idealistic boy of fifteen and teach him to fight. Annon had little natural fight in him, and his attendants hadn't been too pleased with the way Timothy used bare-knuckle brawling and wrestling to draw him out but, eventually, Annon came around. At least he wasn't so hard to look at anymore. He'd make some woman a fine husband, which was what the whole thing had been about. The only worry a second son of an emperor had was holding onto some token post in the army and raising a bunch of fat, happy kids with a fat, happy wife.

Timothy suddenly felt guilty. Clovis wanted more from Annon. The senator wanted Annon to rule. Was he ready? Would he ever be?

"What's wrong?" Annon asked.

"Nothing," Timothy said, forcing his smile. "It's been such a long time. I'm surprised you recognize me."

Annon extended a hand and Timothy took it. "I could never forget you. You've got the hardest left hook I ever ran face-first into." They shared a laugh and a quick embrace before Annon spoke of the inevitable. "About what happened at the citadel …"

Timothy let go of Annon's hand. "It's behind me. As soon as tonight is over, Toria will be, too. I don't want to think any more on it."

"You have enemies here," Annon warned, his voice barely a whisper. "If I hadn't intervened, they would have let you rot in the bowels of the Bloody Keep. The senator you're with? He's not well loved by the aristocracy of Senjele either."

"It's all going to be a moot point after this," Timothy

assured Annon, patting him on the back. "I'll go to Clevennia soon. I'll only come here and look at your ugly face a few times a year. Senjele will be your problem."

"Rebos's problem," Annon corrected with a frown. "I'm to join the executors."

Timothy let go of Annon and stared at him. Annon may have grown but, at nineteen, he was far too young for such an appointment. Some people might have seen it as an honor, but they didn't understand what kind of life the executors led. Annon would be tested, pushed to his limits, much further than Timothy would have liked. "The executors?"

"My mother arranged it. She thinks I'm too naïve to be of use to Rebos when he rules."

"Is it what you want?"

Annon shrugged. "I think it's a punishment for intervening in your situation. I objected to the executors' treatment of you and, therefore, I'll be subjected to some of it myself." Annon forced a smile and patted Timothy on the back. "Don't worry. I'll survive. I've picked up enough stubbornness from you to keep me from dying. Besides, today is your day. I don't want to overshadow you with my problems."

"I'd much rather not do this."

The prince laughed. "That sounds more like you. Well, I had better find my place. If I'm late, Father will be angry."

"Go," Timothy urged. "Come and find me after. I want to introduce you to someone."

Annon left, and Timothy went back to pacing. A short while later, a servant whispered to him it was time. Timothy turned to face the wooden double doors. They opened to trumpets blaring a fanfare. He held his breath and strode out. White and red rose petals rained down on him, littering the plush red carpet and softening his footfalls. The victory cape pinned to his back flew with his quick steps. The floor on either side of the carpet was packed with lords and ladies of the highest order, all stuffed into the finest silk suits and gowns. He barely paid them any mind.

Halfway down the carpet on his right stood the senator, with his thumbs tucked against his armpits. Chaunstance was beside him, calm and composed and somehow as natural here as she was in the kitchen at the estate. She had slipped from one role into the other so flawlessly she might as well have been an actress in a play.

Ahead, the graying emperor stood in front of his throne, with the empress in her golden dress to his right, and his heir to the left. Off to either side, the executors stood guard, the High Executor among them, the emperor's personal guards for the event. If this is a theater, then it is time I played my part.

Just feet from the emperor, he threw his cape out behind him and drew the sword, ignoring the still-fresh pain in his side as best he could. The emperor's guards stepped forward with their weapons drawn. Before the guards could descend on him, Timothy fell to submission on one knee, resting his forehead against the blunt side of the blade, and waited. A moment passed in silence, and then another. His heart raced and he tried to calm his quick breathing. Behind him, a murmur swept through the crowd. Baring steel in the presence of the emperor was an offense punishable by death. Had it been so long since a Val came to the palace to swear an oath of fealty?

Emperor Ludus stepped forward, motioning for his guard to retreat. "You bring ancient customs before my throne," the emperor whispered. "Few here are old enough to recognize the intent behind your gesture, Captain. You are lucky I am so old. My guards might have taken your head otherwise."

Sweat trickled down the back of his neck. *Gods, am I mad?* Timothy groped for words. He should have practiced them, thought this through more. Perhaps he should have waited until court, when there were not so many eyes on him. No, the more eyes the better. "Your Imperial Highness, with your permission, I would give you my oath of fealty as my ancestors before me once did, in the Clevennian custom."

A murmur went up from the crowd like feathers rustling in the wind. The emperor nodded. "If that is your wish."

"I pledge myself to the service of the people of Senjele, to be a sword for the meek and a shield for the weak, to stand where others fall and to remain vigilant where others falter. My sword is yours. My people are yours. The wealth of my land, the salt of my sweat, the blood in my veins is yours to command. I pledge to the people of Senjele my valor, honor and all victories, future, past and present."

The guards tensed as he lifted the sword and drew it across one palm. The blade was amazingly sharp. Blood spilled freely as he offered it in cupped hands to the emperor. They were old words, as ancient as the line of Vals, spoken even when the Vals were kings in their own right.

Some of the ladies in the crowd gasped when they saw the large droplets of blood falling to the ground, and a few fainted. Not to be outdone, more ladies stopped fanning themselves and fell to the floor.

The emperor ignored them and accepted the blood oath, taking Timothy's hands in his own and squeezing them. "You have already proven you are a man of justice and honor. Few men can claim to match your courage. To do what is right in the face of tyranny is a rare trait in these dark times. I hear your oath, Timothy Val, and return one of my own. Give me valor and I will return it tenfold where I may, honor and I will honor you, sacrifice and you will be remembered."

A chill ran through Timothy, to hear the old words. Even he was surprised the emperor knew the old oath so well. It must have been hundreds of years since the last Val had spoken the traditional words of fealty in this chamber, not since Credence Val gave Varren the Conqueror her oath. His father had sworn an oath, but he had used the Senjelian words, foreign words.

A servant rushed forward with a bowl of water for the emperor to rinse his hands before another handed him the medallion. The emperor slipped the medallion over Timothy's head, and let the chain fall heavily onto his neck. "Rise now, Timothy Val, Lord of Castle Valence and governor of Clevennia. Go forth with the gratitude of your people. May you always wear the burden of your station with pride and discretion."

Timothy turned and faced the cheering, clapping crowd. He couldn't resist. He raised the sword in the air and, for a moment, understood what it was like to be loved by everyone.

There was a reception after the ceremony, but Timothy could not attend without slipping into the washroom to bandage his hands. He fumbled with the bandages as Clovis stormed in, red-faced and irate. "You're a madman!" he raved. "A bloody madman! What possessed you to behave like an unbroken stallion up there? Drawing your sword in the presence of the emperor! You're lucky they didn't kill you! Damn lucky! And the fool's oath?

Why not make the one you've been practicing all day?"

Timothy tried to smile as he tightened the bandage with his teeth. "People will talk about it for weeks, won't they?"

"What madness was it?" the senator demanded again, slamming his chubby hands on the sink. "Even Chaunstance believes you are a lunatic. You're no hero to her, Val. It takes more than a little flourish to impress a lady of her caliber."

Timothy finally gave up on the bandages and flexed his hands. A scab was forming but it would be some time before it healed. "It's *Lord* Val, by your own making, I might add. You're not doing your campaign any good now, Clovis. Besides, you're the one who taught me how much power words can have. All the more reason for me to choose them carefully."

Clovis was beyond reason, Timothy knew. He was angrier at having his own game played against him than anything else. The senator would come around by the week's end. A little liquor and a tasteless joke or two and they would be best of friends again.

"This is not the kind of behavior to win you friends in high places, Lord Val. This is how you make enemies here."

"I've already got enemies here," Timothy said in a grave tone.

"Yes." Clovis wore the worry on his face like a mask.

"Sandmen are relentless. They don't give up." Timothy frowned. "There will be another attempt."

"Be on your guard. There is a lot of power here tonight. Were I an assassin, I wouldn't miss this chance." He pointed to Timothy's hands. "Although, I wouldn't worry too much. You're a mess now. A slice in your hands, a hole in your side. You'll likely fall over dead from a dance."

"Chaunstance did a fine job, stitching me up."

"You won't listen to reason, will you?"

Timothy smiled.

Clovis waved his hands at Timothy and stormed back out. The band took up a high-spirited song in the next room and Timothy looked down at the seeping wounds in his hands. *I promised my lady a dance*, he thought, and took up the bandages again.

The guests danced prior to dinner, as was the emperor's custom. The event was the social gathering of the decade, with lords and ladies turning out in their finest faces for the new Lord Val. Senators and minor nobility from the far-flung reaches of the empire came to dance and drink to his success. There was the tall and tittering Fyjokian ambassador in her feather dress and wiry hat. She danced clumsily with Lord Haplan Ambren. Her girth was a problem, for she was twice as wide as he was, and it made for an awkward coupling.

Someone handed Timothy a cup and he sipped the wine as he watched the dance from against the wall. He scanned the crowd looking for Chaunstance but, before he could find her, the dance ended. Lord Ambren bowed to his less-agile partner and turned toward Timothy's corner of the room. Timothy locked eyes with him without meaning to and cursed himself when he realized Haplan Ambren was coming his way. Although the hall was crowded, there was no way he could manage an escape, so he drained his cup before putting it on a passing tray, and waited for what he was sure would be the most awkward conversation of the night.

"There he is," Haplan exclaimed and extended his hand to Timothy who took it hesitantly. "The man of the hour. How does it feel?"

"A little overwhelming," Timothy answered in earnest. He'd always liked Haplan, but they hadn't spoken since he and Nareen went their separate ways. Timothy was surprised Haplan bothered to speak to him at all. "But I think I'll manage."

Haplan nodded and stroked his salt-and-pepper beard. He looked as if he'd swallowed a sour grape. "So, you're Lord Governor of Clevennia, now. I suppose I never thought I'd see the day. I always thought you'd make something of yourself, despite my wife and daughter. But a lord governorship … I'm impressed."

"How are they?" He tried to ask without sounding too interested. The last thing he wanted to do was give the impression he cared, but he had to be polite. People expected it of him now.

"Oh, they're here somewhere." He motioned to the crowd. "Schmoozing eligible bachelors, I'm sure." He turned back to Timothy and leaned in to speak in a quieter tone. "Listen, Timothy."

Here it comes, Timothy thought and scanned the crowd looking for Chaunstance. The dancing had started again, and everyone was moving too fast for him to get a good look.

"Being a lord and a governor is hard work. This climate only makes it harder." Timothy turned away from the faces in the crowd to focus on Haplan. His expression had grown serious but was still pleasant. "If you need anything, anything at all, don't hesitate to ask."

"I promise you'll be the first to know."

Haplan let out a deep breath, then smiled. "Good." There was a long, awkward silence between them. Timothy waited for Haplan to wander off and mingle elsewhere, but the man just stood there, tapping his fingers and staring into the crowd.

Timothy cleared his throat and decided it was best to get everything out into the open, for no other reason than to gauge where he stood with the Ambrens. "You know, I wasn't sure you'd speak to me after what happened."

"You fucked my daughter, Timothy." Haplan grabbed two goblets from one of the serving girls. "If you were any other man, I'd castrate you and hang you upside down to dry." He turned to Timothy and smiled, offering him a goblet before calmly adding, "But I believe the emperor just made it a capital offense. Of course, I happen to know my wonderful daughter is as much a title-mongering whore as my lovely wife. One thing you'll learn about being a man with a title is that you cannot afford to marry for love. We wed for status. It's unfortunate; such arrangements mean you and I must smile and toast our wives as we are cuckolded." Haplan smiled and raised his glass as his wife spun by, dancing with another man. "I love my daughter, Timothy, but I'm no fool. She'd fuck the family dog if she thought it would get her the crown."

Timothy only took the drink when Haplan insisted.

"To water under the bridge," Haplan declared and raised his glass.

Timothy lifted his glass, and the two of them drank together.

Haplan nodded and moved to leave, but seemed to think better of it. "Just one more thing, Timothy, in case it was never clear. All things considered, you've turned into a fine young man. You've brought honor back to your family name, something I wasn't sure would ever happen. Let me say this, because I know no one else will: I'm proud of you. I know your mother would be, too."

Timothy lowered his head. "Thank you. It means a lot."

"I know," Haplan said, nodding. "Now, go. Enjoy

yourself. You only get to be a hero once." Then he walked away.

The dance ended, and Timothy saw Chaunstance standing nearby, her back pressed against the adjacent wall. He passed off his cup and slipped between the few couples standing between them. "My lady," he said, and she turned toward him. He feigned a bow and extended a hand to her. She offered him nothing but a smile in response. "You promised," he reminded her. Her eyes never left his as she slid her hand into his. He led her to the dance floor, and the music began.

Clovis was right. She was quite the talented dancer. At least, she was better than he was. When he missed a few steps, she tried to restrain her laughter. "I'm sorry, my lady. I'm not very good at this."

"You dance like a fish." Though it was an insult, she followed it with a lighthearted smile. He took it as a good sign.

"To say I learned from one wouldn't be far off. To be honest, these Senjelian dances are too complex for their own good. There's too much circling and bowing. Most of what I know are Deynish circle dances."

"I've never heard of a circle dance. What is it?"

"Well …" he laughed at his inability to explain it to her and dance at the same time. "It's something you have to do to understand. It involves a lot of spinning."

Chaunstance raised an eyebrow, mischief sparkling in her eyes. "You must teach Clovis while he's away."

"I'd rather teach you."

A dark shadow appeared beside them. Timothy turned his head to see High Executor Yolen. A chill ran through his chest as he remembered his time in Yolen's care. The High Executor gave a slight bow of his head, to which Timothy had to respond with a bow of his own. Yolen cast Timothy a smug smile.

"Forgive me, Lord Val, but I must insist on cutting in." Yolen turned his attention to Chaunstance and offered a snake-like smile as he extended his hand. "My lady, would you allow me the honor of dancing with the most talented dancer here?"

Her face paled as she stared at his outstretched hand. Even Timothy knew she couldn't deny the High Executor. "If it pleases you," she said and took his hand.

Timothy bit his tongue as he watched him dance gracefully with her, though she was stiff and tense. He tried to convince himself Yolen's interruption was timely, since his palm was getting sore. Just before the dance ended, Chaunstance broke away from the High Executor, the color draining from her face as she gave him a stiff but silent curtsy, before storming to the opposite side of the room. From the dance floor, Yolen glanced over at Timothy and smiled.

Timothy put an arm around Chaunstance as she passed by, matching his step with hers. "Are you all right? What did he say to you?"

"Nothing," she said shortly, and stopped only when they reached the far wall. She turned back to him and searched his face. "When you go to Clevennia, I will go with you."

The announcement should have been a happy one, but Timothy suspected Yolen had said something to drive her sudden change of mind. Even when he'd been bleeding everywhere, Chaunstance hadn't been afraid, but he saw fear in her eyes now. He touched her cheek and she turned away. "What did he say to you?"

"He has the paperwork Clovis filed to free me," she whispered.

"What?" The job was usually handled by lower offices,

clerks working in the citadel, not the chief justice of the empire. How had Yolen gotten those papers?

Chaunstance squeezed Timothy's arm. "He wants information on Clovis and you. He wants me to spy on you. It was the price he asked for his signature."

Timothy turned and scanned the crowd, intending to confront Yolen while there were plenty of witnesses around, but the dancing had stopped, and the band had taken up the dinner procession music. Ludus and Cylene led a parade of guests into the feast hall, hand in hand.

"Come," Timothy said, squeezing Chaunstance's hand. "Tonight, you'll sit with me."

"There will be a lot of talk," Chaunstance protested, even as they fell into place in the parade. "Clovis won't be happy."

"Clovis will have to suffer in silence."

The guests sat according to their station, with the emperor and his empress at the head. Rebos took the seat next to his father while Annon sat next to his mother. Timothy was seated next to Rebos. Even though the servants were a little hesitant, they sat Chaunstance next to him.

Timothy sat, silent in a sea of laughter and voices, chewing contemplatively on his first two courses. It wasn't until Annon interrupted him at the intermediary soup that Timothy paid attention to the conversation around him. Annon leaned forward and gestured to Chaunstance with a smile. "Aren't you going to introduce us to your lady friend, Lord Val?"

Chaunstance looked to Timothy. He wasn't sure what to say. If it came out he'd seated a slave at the same table as the emperor, the night would not end well. They might even escort her from the hall, and he didn't want her to make a walk of shame.

He slipped his hand under the table and into hers before answering, "This is Lady Chaunstance. She works with Senator Clovis."

"It's a pleasure to see such a lovely young lady on a hero's arm," said the empress. She offered a tight smile. "Your necklace is stunning. Where did you get it?"

"It was a gift, Highness," Chaunstance said. Though she was out of her element, she fielded the conversation well enough.

"I have someone to introduce as well," Rebos said, standing. He spoke briefly with a servant who went down into the crowded dining room.

"Who is it?" Empress Cylene asked in an impatient tone.

Rebos didn't answer his mother but, instead, went around to the front of the table. The servant returned and Timothy ground his teeth when he saw who he was escorting.

Rebos took the woman's hand as she fell into a graceful curtsey. "Lords, ladies, esteemed mother and father, allow me to introduce the lovely Nareen Ambren, my future wife."

The whole front of the dining hall went silent. Ludus choked on his food until a servant came and patted him on the back. The empress's mouth fell open and Annon gave a weak smile. They must have been just as surprised by the news as Timothy was. He wondered if Haplan knew. If so, he hadn't brought it up.

The hair on Timothy's arms stood on end when Nareen looked straight at him. She was to be empress one day. Nareen Ambren. Of all the women in the empire, it was her. Even though he had sworn he no longer loved her, seeing her made every wound feel as fresh as the day they'd parted ways.

"Your future wife," the empress repeated.

"Yes," said Prince Rebos, his hand tightening around Nareen's fingers. "And the mother of my child."

The empress rose from her seat, her eyes flashing with rage. As angry as she was, she forced a smile and extended a hand to the girl. Nareen took it with grace. "Welcome, child," the empress offered, and waved to the servants. "Come. Sit with us. Sup with us."

"Thank you, Your Majesty."

Nareen took her place at the head table next to the empress, where Timothy suspected she had meant to be all along.

Rebos returned to the table and inched in beside Timothy, still beaming. "Congratulations," Timothy said, only because he believed it was expected of him.

"And to you as well. You've come a long way."

The prince leaned in close, speaking so only Timothy could hear him. "It's a shame what happened to you on Toria. On behalf of my family, allow me to extend an apology for your unjust treatment."

Timothy reached for his drink and tried to slow his breathing. Flashes of torture came back to him.

"Is there anything I can do to make up for it, Lord Val?"

"You can dispatch a shipment of medical supplies and basic equipment to Toria at once." Timothy reached for the bottle of wine left on the table and fumbled with it. Already, his temper had gotten too hot.

Rebos called for a servant to fill the cup, despite Timothy's objections. When the servant reached for the bottle on the table, Rebos stopped him. "No, not the watered-down swill. Lord Val is a guest of honor. There." Rebos snatched the bottle the wine steward had been filling his own cup with and thrust it at the servant. "This will do."

The servant stared at the bottle blankly. "My prince, that bottle's empty."

"Then fetch another, one from my private collection." The prince laughed as the servant scurried away. "They say good help is hard to find. It seems truer every day."

Timothy stared at his cup but didn't speak.

"Wouldn't you agree, Lady Chaunstance?"

Chaunstance hesitated. "Perhaps you ought to adjust your standards."

Timothy froze, afraid she'd been too blunt.

But Rebos laughed and nodded. "The empire could do with more of your kind of honesty, my lady. It's true! Wherever did you find such a gem, Lord Val?"

The wine steward returned with a bottle. The lad uncorked the bottle and filled Emperor Ludus's cup first, then Rebos's, then Timothy's. Before any of them could take a drink, Rebos rose from his seat, prompting everyone else in the room to do so, and signaled a toast. "Charge your glasses, friends, for the Lord Val and the future success of the Val name. May you remember your oath for as long as you live. To valor, honor and victory!"

Something did not sit right with the way Rebos said his family's motto. Timothy had a terrible feeling in his gut, the same feeling he'd experienced in his bedroom the night before. Timothy's side ached as everyone lifted their cups to their lips. He hesitated to wince and let the pain pass. Rebos lifted his glass high, and swallowed a tiny sip of his finest wine.

There was a sudden, loud crack and the sound of something zipping through the air at high speed. Timothy recognized too late the sound of gunfire. The shot slammed into Ludus's chest with a dull thud. The emperor stared down at a fist-sized hole in his chest, a confused look on his face. The empress screamed as Ludus collapsed and the room erupted into chaos.

Rebos threw himself under the table, pulling his mother down with him. The executors came forward, forming a protective line in front of the head table with their electric batons drawn. It was too little, too late. The assassins came from every shadow, armed with knives and swords. They were dark-skinned, bearing gold and silver tattoos and dressed in rags, just as the assassin at Clovis's estate had been. They moved as men and women possessed, cutting through men, women, children, senators and lords as if they were hogs at the slaughter.

No, Timothy thought as the killers came closer. The assassins weren't dark-skinned at all. Their faces were painted, and the silver tattoos were drawn on. Their clothes were made of the right material, but it didn't look worn enough, and the way they handled their *ikhiri* swords … These were no expert assassins. They were actors playing a role. On closer inspection, he thought he recognized some of them from his time in the Bloody Keep. But why were executors pretending to be assassins?

Metallic silver glinted from a balcony above and a thin, dark shadow fell back. Timothy could only just barely make out the long-barrel shape of the sniper rifle. Whoever had pulled the trigger was slight of build, but he could tell no more than that before the shadows swallowed the assassin.

Timothy shouted for Annon, Cylene and Chaunstance to get down and between them they flipped over the table. It offered little cover, but it was better than nothing. He took Chaunstance's face in his hands. "Stay here," he instructed and then crept out from behind the table without waiting to hear a reply.

His sword drawn, he stood with the executors,

watching the assassins move through the room. The killers did not move toward the front of the room and the executors did nothing to stop them from cutting down the nobility. Oddly, the assassins let some pass untouched while charging relentlessly after others. *They're choosing their targets*, Timothy realized. *It isn't random carnage then. It's a coup.*

High Executor Yolen paced in front of his executors, hands behind his back, as calm and collected as a well-fed snake.

"What is this?" Timothy shouted. "What's happening?"

Yolen regarded him coolly. "Revolution, Lord Val. Now, get back behind the table."

Timothy looked out over the blood-stained floor. He searched for Clovis and Haplan but came up empty. The sword was suddenly heavier in his hand. He gripped it tighter, ignoring the pull of the stitches in his side and the sting in his palm. "I won't let you kill any more people, Yolen! Call them off!"

"You were warned about which side to stand on, Val. Do not step over the line. Not again."

What did he have to gain, pulling a coup and leaving Annon and Rebos alive?

Timothy glanced at the overturned table. A fearful and obedient puppet, that's what.

Now that everyone had seen the power the executors wielded, and how far Yolen was willing to go to enforce his agenda, no one would dare challenge the man he propped up as emperor. In one decisive move, Yolen had not only assured Rebos's ascension while wiping out any resistance, by using 'Erolyian assassins,' he was reminding the people Erolyia was still a threat. This was as much about driving Senjele out of their cold war and into direct conflict as it was about placing the correct emperor on the throne.

Timothy turned and threw himself over the table. Behind it, Cylene held Ludus's body, staring at the blood seeping out of it. Annon had a hand on his mother's shoulder in a protective gesture, while Nareen sat in dazed shock. Timothy wasn't interested in any of them. Instead, he grabbed Rebos by the shirt.

"I didn't know," Rebos said in a panic, shaking his head. "I swear!"

Timothy didn't care. He jerked Rebos from the safety of the table. "Call them off, Yolen," he shouted, pressing the blade of his sword against Rebos's neck.

Yolen turned and took in the situation before smiling. "A sheep never changes his wool, does he, Lord Val?"

"Call off your assassins!"

Yolen sighed but raised a hand and gave a command in Erolyian. The killing ended abruptly, but the wailing and cries of those who had survived didn't pause.

Timothy pressed the sword harder against Rebos's neck. *Now what?*

"I could just as easily put Annon on the throne," Yolen said with a shrug. "I only need one brother. Rebos will have more support, I suspect, but either will work."

"Why?" Timothy demanded.

"You're in no position to question me." The High Executor smirked. "They'll hold emergency elections now. Others will step into the vacuum of power I've created, others who are more open to taking swift and decisive action. Senjele must treat the source of the problem, Lord Val, not just apply a bandage as we did on Toria. Fixing the problem requires drastic action. Power must be taken back from the people and entrusted to those capable of action." He gestured to Rebos, who gritted his teeth.

"Now, let the prince go and I will see to it you die quickly."

"Timothy!"

He glanced down and saw Chaunstance and the others had crawled away from the table. They had found a recess in the wall and slid the panel away, revealing a small passageway. Annon squatted in the entrance while Cylene and Chaunstance crawled to safety behind him. Annon gestured for Timothy to follow. "Come!"

Timothy turned back to Yolen as an executor came to stand next to the High Executor. "Some of the guests fled before the doors were locked," she announced. "Do you want us to pursue them?"

When Yolen turned away to answer her, Timothy shoved Rebos forward, letting the prince tumble over the table. Then, he dove into the passageway.

The passage was narrow, only inches wider than Timothy's shoulders. He was glad Clovis wasn't with them. The fat old senator would have gotten stuck. As soon as he thought it, he felt sick. His quick scan of the floor hadn't revealed Clovis, but it didn't mean he was one of the lucky ones to escape. As Timothy crawled behind Annon to what he hoped was safety, he offered a silent prayer to the gods to look after Senator Clovis.

They crawled in silence and darkness for what felt like forever. Then, suddenly, there was light. They tumbled down a small ramp and into a hallway.

Cylene was the first one up. She pulled Annon up in the same breath, and looked him over before wrapping her arms around him. For his part, Annon still looked dazed, though anger was working its way into the tense muscles of his shoulders.

Timothy grabbed Chaunstance by the shoulders and held her. "Are you all right? You're not hurt?"

She shook her head and choked on tears. "Clovis. Did

you see Clovis?"

"No," Timothy admitted. "But perhaps he got out."

"Where are we?" Cylene asked, looking around.

"Servants' quarters," Annon answered in a growl. "We have to find a way out."

A hand came down heavily on Timothy's shoulder. He turned, fist curled, but paused when he saw it was Haplan Ambren. Haplan looked at his fist, nodded, then said, "The exit is this way."

He led them through several hallways in silence. Timothy never let go of Chaunstance, afraid they might get separated. Somewhere in the distance, there was screaming and wailing. Timothy's vision flashed back to that day on Toria and the sight of helpless men gunned down. It was happening again. He had come full circle. No longer did the capital sleep in silent tension. Nebarius and the palace were war zones.

The corridors were mostly empty, but a few panicked servants ran by. Twice, doors slammed closed. As they passed one, Timothy heard muffled sobbing on the other side.

Haplan led them down another corridor to a side entrance where a transport waited. He paused in the doorway to open an umbrella and handed it to Timothy. "Yolen's men are manning the main gate," he explained. "Take the east exit. The guards there are in Clovis's pocket. They know my transport and will let you pass."

"Lord Val." The empress put a hand on Timothy's shoulder. He turned and saw her grasping Annon's hand. Tears streamed from the corners of her eyes. She tried twice to speak, but choked on her words. "Yolen will kill him," she finally managed, desperation coloring her tone. "You can't let him."

"You must get him off Senjele," Haplan said. "Take

him to Clovis. He'll know what to do."

Chaunstance snapped out of her daze. "Clovis is alive?"

"He is," Haplan said, though his tone was grave. "Our spies uncovered the plot moments before it happened. I got a few people out before the fighting started." He gestured again to the door. "Please, you must go."

"No," Annon protested, and jerked his hand away from his mother's. "I want to stay and fight."

"You don't have the support, Prince Annon," Haplan snapped. "Or the armies. Yolen would kill you where you stood. Now, go. Flee. Live to fight and win another day."

Timothy took the umbrella. "What about you?"

"I'll be fine." He offered a weak smile. "My daughter will be empress, remember?"

"But if Yolen finds out you helped us—"

Lord Ambren gripped Timothy's shoulder and looked him sternly in the face. The rustle of executors' body armor came from a nearby hallway. Haplan squeezed Timothy's shoulder and uttered the motto of his house: "The dragon does not falter, Timothy, especially when he is called upon to act. Now, go." When Timothy hesitated, Haplan gave him a gentle shove. "Now! Before they find you."

As Timothy stuffed Annon and Chaunstance into Lord Ambren's transport, he heard the palace doors closing behind him. The lock turned, and he knew he would never see Haplan Ambren again.

CHAPTER NINETEEN

Rebos

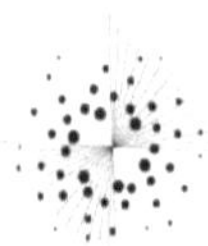

Rebos's fingers trembled as Yolen helped him up. "Are you hurt?" the High Executor asked. The prince fought to find words, but nothing would come. Instead, he looked around at the carnage and tried to understand what had happened.

After a moment of taking in the blood spatters and broken limbs littering the banquet hall, he searched the executor's face. "What are you doing?"

"There were plots against you, Highness," Yolen explained. "Factions were springing up everywhere, vowing to put your brother on the throne. Some spoke the name Timothy Val, and thought Senjele would do better in his care."

"I ..." But what was there to say? Yolen was right. Rebos had suspected there were rebel factions rising. But was all this really necessary? "Surely not all these people were plotting against me?"

"Is that a risk you were prepared to take?" Yolen gestured behind him. "Were you willing to risk your wife and child's life on such a chance?"

Rebos turned. His eyes fell on Nareen. Despite everything, she was lovely. This stress couldn't have been kind to her or their child. He had vowed to protect her, to take care of her. This wasn't what he had in mind.

"You should have warned me," Rebos said, turning back to Yolen. "If I had known what you planned, I never would have brought Nareen up here. You put her in danger!"

"I assure you, she was never in any danger." Yolen made a low bow. "In the future, I will keep you abreast of all things, Majesty. You are the emperor now, after all."

"Yes," said Rebos slowly. He rubbed the sting in his neck and brought his hand away bloody. *The sword cut deeper than I thought. I'm lucky he didn't take my head. How dare he lay hands on me!* "What of Timothy Val?"

"What of him?"

"I want him punished—as he should have been after Toria."

High Executor Yolen offered a half smirk, half scowl. "If you wish to control the people of this empire, Your Highness, you need Timothy Val. The people love him."

Rebos bent and took up the fallen crown, turning it over in his hands. "There will be civil war if he's allowed to go free."

"There will be a peasant's revolt if he is killed."

Rebos tried the crown on his head and found it was too small. Nareen stepped over his father's corpse and put an arm around Rebos's waist. "Timothy isn't an ambitious man. If he's gotten anywhere at all, it was with help. He must have the backing of someone powerful."

Rebos's chest heaved and he closed his eyes, trying to think. Nareen made it more difficult when she kissed his cheek. His eyes snapped open and, when he gave his order, he made certain to do it with added authority. "Search the palace. Find anyone who might have helped him escape. I saw him talking to Lord Ambren earlier. Bring him to me. And Senator Clovis … yes. Bring them to me at once."

Yolen bowed and licked his lips. "As you command." He turned on his heels and barked for his executors to follow him on a sweep through the palace.

"My father?" Nareen said, taken aback. "You can't really believe he had anything to do with this?"

"Your father was conspicuously absent from the banquet hall … as was your mother."

She forced a smile. "I'm sure they just stepped out."

"Then there's nothing to fear."

He kissed her forehead and placed a hand over her womb. She wasn't showing yet, and no one but the people at the head table had heard his announcement, but he was sure Yolen knew. Yolen knew everything.

She put her hand over his and smiled.

Rebos paid her no mind. He was too busy watching a shadow move across the opposite wall. Slowly, the shadow slid away from the wall and became the lanky frame of Reva Tzu in his black and blue floor-length robes. The sleeves hung over his hands and he wore a black, box-shaped hat with a single peacock feather in it that wobbled with each step. His oxygen mask hung around his neck, attached to a portable tank, though he didn't have it on. Reva took two steps forward and knelt in the middle of the banquet hall.

"What do you want," Rebos spat at him.

"Allow me to offer my immediate services, Your Eminence."

"Whatever you want, it can wait."

"My Emperor." Reva dared to lift his eyes from the floor as he addressed Rebos. "Word will soon spread about what happened here. If we release a statement first, we can control the flow of information and preserve your image in the media."

"Make it happen, then."

Reva smiled. "First, there are some things we must discuss. I'll need to know what you intend to do with the empress and your brother. Also, I need to know what you intend to do with the traitors when you catch them."

"My mother has done nothing wrong," Rebos announced. "She fled because she was frightened. Like me, she had no idea what was happening. I don't blame her. When she returns, I will welcome her with open arms, so long as she gives Nareen and I her unwavering allegiance. I don't doubt she will."

"Of course." Reva lowered his head. "And Annon?"

Annon. His brother was a complicated matter. Yolen would want him dead, and for good reason. Unless they eliminated every dissenting voice, there would be whispers of putting Annon on the throne. However, if he had his brother killed, the people would see him as heartless and brutal. There had to be a way to destroy Annon's reputation and credibility without harming his own.

"Annon must be made to look incompetent as both a ruler and a man. Find some of the women he's been with, or pay a few to spread rumors about him. I'm sure there will be footage of him making a fool of himself. Make sure it's released."

"Yes, Highness. And the traitors?"

Rebos took a deep breath as High Executor Yolen slithered back into the banquet hall, his uniform splattered with blood. He wiped his hands with a damp cloth while some of his men dragged in Haplan Ambren, beaten and bloody and barely conscious, and dumped him at Rebos's feet. Nareen pulled away from Rebos, but stayed by his side.

"Did you beat him?" Rebos asked Yolen with a glare.

Yolen shrugged "He resisted."

Lord Ambren fought to his knees to regard Rebos. "A pity your assassin has such good aim, Yolen. A little more to the right and we'd all be better off." He spat a mouthful of blood on Rebos's shoe.

"Father!" Nareen exclaimed. She reached for Rebos's arm and turned, pleading with him. "Please, he doesn't mean it. It's the stress."

Rebos leaned down. "I would be more careful about the words I chose were I in your situation, Lord Ambren."

Lord Ambren locked eyes with Nareen. "I don't have the luxury of being careful. I have a conscience, and I mean every word I said and am about to say." He leaned forward and bared his bloody teeth at Nareen. "You should be ashamed of yourself, sleeping around like a common whore, spreading your legs and opening your womb in exchange for power. Do you think you will find comfort on the throne?"

Rebos drew his hand back and struck him across the face, hard enough to send him sprawling. "You will hold your tongue or I will cut it out of your head!"

Lord Ambren rolled onto his back and laughed.

"What is so funny?"

"You! You think you can rule this empire by force! Brutality will never breed loyalty! You're so blissfully ignorant even I'm surprised!"

Reva leaned in to whisper in Rebos's ear. "If you could get him to confess to being part of the coup and a traitor, and place the blame for these foreign assassins on him, you would be wise to do so. It is always better to be seen as a victim than a victor."

Rebos nodded. "High Executor Yolen."

"Your Eminence?"

"Take Lord Ambren to the dungeons. See to it he confesses to treason and to his part in the conspiracy to murder the emperor. I want a signed deposition within the hour."

Yolen bowed and the executors carried Lord Ambren away.

"Lord Reva Tzu."

Reva chuckled and lowered his head in false humility. "My Emperor, I am no lord. I am a lowly media liaison for House Eflor."

"Nonsense. I think it's high time you were rewarded for your service." Rebos lowered the crown in his hands onto Nareen's head and smiled at how perfectly it fit her. She would look radiant beside him, even when she was old. "My second act as emperor is to award you a lordship for your many years of service and loyalty," he said to Reva.

"Thank you, my Emperor."

"I'll hold a press conference in an hour. I assume you've written speeches before?"

Reva nodded.

"Then you will write one detailing Lord Ambren's confession and tell the people of Senjele I will not allow sedition and rebellion to flourish in my empire."

"As you wish." Reva bowed and took two full steps backward before disappearing into the shadows of the room in much the same way the assassins had when there was no more killing to be done.

Rebos took Nareen's face in his hands. Her jaw quivered against his fingers and he kissed a stray tear racing down her cheek. "I'm sorry, my love. Forgive me for what must be done to your father. I swear, this will not come back on you."

"My father is a traitor," Nareen said, as her voice wavered. "He is already dead to me."

Rebos searched her face, his heart jumping into his throat. "Are you afraid of me, my love?"

"I am afraid for you," she whispered, leaning in close. "If the High Executor can depose your father with such little resistance, what is to stop him from doing the same to you?"

"I won't let that happen," he promised. "I swore I would protect you and our child. I love you more than anything. I would die to protect you."

She touched his face and nodded, blinking away more tears.

"The only reason I am going along with this is because it's best for Senjele."

She turned her face away when he bent down to kiss her. "If you had to choose between my well-being and Senjele's … which would it be?"

"Don't you see, Nareen? You're my empress. You *are* Senjele."

"But—"

Rebos's fingers traveled down her cheek and closed around her throat. She gasped as he tightened his hold. How dare she question him! Her father was a traitor who would have put a knife in his back and another in her belly, if he were given half the chance. Couldn't she see how desperate times were? Didn't she know now was not the time to ask such things?

"Never ask me that again," he said through clenched teeth.

She fought to nod, and he released her, letting her stagger back.

"Find my brother," Rebos shouted. His voice echoed off the walls and high ceiling. "And bring me Senator Clovis and Timothy Val!"

CHAPTER TWENTY

Vyjorin

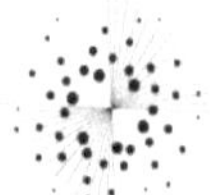

Everything hurt. Laying, blinking, pissing himself, even the ointment that was supposed to sooth him felt like icy acid. He preferred Shireen's touch to the Master of the Herbs, because she wouldn't poke and prod the weeping, seeping wounds on the left half of his body. Whenever Master Goshen came to look at him, the old man would bob his head up and down and insist on peeling away the bandages to have a look, as he was doing now. Every time they took the bandages off, a fresh layer of skin would flake away leaving him red and exposed. Master Goshen pulled the bandage over his arm and forced a clinging bit of scaly skin away. Vyjorin grimaced, or tried to grimace. He couldn't be sure what face he was making. The left side of his lip felt thick and gnarled.

They'd woken him from his fever dreams two days ago in just such a way, peeling away the cloth skin of his bandages to have a look at the monster underneath. He hadn't moved since then, except for when the eunuchs came to change his bed when he soiled himself or when Master Goshen instructed them to rotate him to prevent bedsores on his good side. All of it was excruciating and humiliating but the burns were not the worst of it. The worst part was seeing the Eye of the King dangling between his sister's breasts. When he first saw it, he tried to tell her to take it off, but his words came out as animalistic grunts. He had to strain his lips until they cracked and bled to form intelligible sound.

The herb master bobbed his head. "He's healing nicely. Another week of the cream and I think we may start to see signs of scarring. I have another cream to reduce that but …" he trailed off and drew his bushy, white eyebrows together. "We can't hide them all."

That's barely news, Vyjorin thought, but all he could manage was another grunt.

Shireen quieted him with a gentle pat on the good side of his head. They'd shaved what remained of his hair while he slept.

"Don't talk now, brother. You'll be better soon."

Lies. He couldn't be better, not with those *things* shambling around in the dark. He'd dreamt of Lillith, Fayte, and the twisted child curling around their breasts, feeding. Worst of all, he had no idea whether there were more creatures out there like the one they had made from his Kihran. He pushed the thought of his wife's animated corpse out of his mind. She was dead and her body at peace now, as well as her spirit. Vyjorin should have known better than to challenge finality a fourth time.

"I … am …" he started, rasping heavily after each word. "I … want …" Shireen leaned in closer. "Eye."

Shireen closed her delicate fingers around the Eye. "I'm only holding it for you, brother, so the weight of it doesn't hurt you. You can have it back when you're healed."

"Want … now." It was disgusting, how he had to talk like an infant, but the pain and effort of forming words was too great to waste. He need only get the important words out to get his point across.

"Princess Shireen needs the Eye to run your kingdom while you're on the mend," Master Goshen explained. He had no idea what that thing was, what it could do.

"Don't use."

"I won't use it, Vyjorin. I can't, not like you can."

"Wives?" He'd asked after Kihran's body when he first woke, only to find the rest of them confused. Apparently, when the eunuchs finally worked up the nerve to come in and look for him, they found him alone and burning, lingering close to death. The king tried to relay what had happened, but no one understood him or, if they did, they took it for the fever dreams that made him thrash and claw at his skin. His other wives should have come forward to wail over him. It was their duty. They were too busy quarreling among each other. He needed to dismiss them, as Lillith had ordered.

Shireen shook her head. "None will come."

"Wives … free. Wives … no more. Understand?"

Master Goshen's head rose and fell. "You wish to divorce your wives?"

"Yes."

"Very well. I'll relay the command," Shireen said. She sounded too serious, too womanly for her young age. He should have protected her more. He wondered suddenly if she'd seen the inside of the horrific, black temple. "Is there anything else you need?"

"Mirror." It was the first day he'd wanted to see himself. The damage was extensive, he knew, but he wanted to know what Lillith had done to him, needed to understand the cost of his arrogance. Once he saw it, he could never unsee it.

Shireen exchanged glances with Master Goshen who said, "I think it would be wise to wait on that. Until you've healed a little more."

"No. See now. Mirror now. No waiting. Bring."

Master Goshen looked to Shireen for approval. Why was he second-guessing his commands? Burned or not, Vyjorin was still king. It didn't matter that he was lying in a pool of his own waste. He was king.

Shireen nodded, and Master Goshen lifted a small mirror from his physician's bag.

The face that stared back at him was not his own, but one crusted with waves of black and red on one side, glistening wet with fluid wherever the skin had reddened. His lip was curled into a thick, permanent and scaly snarl. Where once there was a whole nose, now only half of one remained. The other side was just an open hole, dripping and red. He still had his eyelid, though, and he blinked. That was good.

The mirror went away and, with it, the glimpse of the monster he had become. In its place, Master Goshen's head bobbed methodically. "Some of it will heal. We can use surgery and skin grafts to help with the rest, perhaps fill some of the unevenness with collagen."

"No," Vyjorin said sharply. "Leave it." He lifted a finger to point at Shireen. "You. Training?"

"How can I with you like this?"

"Go. Train. Kill. Strong. Win." Didn't she understand that everything hinged on her now?

"All right," she conceded, gently patting his unburnt cheek. "If you will take your medicine and rest."

Vyjorin tried to object but the words came out as spittle and grunts. His gnarled lip was too painful to move anymore. Master Goshen lifted a small vial of ebony milk, straight and strong, and pressed a straw to the good side of his mouth. He drank it down eagerly, not caring when a little spilled down his chin. His sister wiped it away.

The dreams came then, pleasant and quiet. He dreamt of Kihran and the child that might have been, riding on the steps of the mobile palace on their way to the Green Fields, catching torch flies as they moved through the dusk. Kihran sang a soft song in her native tongue to their child, and lulled him to sleep beside her. Even with the babe sleeping beside them, it did not deter their lovemaking. In the dream, she was with child again.

When they woke him, all of it faded, and he was back in the cool room of his palace in Oasis, Shireen gently rubbing oil into his skin. He guessed by the change of her clothes that he had slept an entire day away, maybe more.

"When?" he croaked as soon as he felt strong enough to speak.

"It's been nearly a month since your burns, brother." He noted the absence of the Eye around her neck but felt it sitting somewhere nearby. "I took it off," she told him when she saw him looking at her. "So the sight of it wouldn't displease you. I only wear it when I must. I never use it. I promise." He turned his head away as she rubbed her hands over his chest. "I've been training, like you said. I'm getting better. Even the eunuchs think so."

"Good," he moaned, the word slipping out a little easier than the last time he tried it. He would be able to form full sentences soon. Now ... if only he could stand. "Tell me. How is ... my kingdom?"

The re-animated corpse was all he could think about in his waking hours. He had watched Ki's body die, but he'd revived three others. He'd sent the children to temples, hoping time spent serving the gods would release them from any darkness their spirits encountered on the other side. Still, he worried they were roaming the desert, searching for victims to tear apart.

"Well enough," Shireen said with a shrug. "There has been an increase in sightings of Sandmen, but not near here."

That was good. Most people believed that Vyjorin controlled the Sandmen and, so long as they did as he ordered, he allowed them to do as they wished. It wasn't quite so simple. Vyjorin, as well as his father and his father's father, had needed their services. The assassins kept a strict code. Killing, for the Sandmen, was as much an art as it was a science. They conducted their murders with ritual conciseness. They weren't loyal to Erolyia, however. Anyone with enough coin or a cause strong enough could recruit them. Given the trouble Senjele had with filling their coffers recently, he doubted anyone there could afford them.

He looked to his sister. She chewed on her bottom lip, looking as if she had more to say. "What?"

"The Senjelian emperor was assassinated while you slept."

Bad news. With tensions on the rise, a transition in power would almost certainly propel his empire to war with Senjele. By all reports, Rebos was a warmongering, spoiled brat with delusions of grandeur. At least Ludus had been somewhat reasonable.

Shireen frowned and continued. "The reports I've heard indicate it wasn't a bloodless end, brother. Forty nobles are missing, along with the youngest prince. They say Prince Rebos has arrested them for treason."

Damn Rebos. After all the hell Vyjorin had gone through, the Senjelians might have spoiled everything in their blood lust.

"Prince Annon might even be dead. No one has produced a body, though, so we can't be sure."

Well, he thought. *At least there's hope.*

"Oh, and I almost forgot. Taleed returned this morning and demanded to see you. I told him you were in no condition to …"

Her voice trailed off as he fought to sit. It was no easy task, and more painful than he could have imagined, yet he found the strength to raise his back against the cool softness of the pillows. "I will … see him."

"Vyjorin, you're still so badly burned. Please give yourself time to heal."

With shaky hands, Vyjorin raised his fingers to the thick, white bandages that covered most of his face and half his body like a funerary shroud. They'd hidden most of him away. "I will see … him. Now. Bandage me. I want the Eye."

She didn't wait for him to repeat the order. Shireen knew how to obey. The thick, white gauzy bandages shut out the painful touch of the air, but did little to ease the burning. Sometimes, it still felt like the fire was crawling over him. It was the healing itch, and he had to resist scratching at it.

His sister brought the Eye from a small drawer next to his bed, the crystalline iris casting a shimmering shadow in the dark corners of the room. Vyjorin bit back a scream when she placed it gently over his neck and lowered it to his chest.

"I will send for him," she said, and tapped something into her data pad. "Shall I stay brother? I should attend to you if you … you know."

If I shit myself, he finished, though he felt he finally had some control over his bowels and bladder. Ebony leaf in vast quantities did that to anyone, he told himself. There was no reason to be ashamed.

"Stay," he commanded, but he was more afraid of drooling on himself. The way his lip twisted, he could barely get some words out, and when he did, the spittle was there, dripping down the rawness of his cheek.

"As you command."

Not ten minutes passed before Thein Taleed appeared beside Vyjorin's bed. He didn't hear the door open, but Vyjorin felt a presence by the dark shift in the air, and opened his eyes. That was how the Saleph of the Sandmen always chose to make his entrance, and Vyjorin found it befitted his personality.

Taleed was everything Vyjorin was not. Tall, well-muscled, with an attractive face. He wore dark streaks of paint above, under and around his eyes, that might have made a lesser man look ridiculous. For Taleed, the makeup drew attention to his most expressive feature: piercing, pale blue eyes. He would have every woman in the empire swooning after him if he'd take off that black hood and wear something other than rags.

He regarded Vyjorin with uncaring eyes and did not bow. It was his right. The Sandmen owed him no allegiance.

"Tell me what news you have," Vyjorin managed.

"It was a rogue faction of executors that assassinated the emperor. They had some help from a group calling themselves Nightingales. These Nightingales are under the command of someone my spies have only been able to identify as the Stygian."

"Stygian," Vyjorin scoffed.

"*The* Stygian." Taleed shrugged. "In any case, I believe

him to be someone close to the throne, but an outsider. I haven't yet been able to identify him, but I believe he is working with the High Executor."

It made sense, Vyjorin supposed. Rebos would not have been able to pull that coup off by himself. Had the prince been looking to hire Sandmen, he would have heard about it. This had to be that Stygian fellow, whoever he was. If he was working with the High Executor, why? What could the two of them hope to gain by propping Rebos up?

"Find him."

Taleed bowed his head in compliance but did not move to go. He had something else to say.

"Go on," Vyjorin urged.

"There has been an alleged sighting of the Andraste."

The very mention of the ship made Vyjorin want to growl, though he knew the sound would only serve to make him seem even more inhuman. The Andraste, and her pilot, Jovi Null, were black stains on his kingship, along with that older sister of his. "Where?"

Taleed shrugged as if the sighting meant nothing. "On Senjele, in Nebarius at the time of the murder."

"Is he … involved?" Vyjorin lowered his gaze from Taleed. The well-built man before him only made Vyjorin more aware of how ugly he was. Staring down at the fluid-stained sheets of his bed, he wondered why Jovi would risk being seen.

"I don't believe so. Not with the murder at least."

"If he comes here—"

Taleed gave his king a nod, which was as good as Vyjorin could expect from a man of Taleed's background. "I will notify you if my spies see him again." Taleed eyed him with a frown. "King, there is one more thing. It involves a subject we have spoken on before."

Vyjorin closed his eyes and leaned his head back. There was only one other topic Taleed would wish to discuss with him. "Are you certain it is Shireen?"

"Nothing is ever certain," the Sandman answered, "but many of the signs and portents are right." Taleed stepped closer to Vyjorin, the air around him filled with that disturbingly empty smell that marked his kind. "The spirits say the Shadeem Saleph, the great ender of all things, will come here and supplicate himself to you, Great King. She will need to be ready."

Supplicate himself … That could be anyone. Did Taleed not know how many men bowed before him every day? Vyjorin needed more information, especially now he knew what manner of creatures lurked in the darkness around him. "How will I know him?"

"And you will hear of wars and rumors of wars … Nation will rise against nation, brother against brother and kingdom against kingdom. There will be many prophets in those days, and many false gods. These prophets will produce signs and wonders to deceive you, but you must remain vigilant. You will know him by the sign of the White Wyrm, for it is the Shadeem Saleph, and he alone, that will call and slay her."

Vyjorin snorted at Taleed's cryptic, religious response. He wasn't in the mood for scripture or ancient metaphors involving false dragons. "Not helpful."

Taleed smiled his twisted smile. "That is what I know. To seek the Shadeem Saleph is to seek your own death. The prophecies say—"

"They say he will come," Vyjorin said and tried to ignore the spittle running down his face. "And when he does, Shireen must be ready."

Taleed bowed, low enough for once to suit Vyjorin. "I will teach her the way."

Vyjorin did his best to nod, though it was difficult

with his burns. Taleed was brutal, and would be a harsh teacher for Shireen, but if she was to win the heart of the prophet, whoever he was, she would have to adopt some of that fierceness. *Shireen must produce an heir*, he thought as he watched Taleed leave. *And she must do it with this Shadeem Saleph or else* … Vyjorin reached up with shaky hands to grasp the Eye still hanging around his neck. *Through that union, we shall all be saved.*

CHAPTER TWENTY-ONE

Shen

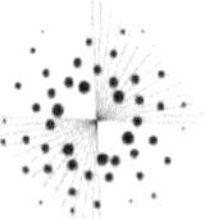

On the other side of Nebarius, in Hangar Twenty of the port, there was a very different celebration. Brek and the rest of the crew had settled into drinks and music aboard the *Rudra*, celebrating the new job and the many zeroes the empress had promised them. There were eight in Brek's crew, but Shen hung back, clinging to the corners of the room and keeping to himself.

The music was too loud. He would have preferred to be on the upper deck, listening to the thunder from the storm echo through the hull. Brek wouldn't let him have any peace, insisting he come down and socialize, as if he had nothing better to do. He didn't want to socialize any more than he'd wanted to take this shady job, no matter how well paid. And, so, he sat in a corner with his knives out on a crate, drawing each one over a whetstone.

A loud crash drew his eyes. He watched as Brek put their newest member, Solomon, into a headlock. Solomon was a big man from Polmira, twice the size of Brek but what Brek lacked in size, he made up for in strength. Mere seconds after his arm closed around Solomon's neck, the bearded man tapped his palm on the floor in submission. Brek let him go and stood, amidst cheers, pointing to Jerute, their youngest member. "How many wins in a row does that make?"

"Six!" Jerute answered drunkenly, and raised his cup.

"Six!" Brek climbed up on Solomon's back and spread his arms wide. "Not one of you bastards can best me, can you? You're a bunch of wet pussies! I've beaten you all!"

Solomon got up and Brek lost his balance, falling, and prompting roars of laughter from the others. "What about Shen? I've never seen you wrestle Shen."

All eyes in the room turned to Shen. The song in the background ended, creating an uncomfortable, heavy silence. Shen finished sharpening the knife he was working on and placed it on the mat holding the others. "I don't wrestle."

"He doesn't wrestle," Brek repeated with disdain. "He doesn't drink. He doesn't dance. He doesn't fuck." Brek wandered closer, tripping on a discarded bottle, but catching himself before he could go down. "Are you some sort of priest, Shen? Have you found a god to your liking?"

"You're drunk," Shen said.

Brek leaned in, stinking of ale sweat. "It's a good thing he can kill and follow orders. Otherwise, I'd have no use for him."

Shen glared at him. "If you've got something to say, just say it."

"You should follow your own advice, Shen. I know it's been eating at you all day. So ask. Speak your objections in front of everyone."

Shen looked over the other six faces in the room. Of them all, only Solomon and Zarah, their lone female recruit, looked bothered by Brek's confrontation. Jerute had been with them long enough to expect Shen and Brek to get into at least one fight over the course of a job. The twins, Ears and Raven, were too drunk to care.

"I've never made my objections secret. I don't kill women, children or idiots. It's always been our rule. I don't see why you'd change it now."

"It always been *your* rule!" Brek drove a finger into Shen's chest. "Not mine. Not this group's. We go where the money takes us. We were paid to do a job and we'll do it."

"The seven of you should be able to handle it without me," Shen said, bending to pick up a knife.

Brek pushed the crate holding Shen's knives away. "You'll come, and you will help with this mission."

"Or what?" Shen smiled. "You'll kick me out?"

"Yes!"

"Come on, Brek," Solomon urged. "Leave him out if he doesn't want to do it."

"It's one less way to split the money," Zarah added, twirling her raspberry-colored hair on a finger. "We all get richer and he can sit on his fine ass and do nothing. Everybody wins."

"No. We go together. All of us," Brek insisted. He bent and took up a knife Shen had finished sharpening and pointed it at Shen. "Do you think you're better than us? Are you above following orders? I am captain here. I give the orders! You follow! That's how it works!"

Shen stood, eying the drunken way Brek held the

knife. "If that's how this is going to be, then let me save you the trouble of kicking me out. I'll leave."

Brek sneered. "I won't let you."

"Brek." Solomon's hand came down on Brek's shoulder. "Let's sleep it off and talk about it in the morning, huh?"

Brek shoved him away and swung the knife at him. Solomon's forearm caught the blade. Solomon fell back, grabbing the wound and cursing. Ears and Raven sobered a little at the sight of it and jumped up, blinking starry eyes. Zarah lowered her foot from the barrel it was resting on and frowned. Brek turned back to Shen and threw the knife at him. The handle struck the metal wall beside Shen's head and then clattered to the floor.

"Do you see what you've caused?" he snarled at Shen. "You and your morals."

"Shut up, you drunken bastard," Zarah said, standing. "You know full well you can't kick Shen out, not without losing half of us."

"'Sright," Ears slurred. "He goes, we goes."

Brek eyed his crew, and swayed back and forth. Then he marched across the room and grabbed Zarah by the chin. "We're doing this job."

Zarah sucked in a deep breath and jerked her head forward, slamming her forehead into Brek's nose. There was a resounding crack and blood poured down Brek's face. He stumbled back, crashing into a few crates.

"No one said we weren't," Zarah said, standing over him, looking like she'd just swallowed a whole pickled egg. "But if you put your fucking hands on me again, I'll rip your dick off and feed it to you."

Ears tittered with laughter when Zarah stepped over Brek and went to Shen. She threw an arm over his shoulder, grabbed his crotch and planted a big kiss on his cheek. "Come on, Shen. I could use a little company." She pulled him toward the crew quarters.

Shen didn't dare voice an objection. This was her version of a rescue. He went with her through the hallway, the two of them keeping up the act as far as the elevator. When they stumbled inside, and the door closed behind them, Zarah let him go and both of them laughed.

"Brek will shit an egg!" Shen said, grinning from ear to ear. "He'd give his left testicle to see you naked, let alone sleep with you."

"Well, he can keep on waiting. I'll sleep with Brek when dogs lie with cats and the hen eats the fox." She bent down and unbuttoned her boots.

"Is that prophecy, Zarah?"

She smiled up at him. "Where I come from, they read the entrails of sheep for prophecy."

The elevator door opened on a narrow hallway and they both stepped out, heading for the crew quarters on the right. The corridor wasn't well lit, but they'd been this way enough times they could have found the quarters in complete darkness.

Once they reached quarters, Zarah kicked off her boots and unlaced the leather bodice she wore as armor when off duty. Shen couldn't imagine seeing Zarah without armor of some sort. It was a second skin to her, perhaps even more natural than the first. But she took it off, disarming herself of several small pistols and two knives.

"So tell me," she said, pulling off her shirt. "The empress. Was she beautiful?"

"Common enough," Shen answered with a shrug, pulling off his belt and tossing it aside. "But not your type. She was too willing a whore. You like the chase, even if it is pretend."

"I like to chase and catch," she laughed. "I hear she has small tits anyway."

"I think the Senjelians like their women with small tits. Haven't seen many well-endowed women since coming here."

"A pity. What was the world where we found the woman who could lift transports with her tits?"

"Weifeld, and it wasn't transports, it was boats."

"That's right. I remember now." Zarah plopped down on the bunk across from him. "What else did you see at the palace? Anyone that tickled your fancy?"

"The only other person I saw, aside from some guards, was the empress's advisor. He was Amasian."

Zarah leaned forward, eyes wide. "I've never met an Amasian, but I've heard the stories. They say they are beautiful and open to all kinds of things. Even some of the kinky shit you're into, Shen."

Shen shook his head. "He wasn't what you would call beautiful. I would call him … unsettling. He's the man behind this mission, Zarah, and I don't trust him. Brek was too blinded by his dick to think it through, even though I tried to tell him. This isn't the kind of job you walk away from. They don't hire you to kill royal bastards and let you live."

"Is the great Shen Gravel afraid to die?"

"You know I'm not –– but I don't want to die with dirty hands. I can't change my rules to fill Brek's wallet."

She reached out and put a hand on his knee. "If you don't, you'll just piss him off more."

"I can handle Brek," Shen said, falling back into his bunk and putting one arm behind his head.

Zarah sighed. "You're worried about him."

"Brek is a prick. But he's my brother. We might not share blood, but we've shed enough together, and been through enough, that I don't want to see him do something stupid. I especially don't want to see him drag all of you into it. We should have turned the job down."

"It's too late now. The men have seen the credits they'll pull in."

"What about you?" He turned his head to look at her. She'd laid down in her bunk, and was staring at the bottom of the one above her. "Are you okay with killing children who have done nothing but be born a bastard?"

"I should object to killing children because I'm a woman?"

"Come on, Zarah. You know me better than that."

She turned to him and smiled. It was a sad smile. "I do, unfortunately," Zarah said, and rolled onto her stomach. "What if there were a compromise? What if you could come with us without killing anyone?"

Shen frowned. "I don't see how it's possible."

"Volunteer to do the recon for the mission. Find the bastards before Brek and the rest do. Scope them out, decide if they're worth killing or saving. If your opinion doesn't match up with the credits the crown is offering, walk away. Let Brek and the others do the killing."

He turned his head and stared up at the bottom of his bunk. There was a list of names written there in black marker. Every night before he went to sleep, he uttered each one in a prayer for forgiveness. Even though the list was short, it weighed on his mind. Shen couldn't let himself forget the men who had died needlessly because of his greed. Now Brek was going down the same path. He was letting credits and material possessions and desires blind him. This was supposed to be a life free of all ties of loyalty to king and country, free of judgment and hate. Wasn't that why they had started their band of mercenaries? As long as every man—or woman—could pull their weight and contribute to the job, they were welcome to share the spoils. They used to turn down jobs all the time when it didn't fit their way of doing things. Where had they gone wrong?

"I don't know if I could live with myself," he said at length. "Once Brek realizes what he's agreed to, I'm not sure if he can, either."

"You can't save Brek from himself, Shen, especially if you're not around when he fucks up."

"I'll meditate on it."

"Meditate?" She raised an eyebrow. "You sure that's all you want to do?"

Shen shook his head. "I'm not really in the mood for anything else. I'd rather just think it through."

"That's why woman learned to pleasure herself," she said with a wink.

Shen rolled over to face the wall. Thunder echoed through the hull of the ship like a distant gunshot. Rain pounded against it as if it were a war drum. He fell asleep, but he did not dream of rain and drums. Shen's dreams were filled with the same nightmares as always: gunfire. Explosions. Death.

When he woke, it was to the sound of Brek shuffling into his bunk above. Shen lay there for a long time, thinking about what, if anything, he should say. He could stay out of it and let Brek go off and get into trouble. How was he to learn his lesson if he didn't make a mistake or two? But Shen worried this was a mistake his brother wouldn't walk away from.

"Brek," he whispered. Brek's response was a grunt. "I will go with you."

"Change of heart, huh? Did Zarah help you get that stick out of your ass?"

Shen smiled. "I want to do recon for the mission.

That's my condition. I won't kill children."

Above him, Brek shifted and, after a moment, his head and shoulders appeared upside down, hanging from the bunk. "We're leaving for Yoris in the morning," he announced. "And recon gets half the pay of everyone else. You good with that, brother?"

"How is your nose?"

"It's fucking broken, that's how." Brek settled back into his bunk. "By the way, the emperor of Senjele is dead. News says someone fucking assassinated him. Erolyians backing a coup, they're saying."

"The empress has excellent timing, looking to eliminate the bastards now," Shen said.

Brek didn't answer. Maybe he was too drunk, or his face hurt too bad. Maybe he knew Shen was right.

"I don't think it's coincidence," Shen said after a long silence.

Brek sighed. "Maybe not, but you can't beat the price tag. Not by a long shot."

"What about after the job's done? You think they'll let us ride into the sunset with our spoils?"

"After is after," Brek said with a yawn. "We'll worry about that later."

Shen read the names written on the bunk again, knowing the cost of waiting until later. Brek had already proven he wouldn't listen to reason, and that settled things. Shen had to go with him if Brek was to get out alive.

CHAPTER TWENTY-TWO

Chaunstance

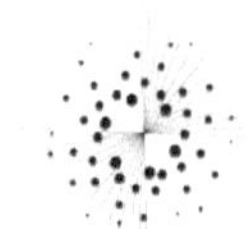

Chaunstance sat in the transport across from Timothy and Annon on their way home. They rode with the windows up and the screen that separated them from the driver locked tight. The only sound was the patter of raindrops. Chaunstance watched the rain splatter and streak the glass. Against the red city lights, the rain looked like tears of blood.

"Clovis is alive," Timothy repeated for the third time.

"I know."

"We are alive. It could have turned out very differently."

"I know," she said again, and finally turned to face him.

"Then why do you look so worried?"

"Things are changing and I ..." Her voice trailed off, and she turned to watch the city lights pass in a blur.

Her throat constricted and her eyes watered. Even as she tried to swallow, she found she couldn't. When she opened her mouth, a stifled whimper belonging to someone else came out. It belonged to a scared little girl, the one she had left behind the day the slavers raided her settlement. Everything was suddenly too tight, the air so thick she thought she would choke on it.

"What is it?" Annon asked, but she could barely make out his voice for the ringing and pounding in her ears.

Timothy jumped out of his seat and slammed a fist against the plastic partition of the car, shouting something incomprehensible at the driver. The car screeched to a stop. Blinded by tears and driven by a sudden, intense need for air, Chaunstance clawed at the door handle. It gave way and she flung herself into the rain, landing on her hands and knees. Bits of gravel dug into her palms, but the pain didn't register. She needed earth and grass beneath her, and sky above. Nothing else mattered.

She clawed her way across the road, rain pouring over her in heavy sheets, and stopped when she reached the median. Wildflowers stood vigil, their petals heavy and bent. Chaunstance grabbed handfuls of dirt. Every gasp for air brought in icy rain water. Some part of her was aware she wasn't getting enough oxygen and made her fight all the more for it. Her face and fingers were numb.

Behind her, Annon and Timothy climbed out of the car. "What's wrong?" Annon shouted. "Should we call a doctor?"

Timothy sank into the grass next to her. Chaunstance didn't wait for him to speak. She needed to get the words out now, while she still could. "I can't—" She gestured to her throat. Her words came out slurred and broken. Gods, what if he didn't know how to help? What if she couldn't be helped? What if she died and didn't get to see if Clovis was safe?

"Breathe through it." Timothy grabbed her hand. "In through the nose, out through the mouth when I squeeze. That's good. Do it again."

After a few minutes, the ringing in her ears stopped, the pounding in her head lessened, and some feeling came back into her fingers. The panicked, tight feeling in her chest dulled. "What's wrong with me?" But she already knew the answer. It had been a long time since an attack had crept up on her. Not since Clovis took her in. But every time she heard the creak of metal on the slavers' ship, every time a shadow passed over her, or one of them grabbed her from behind it would be like that. She would be small and helpless, broken and afraid. No one had wanted her because the attacks made her sickly. If Clovis were gone, no one would want her now either.

"Nothing is wrong with you," Timothy said. He sounded so calm, so confident. She hated him for it. How could he be sure of anything now? The entire universe was upside down.

His fingers tightened around hers and he pulled her up. Chaunstance wasn't sure she could stand. Her legs were wobbly and breathing was still hard. The only reason she stayed upright was because she leaned on Timothy. "I—I'm sorry," she stammered. "I shouldn't have made the car stop."

Annon shifted his weight and looked around. "Isn't that Clovis's villa over there?"

"So it is," Timothy agreed and wiped rain from his face. He put an arm around her. "Come on. Let's get you inside."

Annon jogged back to the car and returned with the umbrella, handing it to Timothy. "Go around the back," Timothy instructed. "Wait for us there. We'll be along."

He opened the umbrella and handed it to her before taking off his jacket. When he slid it off his shoulders, she caught sight of a smear of blood where some of her stitches hadn't held as well as she'd hoped. She'd been terrible to him. *He's been nothing but kind to me. Everyone has treated him so poorly and he has done nothing to deserve it. Even Clovis is using him.* All he wanted had been taken from him. The two of them may have come from different walks of life, different solar systems, but they were cut from the same cloth.

"You're bleeding," Chaunstance said, and reached out to touch his side.

Timothy glanced down. "I suppose I am."

When he placed the jacket around her shoulders, she turned her head and pressed her lips against his. The movement was so quick, she didn't even stop to think about it. She barely knew it had happened before it was over. Timothy froze, the jacket half on her, the umbrella tilted to the side, icy rain pelting both of them. He looked down at her, as if a thought was caught somewhere between his throat and his lips. "I'm glad you're here."

He finally seemed to realize he was getting soaked for no reason, and adjusted the umbrella over both of them.

They trekked through the grass toward the back end of the estate, where Annon waited. The senator met them in the rain, struggling with an umbrella of his own, a worried look on his face. When he saw Chaunstance and Timothy, his face lit up. He rushed out to greet them, splashing through puddles, getting his best trousers dirty. "Gods, what are you two doing out in this downpour? Don't just stand there gawking at each other! Get inside! Inside!"

They gathered in the cramped space of Clovis's office and waited for the senator to pull the shades and lock the doors. When he spoke, it was in a whisper. "I apologize, Your Highness, but for your own protection, we'll have to keep you hidden. Perhaps even move you off world. Your life is in danger. Rebos will do anything to secure his claim to the throne."

Annon frowned. "Claim? It's his birthright."

"It's his by tradition," Clovis explained. "A unified decree from the Senate and the lords of Senjele can override that."

"But ..." Annon's dark eyes looked to Timothy. For the first time, Chaunstance realized Annon did not know about Clovis's plans to make him emperor of Senjele.

"You will replace him," Clovis said when Timothy looked away.

Annon didn't balk at the idea, as she expected he might, but he didn't seem pleased either. Clovis probably thought of Annon as a tool, as he did Timothy. Perhaps Annon thought the same of himself. His only reaction to the news was to tighten the muscles around his jaw and straighten his posture.

"Once the vote goes to the floor, I'll have no trouble passing it." Clovis went to his desk and unlocked the top drawer, which he removed. Behind the drawer, there was a secret locker, one even Chaunstance did not have access to, though she was aware of its existence. From the locker, Clovis lifted a thick, official-looking binder, and placed it carefully on the desk. "Until this document is ratified by two-thirds of the noble houses, I can't bring the vote to the Senate." The senator rose from his seat, pen in hand, and held it out to Timothy.

Timothy didn't hesitate. He came forward, took the pen and put it to paper. The moment had been weeks in the making, yet it passed quickly and quietly. There was no fanfare, no applause, and no slogans or speeches, just the sound of a ballpoint pen moving freely across paper. Timothy handed the pen back to Clovis.

"So, what do you plan on doing with me until then?" Annon asked.

From the blank look on Clovis's face, Chaunstance knew the old man hadn't thought it through yet. The fool had planned everything so meticulously, yet he had neglected to account for a sudden assassination.

Clovis cleared his throat. "I was making those arrangements last night. I had hoped I would have more time to finalize things. As it is, you will have to leave Senjele. I had thought to hide you on Clevennia but—"

"Then I will go to Clevennia with Timothy," Annon offered.

"No." Clovis leaned forward, resting his palms on the table. "We cannot all be in the same place, not for quite some time. We are likely to become targets. To increase the odds of each of us surviving, we must separate. You must be moved out of the empire, to a place where not even High Executor Yolen can reach you."

A glimmer of realization flickered over Timothy's face like sparks on steel, but they didn't take light.

"There has been talk. The Erolyian king, Vyjorin Thagg, has a younger sister who has come of age. I'm sure you've heard the rumors. He means to offer her to Rebos as a bride to ease hostilities," Clovis said.

Timothy met and held the senator's eyes. "I expect Rebos will decline."

Clovis frowned. "Why is that?"

"Rebos intends to marry Nareen Ambren. She's carrying his child."

Silence echoed through the room. Both Annon and Clovis shifted. Timothy brought a hand down on the table, the smack echoing through the room and making everyone jump. "You mean to marry Annon to the Thagg girl instead."

Annon shook his head but Clovis continued as if the prince wasn't even there. Chaunstance recognized the defeated look of disbelief in Annon's eyes. He still believed he was powerless.

"You'll go in an unmarked transport and surrender yourself to King Vyjorin as a hostage. Out of duty, he'll be obligated not to harm you. Out of spite, he won't return you. Once they've accepted you as a hostage, you'll propose the idea to the Erolyians."

"You'd throw me into a pit of vipers, make me crawl into bed with one, possibly bow to another, so I can make war on my own brother?"

"It doesn't have to be so dramatic, Annon! Negotiate with their king for peace, marry the girl, and get her with child as quickly as possible. By then, all will be taken care of here and we can fly you back. You can prevent a war and unite the empires without firing a shot."

Timothy nodded. "It could work."

Annon clenched his fists. "If I refuse?"

Timothy tried to comfort Annon with a hand on his shoulder, but the prince pulled away. "You're not safe here, Annon, nor anywhere in Senjele." Timothy sighed. "Even if you could hide, I couldn't protect you without making you known. You need an army between you and your brother's followers. Erolyia might not be big enough to hide behind, but it's the best we have. Vyjorin will make you a hostage, but he'll make every effort to keep you alive if you can put a child in his sister's belly. He can't kill his own blood. As soon as yours mixes with hers, you're untouchable. Not to mention the lives this union would save on both sides."

"What about my life? My freedom? What if I don't want to marry this foreign girl?"

Clovis furrowed his brow and pointed an accusatory finger at Annon. "Your blood makes you a prince! Your duty is to Senjele, not to romantic whims. This empire can't afford for you to mull over whether you like blondes or brunettes! Lives are at stake! Your father understood—"

Chaunstance couldn't take it anymore, all the fighting over who would run this ridiculous empire. She stepped into the narrow space between Timothy and Annon. "Doing what is right sometimes comes at a great personal cost."

Annon regarded her angrily.

"I know the anger you feel toward your brother. Despite what everyone tells you, it will not go away. It will not get better. It will hurt for the rest of your life—the life your brother stole from you. Night after night, you'll lie awake looking at the stars and wondering how things might have been different if this had never happened."

She took a step closer and dared to look into Annon's, dark blue eyes. He took a step back from her. The air between them was thick and charged as if lightning were about to strike. "He will kill you, Annon, unless you find a way to kill him first, and you will not do it without the army we are prepared to give you."

"Fine," Annon muttered, and stepped away before turning his back on them. "How am I supposed to get to Erolyia?"

Clovis clapped his hands together. "I have a ship

waiting," he said. "But it will have to be tonight, before Rebos searches door to door." Clovis turned to Timothy and pointed. "You need to go as well. You should get to Clevennia. He wouldn't dare move on you there."

Timothy shook his head. "We'll be even more of a target if we move together. It would be best if Annon and I were on separate ships."

"You will take my personal shuttle," Clovis said, rifling through another drawer. "Chaunstance, pack your things. You're going with him."

Chaunstance suddenly felt cold and lightheaded. Part of her wanted to see Timothy's world, yes, but she didn't want to be away from Clovis. He wouldn't know what to do without her. What if Rebos found Clovis before he got to safety? Her throat tightened.

"Me?" She barely recognized her own voice; it sounded so small. "But, Clovis, who will take care of you?"

"You'll be safer there," Clovis said, and pulled out the folder of authorization codes for his personal shuttle.

"That's not what I asked." She marched up to the desk and put her hand over his as it rested on the folder.

"I suppose," Clovis drawled. "I must look after myself." He cleared his throat and pulled his hand away. Then he retrieved another folder and handed it to her. "Your freedom."

Chaunstance stared at it. "But I thought—"

"The High Executor was holding it up?" Clovis's eyes sparkled. "Oh, my dear woman, the beauty of bureaucracy is that there is more than one way to get something done if you have the capital."

Her hands shook as she took the papers from Clovis. They felt so light. Until she was holding freedom in her hands, she did not understand how much she wanted it. No longer could she be bought or sold from under Clovis should his assets be seized. Her throat tightened, but the panic wasn't there. All she felt was … free. She was free. Gods, what did it even mean?

"My dear, don't look so upset. It's only for a few days, a week at the most. By tomorrow, I'll have lords crawling to me on their knees, begging to sign this deposition. Think of it as a much-needed vacation, your first chance to go and enjoy yourself as a free woman."

Timothy put an arm around her shoulder. "I have to agree with Clovis, Chaunstance. The more we split up, the safer we are, at least until things calm down."

Chaunstance wiped away a tear. Twice she tried to speak, but couldn't, so she threw her arms around Clovis and wept.

"Now, now …" Clovis patted her on the back and peeled her arms away. "Don't worry about me. I'll be fine. I'm much too stubborn to die."

She nodded, even though she didn't believe him. He was a man of flesh and bone, as fragile as any other.

Clovis held the envelope of codes out to Timothy who took it. "Don't try to contact me," he instructed. "It would be best for you if you stayed out of the public eye for a while, I think."

Timothy gave Chaunstance's shoulder a squeeze.

She went with Timothy, his arm still wrapped around her shoulder. Timothy paused at the door to extend his hand to Annon, who stared at it despondently.

"I'm sorry," Timothy said.

Annon finally clasped Timothy's hand. "So am I." The two men stood and stared at each other, hands in a tight grip.

"Be well, Timothy," the prince added after a time. "You've been given a second chance to serve Senjele. Don't waste it."

Timothy nodded and Annon let him go. As they passed, Timothy gave Annon a clap on the shoulder, as if they were still good friends.

Chaunstance felt sick, as Timothy helped her into the transport, and all the way to the port, where they found Clovis's private shuttle. Timothy assured her over and over that everything would be fine. He promised he was a capable pilot, having received honors for his maneuvers during the Nautis Blitz. Chaunstance believed him, but she wasn't sure she was doing the right thing, leaving Clovis behind. *There's no going back now*, she thought as she buckled into the shuttle. She'd ridden in it a hundred times before with Clovis, but the space was so much smaller once Timothy climbed inside and started the automated launch sequence. Her heart sped in her chest as the engine whirred to life. Chaunstance held her breath and watched the empty patches of stone and grass fall away with the take-off, replaced quickly by clouds and stars. To keep her mind off it, she switched on the small monitor on the dash between them. The fuzzy image of a man, bloody and beaten, appeared on the screen.

"Gods," whispered Timothy when he looked at the screen. "That's Haplan." He reached over to adjust the volume.

Rebos's voice boomed over the airwaves while the camera held Haplan's bloody face firmly in its lens. "And behind that murder was the same power responsible for the deaths of our countrymen on Toria, on Illion and Nautis, the same power responsible for the death of our illustrious and beloved emperor. Behind the murder of our innocent brothers and sisters, women and children, were other brothers and sisters and their children, incited to these dark acts of tyranny by this band of rebels. These rebels, to whom our empire had done no harm, have sought tirelessly to subjugate and conquer the Senjelian people and make us their slaves. They may call themselves liberators, revolutionaries … whatever they wish. They may promise you equality and freedom, but know this: they do not intend to deliver. These rebels seek to dominate and destroy Senjele. Their existence threatens our very way of life. I swear to you, as your emperor, I will return treachery with vengeance. No longer will sedition be allowed to flourish here."

There was a long, dramatic pause. Haplan's face shifted and Chaunstance was sure she saw his lower lip quiver, but he never took his eyes from the camera. "I have brought before you, for the first time, one of the monsters responsible for these unnecessary deaths. He has given us a full confession, naming in detail those who conspired to bring down Senjele. Lord Ambren has accepted responsibility for the death of the emperor. As a lord sworn to the service of the crown, he knows the punishment for his crime is death."

Chaunstance glanced at Timothy. He was no longer watching the screen as he piloted the tiny shuttle toward the gate. Even so, Chaunstance saw his fingers tighten around the steering wheel. She watched his chest rise and fall quicker, and his knuckles turn white, as he listened to the gun charge and fire against the back of Haplan's head. She looked back at the screen as the camera panned away from Haplan's lifeless body to Rebos's reddened face.

"Lord Ambren did not act alone. There are still those among us who would pit brother against brother in bloody war for no reason but their own gain. There are those who would rather see this great nation engulfed in a civil war than enjoy a time of peace such as we have never known. I tell you, we will hunt them down, each and every one. We will show these traitors no mercy. In the name of all that is good, in my father's memory, in honor of those who fell in meaningless bloodshed across the empire, I swear to you, we shall live to see a day when the swift sword of justice avenges the sons of Toria and the daughters of Illion. There will be peace. There will be unity. Senjele will endure."

They lost the signal as the shuttle slipped into the swirling, blue vortex of the gate. Chaunstance slid her hand into Timothy's. He squeezed back.

CHAPTER TWENTY-THREE

Jovi

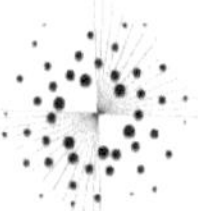

Jovi laid out two kings and three queens, took the cigar from his mouth, and announced, "Read 'em and weep, ladies." The women exchanged glances. He had the brunette, Jeanie, down to one of his button-up shirts, a black pair of panties with lace on them, and mismatched socks. The false blonde, Meg, still had her jeans but, with his luck, those wouldn't last long. They dropped their collective hand to reveal the last two kings and three emperors. "Damn. You ladies are hot tonight." He bit the cigar and stood to drop his drawers. They'd robbed him of everything else. Jeanie lifted an eyebrow. Meg giggled and tossed her pigtails. "You want to go another round?"

Jeanie leaned across the table. "You have nothing else

to take, Jovi."

He looked down, rubbing his chin. "I got socks." She sat back down. "Unless you ladies got a better idea?"

Jeanie put a firm hand behind Meg's head and pulled the other girl into an open-mouthed kiss.

"Now this is a game I know how to play." Just as he was about to climb over the table to join them, the ship's communication system kicked on. "Jovi. Jovi? Damn this thing. Is it on? Jovi!"

"Not now, Senator." Meg was unbuttoning Jeanie's shirt. "Call back later."

"Jovi, this is important!"

Jovi sighed and pulled his pants back on. "Carry on," he told the girls, who didn't seem to care he was going. He'd already paid them. *Might as well let them have their fun.* "But don't get nothing on my seats, you hear?" Jovi prowled up to the cockpit, cigar still in his mouth, and took up the private terminal. "You've got the worst timing, Clovis."

"Start the engines," the senator huffed.

Jovi leaned forward, peeling his back off the leather seat. Clovis sounded winded, and there was a lot of noise in the background, though he couldn't make out what kind.

"Man, I got company! Don't do this to me," he whined, but his fingers worked over the switchboard anyway. Clovis paid him good coin to be ready at a moment's notice. He should have guessed the old fart would come running at the worst possible time. He flipped on the warm-up sequence and took up the intercom. "Attention, passengers: this is your captain speaking. Party's over. Get the hell out."

Jeanie poked her head into the cockpit. "It's after midnight."

He turned in his seat, irritated to see her this far afore. It was bad luck to have a woman in the cockpit. "So?"

"So, you owe us another sixty each."

Jovi stood and squeezed between the narrow seats, pushing her back with as much gentility as a man in his position could afford. "Put it on my tab," he said, and walked them brusquely to the door.

He forced Jeanie out half-dressed and she threw a shoe at him. "Cheapskate!"

"Don't you forget it, babe," he shouted back and slammed the door shut, winding the pressure lock after her.

He returned to the cockpit to finish the pre-launch sequence. There were a hundred things to do in a normal launch: a launch trajectory to calculate, a last-minute check of weapons, life support, gravity control, heating, ventilation, pressure control … most chumps bought a computer to do it for them, but Jovi knew better. Computers not only weighed a ton, they couldn't judge things like he could. Sure, they could make split-second adjustments and do all the math. But once a man let a machine think for him, he was no longer captain of his hold. Still, Jovi didn't mistake himself for a mathematical genius. He'd still flip on the old standby to check his calculations.

He caught the switch to the standby module as he jumped back into his seat. "Computer, check my calc." A correction flashed on his control screen, an impossible ascent trajectory even the *Andraste* would have trouble reaching inside the atmosphere. He smacked the module. "Verify and explain."

"Gale force winds detected," the pleasant computerized voice chirped. "Safety hazard detected. Warning. Hazardous weather conditions. Aborting launch sequence."

"The hell you are." Jovi flipped off the module and unplugged it from the dash. Every time he unplugged it, he imagined killing the computerized voice in his ship. It made him smile.

He turned to another screen and scrolled through a series of reports with one hand while the other moved across a dashboard of flashing red lights, turning them all green. The gale force winds looked to be true enough. A massive storm was slamming into the coast just north of Nebarius and this was just the front end of it. The port authority had grounded all ships and put out a notice that every hold was subject to random searches.

"No good, Senator," he said, knowing the senator couldn't hear him. "Come on, give me something to work with."

Green flashes of light lit the dash. He unrolled a keyboard and hacked through the port's security. It was easy enough to do, since the Senjelians had shit for firewalls. They had the port locked up tight, though, and there was no way he could bypass the hood holding the Andraste's docking bay closed. He could ram through, but then he wouldn't make the crazy ascent trajectory they needed to clear the storm without damage. He would have to open the launch hood manually.

Jovi jumped out of his seat and went back to the door, hoping Jeanie and her friend weren't still down there, waiting to jump him when he came out. He had a rule about not hitting a lady, but whores were different. *A man has to defend himself, after all.* He unwound the pressure lock and threw the door open, relieved when he found the bay empty. He locked his feet on the sides of the ladder and slid down, rubbing his hands on his shirt as he looked for the controls. What he wouldn't give to have his co-pilot back. The kid was a crack hacker. He could have gotten through and opened the hood without leaving the ship or breaking a sweat.

While he stood, surveying the mess of the bay, the door slid open. Senator Clovis stumbled in, hanging heavily on the arm of a twenty-something male wearing a dark hood and a set of clothes too loose in the chest for his scrawny body. They hung sopping wet off him. As the two of them tumbled in ahead of the rain, the kid turned and fired two shots. Clovis fired a shot of his own, and the two of them fell behind a set of crates.

Several executors, who had filled the doorway, guns drawn, went down. The rest opened fire on the bay. Hot plasma struck the walls and hull of the ship. Jovi pulled his pistol, spun it once and discharged it from the hip, hitting the door panel. The panel sparked, and the heavy, plasma-proof door came down. One of the executors following them slammed into it with a satisfying thud.

Jovi spat on the ground. "Fucking executors."

He caught sight of the manual hood controls in the corner, a big, hulking cog with a chain wrapped around it. "Huh. There it is." He strode over to it, the senator popping up to join him. "Where's your urgent cargo?"

"This is him." Clovis motioned to the kid, who threw back the hood, as if Jovi should know or care about his baby face.

Jovi looked him over as he grunted and tried to pull the cog. Damn thing wouldn't budge. "I don't transport people, Senator. I told you. Not unless they're good with a ship or a gun."

The kid pulled his gun back out and fired without aiming, hitting the cog so it would spin. The sudden shift in movement threw Jovi on his behind with another grunt. Then, he spun the gun as Jovi had done and dropped it back in its holster. "Good enough for you?"

"Where do you find these people, old man?"

Clovis extended a hand to help him up and he took it gladly. The pounding on the door was getting more insistent.

"And why in the hell are executors shooting at you?"

"Can we work out the details when people aren't shooting at us?" the kid asked.

As they made for the ship, Jovi explained, "Engines are hot, but I don't know if I can make the trajectory in this storm. It's a hell of a mess out there." Once aboard, he didn't wait to hop back into the pilot's seat and finish the abbreviated version of his pre-launch, checking the weapons and bringing up a barrage of maps and scanners. "Strap in," he told them without looking back. "We're flying blind."

"Is this a good idea?" the kid asked the senator.

"No," Jovi answered. "But Clovis don't pay me to have good ideas, and if you value your life, you'll keep yours to yourself."

Clovis put a hand on the kid's shoulder. "If any ship can get out of this, it's the *Andraste*."

"Damn straight." Jovi pulled his seat belt across his chest as the launch pad rotated the *Andraste* into his pre-programmed trajectory. They would barely clear the hood, but there was no reason to tell his passengers that. Until they cleared the storm, they were a mobile lightning rod. If they got hit, the whole system would fry. Taking off in a lightning storm was about the dumbest thing he'd ever done. "Nobody pukes, understand? I just reupholstered in here."

Before either of them could protest, the *Andraste* blasted forward, five g's of gravity pushing them hard into the seats. They cleared the hood with inches to spare, and shot into a mess of swirling black and gray, raindrops the size of fists pounding against the view window and hull. Hail an inch in diameter bounced off the plating as they approached trajectory speed. His baby could take a little pounding, but one good jolt of electricity and they'd fall like a rock. He watched the lightning strike radar light up like an Amasian whorehouse, nervously moving his fingers across the board. Everyone said the *Andraste* was faster than lightning, but he'd never tested the theory until now. An arm of light snaked across the sky close enough that a few sensors went blank, and the board flashed red for a moment, but came back up without incident.

When they cleared the storm and sped into the upper atmosphere, Jovi let out a loud sigh of relief. The beautiful blackness of space rushed up to greet them, and the *Andraste* fell into it, more graceful than a swan. Jovi moved them into orbit before swiveling the chair around.

Clovis had never looked so fat and ugly in all the time he'd known him as he did sitting strapped in the cockpit chair. The kid wasn't faring much better. He looked uncomfortably green.

"Now," said Jovi, eying the two of them. "Talk."

Clovis scratched his balding head. "The emperor is dead."

"So? You Senjelians always shoot at each other when someone dies?"

"This," continued the senator, motioning to the kid, "is Prince Annon."

Jovi leaned back in his seat and rubbed the stubble on his chin. The intricacies of Senjelian politics weren't completely lost on him. He knew there were only a handful of reasons the Senjelian senator would ask him to transport a prince off the planet, no questions asked. The list was even shorter since the emperor was dead.

Given their earlier conversation, Jovi narrowed the purpose of their trip down to one thing.

"Great. Just great." He turned his seat around and crossed his arms. "So kind of you to dump a civil war in my lap, Senator. Now I'm wanted here and in Erolyia. You better hope those F.O.F. codes you gave me are still good."

"They're good." Clovis was smiling behind him. He just knew it. "I had a friend of a friend pull the codes from Yolen's ship. Trust me; they're the best."

"Hacking into the High Executor's warship? I like your style, but you got no sense."

"He's Rebos's dog," Clovis explained it as if they were talking about sheep and grain, not princes and treason. "He's sure to send someone after Annon. It will slow him down and get you passage anywhere you need to go. Best of all, no one else has the authority to block the codes. I doubt Yolen will block his own codes, especially if you're not liberal with their use."

"So what am I doing with you, kid?" Jovi moved one screen through a series of breaking headlines. Most channels focused on the public execution of some nobleman he'd never heard of, praising it as a bold and decisive first move by the emperor apparent, Rebos Eflor. "I assume you have some destination in mind?"

"Erolyia."

Jovi spun his seat around again, hoping the kid was a joker, but his face was straight, so he looked to the senator. Neither of them smiled. "You're joking." Then, he remembered the message on the crystal. "You can't be serious! Do you know the first thing about Vyjorin Thagg? He'll eat this kid for breakfast and use his bones to clean his teeth. And that's just Vyjorin. Who knows how batshit insane his little sister is? He's dead the moment he sets foot in Erolyian space, and that's if we're lucky enough to get that far. Getting there with a ticking political time bomb on board and stolen codes will be one hell of a thing to pull off."

"How do you know anything about the Thaggs?" Annon asked. "Erolyia's communications blockade is ironclad. No information is getting through."

"Suffice to say, I know the Thagg family better than I care to. I'm serious. The minute we enter Erolyian space the Swift Fleet will have me pegged. They'll board us and haul us back with the trash. What you're paying me, Senator, isn't worth my ship or my skin."

"Just how much is a wanted smuggler's skin worth these days, Jovi?"

Jovi scowled. "Less than a traitorous senator's, I hear. I make this run, I want more than gold."

"Name your price." Clovis patted Annon on the back. "The future emperor of Senjele is a generous man."

Annon shifted uncomfortably at the title.

"A pardon, here and in Erolyia, for me, Skan and Rekelle. If you're marrying a Thagg, you'll have the power to make it happen. That, the gold, *and* a guarantee you'll cover my expenses, including any ransoms, ship damage and port fees. You get me those things, I'll get you to Erolyia. Once you're there, though, no promises on a ride home."

Jovi spit in his hand and extended it to the prince. "I don't consider nothing done without a spit shake." He leered when the kid hesitated. "Go on. Even a prince can spit in his hand. You wipe your ass with it like the rest of us, and don't you pretend you don't."

Looking disgusted, Annon made a pathetic attempt at spitting and grasped Jovi's hand. The princeling's hand was more calloused than Jovi thought it would be, a good sign, but he squeezed the kid's fingers tightly enough to convey his message: *I don't like this.*

The way Annon shook his hand said, *I know. Me either.*

Jovi wiped his hand on his pants, suddenly realizing he was still shirtless and shoeless. Well, he still had his socks. "So, where can I put you down, Senator Clovis?"

"Toria," Clovis answered quickly. "Quick and quiet, if you please."

The senator gave Jovi a knowing grin, telling him he didn't want to ask any more questions. He'd live longer. So, instead, Jovi turned around and plotted their course.

The *Andraste* glided through space, gentle as a cool wind on a hot day. It was a single jump to Toria, and five dangerous ones out to Nautis, where he could ride the blue wave to Erolyia. If Lady Luck was on his side, he could be back playing a game of Kings and Emperors with Jeanie and Meg by the end of the week.

CHAPTER TWENTY-FOUR

Vyjorin

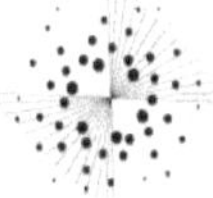

When he was well enough to sit and wear the Eye—and when he was certain his bodily functions were back under control—Vyjorin braved a mostly empty throne room to watch his sister practice. The throne in the capital of Oasis was much more accommodating than the one on the mobile palace would have been, with its softer cushion and all the furs draped over it. Vyjorin barely felt any pain sitting there. By now, most of the bandages had come off, and the doctors said he was healing well, though his face was thick with knots of tissue.

It made him glad that his wives had agreed to divorce him with minimal complaint. Nira, his eldest wife, a smooth, round-cheeked woman of thirty, sent a recording of her voice, promising that she still loved him and would be available and fertile should he wish an heir. Nira was jealous of Kihran and had been from the start. If he hadn't whisked her out of Oasis the moment they wed, Nira's knife might have found Ki's belly in the dark.

Women are like that, he mused as he watched Shireen swing the wicked, curved *ikhiris* at a mannequin made of thick reeds and cloth. The blades sliced through the green stalks in the neck with ease, but she kept hacking at it, taking fingers, arms, and legs. *Vicious, territorial creatures full of spite and murder.* They were far more sadistic killers than men, his Kihran no different. The memory of her after her victory in the temple rite was as sweet now as it was bitter. She stood only to his neck, thin with sun-darkened skin. The long, platinum hair common among her people was red with blood, the same blood that splattered over her cheeks and across her bare breasts. She raised her *ikhiris* high and gave a high, eager shout as the last of the other women, some twice her age, groped in desperation at her entrails spilling out into the sand.

Vyjorin shifted on his reclining cushion and pushed the memory away. The wound was too fresh, the memory too vivid, his sister's plight too similar. Vyjorin hoped Taleed would be gentler with his sister than he had been to Kihran. His sister was not the fierce female that his wife had been.

"Harder," he instructed her. "Reeds are not flesh and bone."

Shireen lowered her blades and turned back to glare at him. "Harder will make them split just the same. The force of my strike will matter little if I've no arm to wield it."

Taleed stroked the thin line of hair curling down from his long chin. "They will take more than your arm if you are weak."

Sometimes, the rites meant a maiming, but that was rare. It was kinder to kill. Shireen was Vyjorin's blood, his *only* blood, and she could not lose.

She swung one *ikhiri* and split the river reed dummy in two, sending the stalks flying. Then, she stormed at him with such anger in her eyes that two of his eunuchs stepped between them, blades at the ready. Shireen halted but not before threatening Taleed from afar. "I am not weak!"

Taleed stood.

Vyjorin leaned forward. "Taleed," he hissed in warning. Sandman or not, he wasn't going to let Taleed harm his sister in front of him.

"Relax, Great King," said Taleed as he stepped forward, taking a *ikhiri* from each of the eunuchs as he passed. He spun them with ease as he took up a stance opposite Shireen. "It is natural for a woman to bleed."

Shireen turned to face Taleed. Vyjorin could almost make out the outline of her face through her veil. He hadn't seen Shireen's bare face since before he sent her away to study with the Red Priestesses. She'd been a girl of seven then, still fat in the face. Now, her cheeks seemed trim and attractive, the body beneath not unappealing. Most importantly, she had good hips and a womb as fertile as farmland, or so the physician assured him. After the rites, he would find out quickly enough. Her husband would not have the luxury of waiting—and why should he want to? Even the Senjelians had heard stories about the Red Sisters. The Amasians had stolen a few away to teach a corrupted form of the art to their whores. The whores wasted it. They lacked the discipline to wield such a weapon gracefully. Shireen, though, would have to work her charms on the prophet that came to her, and quickly.

Any thought of leaving would vanish the moment Shireen learned to kneel.

Vyjorin tensed as Shireen moved stiffly into the stance the priestesses had taught her. *She actually thinks she can fight him*, Vyjorin realized, and wondered if the session was not a mistake.

Shireen stood across from Taleed, all the rage of a sandstorm in her eyes. It could be her power, if she would embrace it, or her undoing if she shunned it. Her anger did not strike fear into the cold, guarded heart of Taleed.

The fight was quick. Shireen lunged forward clumsily and Taleed shifted away and let her fall on the ivory hilt of the eunuchs' blades. She stumbled back a step, but not out of Taleed's reach. The flat of his hand found the back of her neck and gave a quick strike when she bent over in pain. She sank to her knees, but Taleed did not let her rest. He kicked her onto her back and stood over her, the points of the blades resting gently against her throat. Taleed did not take his eyes off his prey even as Vyjorin found his feet.

"Yield!" Vyjorin shouted to Shireen. "Yield, damn you!"

Shireen knocked the threatening *ikhiri* away and sprang to her feet. She and Taleed circled each other, and Shireen put a hand to her neck, pulling it away to find it bloody. If this had been a real fight, she would already be dead. As they circled, Taleed tossed aside the borrowed *ikhiris*, intending to take her on with nothing but his fists. This time, he danced forward first. She swung at him wildly, but she was not fast enough to catch him. He slipped through her advances like grains of sand in an hourglass and, soon, almost too quick to follow, he was behind her again. Taleed grabbed her by the hair and kicked her legs out from under her. Shireen let out a screech of rage that Taleed silenced by wrapping his hand around her throat. She let her swords skitter to the floor and tried to peel his fingers away, but it was no use. Taleed was a large man, strong even for his kind. There was no chance that a fifteen-year-old girl would overpower him.

"Yield!" Vyjorin screamed, but the stubborn bitch held her jaw tight in refusal.

Taleed let go of her throat and held Shireen against him with such force that she whimpered. He used her hair to yank her head back further. Taleed's nostrils flared as he took in her scent. Shireen shivered and tried to turn her face away. He snapped his teeth loudly by her ear.

"Taleed … what are you doing?"

"Patience, Great King," cooed the Sandman. "This one needs a lesson. The Red Priestesses have made her soft, supple, and scented of nectar and honey. Be still, and see how a warrior is made."

Taleed tore away her veil, and Vyjorin watched it flutter, weightless, to the floor. Shireen's eyes went wide with fear and they slid up to meet Vyjorin's. Vyjorin felt he should interfere, but it was too late. He'd already made his promises, and Shireen had yet to learn.

"Do you know what I am, girl?" Taleed asked, and Shireen shook her head. "Pain is the one thing common to all living, breathing beings. It unites us in ways that no other feeling can. Pain is the path to enlightenment, child, not pleasure." He rested the knife over her left breast, closed his eyes and took a deep breath. "Do you feel that? That pounding in your chest? Do you know what that is? That is fear. Fear is the great inhibitor. It blinds us from what binds us. Did you know that, little girl?"

A tear trickled down Shireen's cheek and into the corner of her mouth.

"Are you afraid now, Shireen?"

Vyjorin did not hear her answer but he read the whisper on her lips. "Yes."

Finally, Taleed let her go, and she fell limply to the palace floor, weeping. "To know fear is the first step toward conquering it," he said, and approached the throne. "This girl is not fit for a bed, Great King, let alone the arena. Give me a month with her and I will turn her soft, woman's heart to stone."

Vyjorin turned away. He didn't know if he could stand thirty days of watching Taleed torture Shireen. He didn't know if Shireen could stand it.

He thought of Fayte, Lillith, and the terror they were raising in the Black Temple. The holy books of the Sandmen predicted this, Taleed had told him. They spoke at great length of the creatures that would rise to devour his land. Only the Shadeem Saleph, the prophet that was coming, could save them, and only if wed to a Thagg. The prophet could purge his line of the infectious madness that ailed Vyjorin.

Vyjorin made a slow turn and trudged back to his throne. "Teach her," he commanded. "Do as you wish with her mind. Just make sure her body remains intact."

Taleed bowed, turned and went to scoop Shireen off the floor. "Come, child," said the Sandman, throwing the girl over his shoulder. "Dry those tears. They will not save you from the truth."

Vyjorin's eunuchs brought him his milk, and he sipped at it from the good side of his face, recalling the rest of the prophecy, the part where the prophet purged the Great King's madness from the world in a torrent of blood and fire. *Let him come*, Vyjorin thought. *Let him rain his fire down on me. I am the mad king, marked by fire, tainted by blood! Come and taste my sweet sister, prophet of destruction, and I will go freely into the eternal, dark night.*

CHAPTER TWENTY-FIVE

Reva

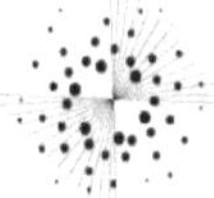

Reva Tzu refilled his crystalline wine goblet with milk and watched yet another storm pouring its fury out in the distance. The eighth-story balcony window of his bedchambers towered above the sleeping city of whitewashed stone, only a small distance from the lightning looping and clawing its way across the sky. Clouds heavy with rain rolled against one another, the warm front of summer butting heads with the distant chill of Senjele's winter. The cool breeze carried the sweet, flowering scents from the temples of pleasure below. He stepped through the sliding glass doors onto the balcony in his robe and lit up the brazier, throwing handfuls of jasmine and kindling into the fresh fire before leaning against the iron railing to sip his milk. Above the clouds, dawn was breaking, rosy pink and proud. Not down there; in the city, the dawn came gray and heavily charged. An arm of red lightning raked out of the clouds to kiss the top of the trees, the electrical jolt so close it made his hair stand on end.

If this were any other dawn, Reva would have chanced to stand naked on his balcony and let the lightning come as close as it dared. Few things excited him more than the electrical tingle of limitless power crawling through his nervous system. *If I am to die*, he thought, raising his cup to the storm, *let it be in a storm such as this*. He drank the milk, wishing he'd thought to warm it first. In the gathering wind, he could have used a little warmth. *The winter will be worse. I hope the cold doesn't kill me.* Even in the mild chill, he could feel his stunted lungs tightening, squeezing and contracting to fill with air.

His Great-Aunt Elyise argued it would have been kinder to kill him than let him struggle every day of his life, measuring each day by counting the hours between medications and treatments. Perhaps she was right. His lungs were too small and weak to work at full capacity in Senjele's thicker atmosphere. Adjusting his body to the new climate and pressurization had taken weeks of careful planning and monitoring by his personal physicians. Zaied, his great-uncle, and the leader of House Tzu, had landed him the initial posting as the media liaison for House Eflor.

With Senjele headed toward civil war, he was glad to be in a position even closer to his goal. Getting his seat in the small council wasn't so difficult. Reva won it easily once he knew which strings to pull. He needed to be close to Rebos and Yolen for his plans to work.

He turned his head as the door behind him slid open.

His husband was a middle-aged man with salt-and-pepper hair, broad shoulders, and a deep and naïve love for justice and truth. Konstantis—Stantis for short—was an attractive man, but the straight-pressed lines of the executor's uniform did him no justice. It was almost a shame he'd have to put the uniform back on and go to work. For now, he was content to wander around Reva's quarters in the nude.

Stantis crossed his arms and leaned against the doorway. "The briefing said they see storms like this all the time on Toria. It floods there, too."

Reva watched another arm of lightning split the sky, then branch into half a dozen smaller arms. He took another sip from his milk. "So, you're still going, then? There's nothing I can say or do to change your mind?"

"Yolen asked for me personally. If I turn him down, it will tank my career. You know it will."

"Who is going with you?" Even though Reva already knew the answer, he had to ask. Stantis knew nothing of the underhanded dealings Reva had in the empire. He'd gone to great lengths to keep him away from it. As far as Stantis knew, Reva was just a busy royal advisor, and his secrets were matters of state. It drove him mad Stantis didn't inquire anymore.

"Fraila Kaarsgard. She's young but a hard worker. I think we'll pair well together." He came forward and massaged the gnarled skin on Reva's shoulders. "It almost seems an exercise in futility, investigating Toria now. But the High Executor is sure there's still resistance. Things didn't end well."

"No, they did not. Be careful, Stantis. Even if you find something there, think hard about revealing it."

"I know what I'm doing, Reva. I promise."

Stantis kissed Reva's cheek and smiled against his skin.

That fool. He didn't understand what he was getting into. What was worse was that Reva was powerless to warn him without destroying the life they had built. If Stantis knew what he had done, he would leave him.

A buzz at the door surprised them both. Stantis frowned. "Who would call now? It's dawn!"

Reva squeezed Stantis's arm. "I'll take care of it. Why don't you get in the shower? I'll make you something to eat on the shuttle out."

Stantis frowned and touched his fingers to Reva's forehead. "Are you sick again? Or have aliens kidnapped my husband and replaced his brain with one that likes to make sandwiches?"

The door buzzed again, and Reva opened the balcony door for Stantis. "Go. I'm only being nice because you'll be gone for so long." He gave Stantis a pat on the butt and sent him along.

As soon as he heard the bathroom door close, Reva went to the door of their apartment and unlocked it. It slid aside with a whoosh to reveal a woman covered head to toe in curling, silver tattoos, visible even in the dark.

"What are you doing?" he snarled, and grabbed her by the arm, dragging her into the apartment. "What are you doing ringing my doorbell? Why have you come to my home?"

"I thought the doorbell was appropriate, since you had a guest."

"Lower your voice. My husband is here."

"I apologize."

He paced to the bottle of wine Stantis had opened earlier to relax with, and put the cork back on. "Why are you here, my Magpie?"

"The High Executor is monitoring your call channels."

"That bastard," Reva growled. "He's probably bugged

my office, too. The only reason I can be sure he hasn't done it here is because I have been here most of the night. Please." He gestured to a chair, and she sat. "I assume you have important news?"

"The *Andraste* took off during the storm."

"Jovi Null was here. The rumor isn't news to me. He was likely carrying Prince Annon, Timothy Val and Senator Clovis. They will go to Clevennia, where they will plot to overthrow the emperor and place Annon on the throne."

"You seem certain."

"I did not have Torbin Val murdered so Castle Valence could sit empty. I certainly didn't conspire with the High Executor to murder the emperor so Rebos could rule, however."

The woman pursed her lips and eyed him as he put the bottle down and adjusted his robe.

"You have a question," Reva observed. "Ask it."

"If you wanted Annon on the throne, why not kill Rebos? That seems the surest way."

Reva smiled. "Have you not heard the prophecy? It must be one not of royal birth who sits on the throne, both on Erolyia and Senjele."

"Then who would you have rule?"

"That is for me to know, and no one else. Senjele must prepare itself for the true threat."

"You speak of the Darkness. Of Drelè."

"Do not speak that word here!" Reva snapped, rising to look out the window at the coming dawn. "Have you any new information about it?"

"Sailor's stories mostly. Sightings of massive ships in hyperspace. Whole worlds gone from the grid. At first, pilots were reporting it was just the gates, but now—now there is empty space where once there were populated worlds."

"How many worlds?"

"Three, so far, each one closer to the Erolyian empire than the last. Whatever is responsible, it will strike there first. If it is the prophesized Darkness, we will not have much time to act."

Reva closed his eyes. If only Toria had not been such a disaster. The blight was one thing. It was an unintended side effect of the research there, but it was necessary. What he hadn't counted on was Timothy Val and all the media attention he had brought. So far, Reva had manipulated everything to his advantage, but the investigation the executors were launching could be his downfall. If they traced the source of the blight back to his people's research and found the weapon before it was ready, he didn't know how he would recover.

"How is the weapon?"

Magpie shrugged. "The rebellion slowed progress."

"Then we must move forward with Plan B." He turned away from the window. "As of this moment, I am green-lighting Project Hourglass. Go to Yoris and ensure it is completed and stays on schedule."

"What will you do with the facility on Toria?"

Reva sank into his seat and sighed. "It hasn't been compromised yet. If it is, I will deal with it. We must place our faith in the progress of science and the power of the mind, Magpie."

The woman narrowed her eyes, which did interesting things to the lines tattooed on her face. "It is written no weapon can strike the Darkness. The people prayed to their gods, but the gods were dead. No one heard their cries as they burned. Only the Nameless One knew their suffering, and he delighted in it."

Reva dismissed her words with a wave of his hand. "I

know the scripture."

"Yet you do not believe it."

"I believe in the power of man, not of winged gods, or dark lords of destruction." When he saw she was disturbed, he reached forward and put a hand on her leg. "Don't worry. I happen to believe when your religion speaks of a magic sword, able to slay demons, and even in the Darkness itself; it's likely an allegory for a real thing. If I didn't believe, I wouldn't fund Project Hourglass."

The running water in the bathroom stopped, and Reva stood. Magpie stood with him. "You must go," he said and ushered her to the door.

"There is more we should speak of," Magpie insisted. "What about Timothy Val?"

"He is exactly where I need him to be." Reva pushed her out the door. "Do not come back here. I will contact you if I need anything further."

The door slid shut and he put in the code to lock it.

"Who was that?"

Reva turned away from the door. Stantis was drying his wavy, graying hair with one of their good towels. "No one."

"I heard you talking to someone."

"Just a messenger with an update from the palace. I have to go in early today. The emperor-to-be seeks my council. Not surprising, considering all that's happened."

Stantis came forward, took Reva's face in his hands, and kissed him. "Advisor to the emperor. I'm a little jealous."

"Your work is just as important." It was a lie, but Reva forced himself to say it. Stantis liked to hear how important he was. It made him smile and kiss Reva on the cheek again.

"I have to get dressed. You promised me breakfast."

"Of course. Your uniform is hanging in the bedroom."

As Stantis dressed, Reva watched the storm roll in on top of them. Stantis was a damn good executor. If Stantis and Fraila found out about the Phalanx Facility, they might expose him. The enemy could already be on Senjele. There were spies everywhere, hiding around every corner, just waiting for the chance to stop him. The Darkness lived in the hearts and minds of men, twisting their will and desire until they served its purpose. There was no way Reva could tell friend from foe. If he was at risk of being exposed before the weapon was ready, he might have to kill Stantis.

A lesser man might have spent the morning agonizing over whether he could murder his husband to save a dying empire. Reva only wondered how he might arrange it so Stantis never saw him coming.

CHAPTER TWENTY-SIX

Timothy

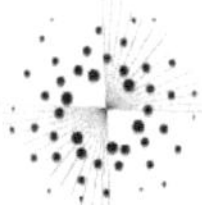

Timothy Val's shuttle dipped below the clouds and within range of Castle Valence's anti-aircraft guns. The on-board computer assured him that the guns had not targeted him but that didn't settle his unease. Timothy's stomach should have been calmer. He'd spent more time in the pilot's seat in the last decade than on solid ground. Most of that time, however, had been spent in the dead of space.

The computer showed a low priority warning about wind speed. Timothy adjusted the shuttle's flight path accordingly and stole a glance at Chaunstance. She'd curled up in the seat next to him, chest rising and falling in a slow rhythm against the low neckline of her dress. A spatter of dried blood spatter marred the otherwise flawless blue fabric. They hadn't had time to change, such was their hurry to escape the capital. Her dark hair had fallen from the formal arrangement piled on top of her head to rest over her neck and shoulders. Even exhausted and bloodstained she was beautiful.

The journey had been hard on her. She wasn't used to space travel and it made her feel sick, though she hadn't thrown up. She didn't complain either. Once they'd hit the jump she fell asleep with her head against the side of the shuttle. In the eight hours they'd been traveling she hadn't moved once.

Chaunstance stirred when the computer chirped its warning and her eyes fluttered open, struggling to focus. She turned her head, looked at him, and sat up with a yawn. "Morning."

"Afternoon, actually." Timothy flipped the first switch of the pre-landing sequence. "Clevennian time runs on a thirty-six-hour day. It's fifteen hundred hours here."

She frowned at him and arched one brown eyebrow.

He smiled. "Three in the afternoon to off-worlders and civilians. Both of which you will find are in short supply here, my lady."

"Your home world is unfriendly to outsiders?"

Timothy doubted she had heard much about Clevennia, having grown up a slave on the capital of Senjele. Senjelians liked to believe every planet in the empire was much like the capital, even though some worlds didn't even share a language. Thankfully, Clevennia didn't provide such a barrier for Chaunstance, but her accent, mannerisms and dress would make her an obvious foreigner.

"Not unfriendly," Timothy said, moving his fingers across the board to slow the craft and lock onto the landing pad at the castle. "Clevennians are a proud people, is all. Not fond of politicians like Clovis."

Chaunstance's brow creased and she looked down at her hands. She hadn't been happy to leave Clovis, but he would be joining them on Clevennia as soon as his other work was done.

Timothy didn't like the idea of Chaunstance being sad, so he adjusted the viewing screen to enhance a tiny square on the horizon. "There it is," Timothy said, pointing. "A dozen generations of stone and sea, blood and sweat. The heart of Clevennia. Castle Valence."

Chaunstance leaned forward and squinted into the distance where a stormy, green-black sea pounded against a craggy cliff. Timothy pointed to one side. Resting against the cliff stood Castle Valence—an impressive fortress of dark gray stone. The sight of it made her sit up and lean toward the window. Five towers, each the size of Clovis' villa, and thrice as tall, swept against the sky like fingers grasping for clouds. Between each stood a wall of two stories, wide enough for four to stand abreast. The keep branched from the center to each tower over a great, curving stone ramp. A dozen ancient evergreens rested their boughs against the towers furthest from the sea, dwarfing the reddening maple and ash trees that grew in their shadow.

"The place is excessively large."

Timothy smiled at her bored tone. It was in contrast with the excitement that touched her eyes. Everyone who saw the castle for the first time was surprised by its size. Only the emperor's palace in Nebarius could have bested Castle Valence in size and grandeur.

"It must take a day just to walk the walls," Chaunstance continued. "I didn't think castles like this existed outside of the old tales."

"It's old," he assured her and steered the shuttle

toward it. "And there are tales about Castle Valence. Songs, even. I have no doubt that you'll hear them soon enough."

The shuttle touched down inside the landing bay attached to the castle.

The wind struck them hard, cold and damp. The sky above hung a cool slate of gray with thick, billowing clouds. Beneath their feet, the mossy ground was thick and wet. A storm brewed somewhere nearby. They'd see the first signs of it by nightfall.

Chaunstance looked up at the sky and rubbed her arms as the wind whipped strands of her hair out in front of her. Worry touched her features.

Timothy smiled and took her hand in his. "Come, I'll show you around." He tugged gently on her fingers.

They passed under the stone arch entryway decorated with the sigil of House Val— a sword crested by five stars—to the castle grounds. Inside the courtyard, paths of polished stone led from the wooden doors of each tower into the keep which stood in the center. The old stone structure stood tall, dark and foreboding, the many windows dark.

Timothy stood below it and swallowed. How many of his forefathers had ruled before him? They had probably been greeted with fanfare and whole armies of men. Yet, no one heralded his coming. The yard, the towers, and the land all stood a silent vigil.

He turned his head to one of the surrounding towers and pointed, naming the towers for Chaunstance. "Speardant, Deyne, Seaward and Yok, after the banner men sworn to House Val. In the mid-levels of the towers there are three bedchambers for guests of high rank. The upper level is a guard bunk with a kitchen in the top and a cellar in the bottom. Tower Deyne houses the dungeon,

Speardant the armory, and Seaward has a tunnel that opens to the sea."

He pointed out the empty stables and promised to fill them with fine horses, the hole in one wall where he planned to build a covered entryway for transports and shuttles as there was in his youth. When he turned back to Chaunstance she stood alone in the center of the courtyard hugging herself and rubbing her arms. The cold and damp was refreshing to him, but it must have been a shock to her after living so long in the warmth of Nebarius on Senjele.

You idiot, he thought. *You should have taken her inside first to warm up.* Timothy went back and placed an arm around her. She stiffened under his touch so he retracted it. "Come, my lady. Let's get you inside and in front of a fire."

Timothy halted on the steps of the Lord's Keep, his face darkening under the heavy clouds as he placed his right hand on the door to push it open. "The last time I was here it wasn't this empty. My father had passed but my brother, Torbin, held the Lord's Keep. The last time I saw him, we stayed up and argued late into the night. I left in the morning, not knowing that I would never see him again."

Would things have been different had he known? He might've repaired things with Torbin at least.

Torbin was dead. Murdered, if Senator Clovis was right. He had never been close to his brother but Torbin was the second Val in a row to rule Clevennia and meet a violent end. Given the current climate in the empire, Timothy could easily be the third.

Chaunstance tightened her fingers around his. "We'll go in together."

They pushed the door open, expecting to find cold

darkness waiting for them but instead found warm firelight. Hearths decorated with medals and pins lined either side of the room, six in all. A long, narrow carpet of steel blue ran through the center of the hall, ending in a circle that surrounded two lord's chairs of stained cherry wood: gold leaf over the back illuminated the Val crest. To the right and left, stone stairs curled around and up into the heights of the keep under flickering gas lamps.

It wasn't an exact replica of how Timothy remembered it, but it was close. All that was missing was his brother, tall and slightly heavier with a golden, single pointed crown on his head. The same crown, or perhaps a slightly more graceful replica, rested on the cushion of the raised seat on the right. Timothy went to the seat and took up the crown but did not put it on.

Footsteps echoed down one of the stone stairways and a tall, rake of a woman with dark hair and plump, pink lips came from the tower with her hands folded behind her back. "A simple crown, such as the Lord and Lady Vals have worn for half a thousand years and then some. As you requested, even though I disapprove. This is a lordly castle with no rival. Its rulers should wear something more...lordly. A crown of swords, perhaps."

Timothy took in the woman's long, gaunt features, stiff posture and hook nose. She was one of the Speardants. Aliah, if memory served, though it looked as if the last decade had been hard on her. He had been corresponding with her by coded message for the last few hours, setting things in place for his arrival. While the people of Clevennia knew of his appointment, they hadn't expected him to arrive for several more days.

Timothy let the crown drop back to the cushion. "This will do. I thank you for the fine work, Aliah, and apologize for the short notice."

Aliah lowerd her head into an exaggerated bow, making her oversized nose look more like a beak. "It is my pleasure to serve house Val, as it was my father's before me. I have word from the other banner men, if it pleases the lord and lady of the castle to hear it."

"Oh, I'm not—"

Timothy cut Chaunstance off with a gesture. "This is Lady Chaunstance, a dear friend and an honored guest. She is here to assist in the transition of power and to help me order the estate."

Aliah lifted her head, the shadow of a smug smile on her features. She had known all along. "My mistake. I just assumed."

Timothy waved a hand as she straightened unbidden. "Think nothing of it."

"It does not change my purpose, lord governor. The Deynes and Seawards stand ready to offer an official renewal of their pledge to house Val and their liege lord. I have men at the ready to take up arms to defend your walls should the need arise. There is a small force of guardsmen here already. I've placed them about the treasury, the armory and your chambers. Let us be the first to welcome you home."

It seemed as if she were being polite but Timothy knew better. Aliah more than anyone had reason to manipulate him to her benefit. Had he not been appointed lord governor the keep likely would have gone to her. The Speardants might have ruled. His appointment had robbed her of a title. She—or one of her kinsmen—were his primary suspects in the assassination of his brother.

"If any craft come within threatening distance of the castle I expect the token force you have stationed here will do little more than irritate the invaders. You and your men may retire, Aliah. I will call for you if your services are needed."

She placed a fist to her chest and bowed again. "Yes, Lord Val."

"You mentioned the Seawards and the Deynes. What of the Yoks?"

"Notably silent, lord governor, but the storm may account for that. Communication through high winds and rain is difficult."

"And what about Torbin's murder investigation? Who is heading that?"

Aliah stiffened. "Murder? The initial investigation concluded natural causes."

Timothy narrowed his eyes. "He was only thirty-seven."

"With respect, he was thirty-seven with a love for food and drink as well as a hatred of exercise. He strained his heart and it simply gave out."

"I'll want to see all the reports and the results of his autopsy."

"There was no autopsy, Lord Val."

"No autopsy?" Timothy rubbed the slow healing wound in his side. He'd need to see to the dressings soon. He was healing well enough, but he would bear the scars of the Sandman's attack forever. "Why not?"

"The death wasn't ruled a murder," Aliah said, straightening.

"Then we will have to exhume the body."

"In accordance with his last will and testament, and Clevennian custom, Torbin's body was cremated."

Timothy sighed and rubbed his head. How curious that they'd been so quick to dispose of his body and to declare his death natural. No matter. He would get to the bottom of it and speak with someone who was not a Speardant. "Are the kitchens stocked?"

"Minimally, Lord Val, but I can have men bring provisions from Speardant Hall if you require it."

"No." Timothy's tone had grown as harsh as Aliah's. If she called him Lord Val one more time, he thought he'd lose his temper completely. As much as the title was his, he wasn't used to it yet. He'd never wanted it and now that he had it, he didn't know what to do with it. "What I require is time to process this. Alone."

"Of course, sir."

"Thank you. Do you need lodging for the night?"

The Speardant woman wrinkled her crooked nose. "I thank you for your offer, but I will sleep elsewhere tonight. If I may have your leave?"

He waved her away. The woman turned, gave a curt nod to Chaunstance and made a hasty exit.

"Sorry you had to see that." Timothy sank into the lord's chair with the crown in his hands. "The Speardants are still a little sore about the castle. They stood to inherit it if no one came forward with a claim. I hope Clovis' boldness doesn't cost me my head. They're fierce fighters."

"As are Vals, I hear. Why the Speardants and not one of your other banner men?" She had to raise her voice in such a large room. The walls ate the sound.

"Torbin was promised to a Speardant woman. Though I think that's why he never married. Imagine the noses on those children!" He laughed, but it was cold and empty laughter.

Timothy turned the crown in his fingers and stared into the cold steel. "I'll have to hear oaths of fealty now, petitions and collect taxes."

"Such is the duty of a lord governor," Chaunstance said with a shrug.

"But, before all of that, I need to know who I can

trust. My father was murdered in this very chair. If it turns out as Clovis suspects, that my brother was murdered, I may become their next target. And then there's Rebos." He stared down into his reflection in the cold steel of the crown. "If Clovis means to prevent Rebos from tightening his strangle hold of power over the empire, he will have to move fast."

Chaunstance moved a short distance away from the thrones. The room lit up with her smile as she thought of the old man. He wondered how Clovis was doing and what he was up to, but most of all, he wished she would smile like that when she thought of him.

Thunder rumbled through the hall, pulling Timothy from his thoughts. "There will be a feast," he declared, placing the crown on the adjacent chair. "Probably music and dancing and celebrations. You'll want to get settled in before then, my lady."

"I'd like to get in contact with Clovis as soon as possible, Timothy. I'm worried about him."

"As would I, but the storm will make ordinary communications difficult, let alone off-world. I don't know where Clovis is, nor do I wish to alert Rebos to his location. His spies could be monitoring transmissions from here."

She clutched her hands to her chest. She didn't say it nor did he, but he was certain they were both wondering the same thing. How far would Rebos go to tighten his grip on Senjele?

"And if Rebos demands your fealty before Clovis is ready to move with his vote in the Senate? Then what?"

Timothy's fingers tightened around the delicate metal band. "I must do what is best for Clevennia. The will and well-being of the people must be my first concern. I will not bow, Chaunstance, not unless I have no other choice."

"You know that will make you a rebel, Timothy? A traitor in the eyes of the empire."

He raised his eyes to hers and forced a weak smile. "It would not be the first time I've been called that."

She smiled and they shared an uneasy laugh.

Timothy's smile faded as his eyes drifted to House Val's banner hanging over the door of the keep, their motto sewn in gold at the bottom: valor, honor, victory.

.

ACKNOWLEDGEMENTS

There are so many people to thank for this one, but first and foremost thanks goes to my husband, Jon, who never let me give up on this one, and my son Matthew who is my go-to guy for space questions. My wonderful team of editors at Bolide, my amazing cover artist, my countless beta readers, ARC team and critiques… You guys all rock. Lastly, I have to give the biggest thanks to my sister and best friend, Anne Young, who is at least partly responsible for the creation of these characters and this world.

ABOUT THE AUTHOR

E.A. Copen is a prolific speculative fiction author living in beautiful Southeast Ohio with her three kids, three cats, a dog, and a husband. She writes everything from space opera to weird west and all the strange genre mashups in between. When she's not chained to her keyboard working on her next novel, she enjoys exploring old graveyards and other creepy places. On weekends, you can find her time traveling with her SCA friends, at least until she saves up enough money to leave the Shire and become a Jedi.

eacopen.com
@authoreacopen
facebook.com/EACopen/

RENEGADES

BOOK TWO OF BROKEN EMPIRE

COMING OCTOBER 2018

BOLIDE
PUBLISHING LIMITED